Seasons in Pinecraft

A PATH MADE PLAIN

LYNETTE SOWELL

Abingdon fiction™
a novel approach to faith

Nashville

A Path Made Plain

Copyright © 2014 by Lynette Sowell

ISBN-13: 978-1-4267-5365-7

Published by Abingdon Press, P.O. Box 801, Nashville, TN 37202

www.abingdonpress.com

Published in association with the MacGregor Literary Agency.

Macro Editor: Teri Wilhelms

Scripture quotations are from the Common English Bible. Copyright
© 2011 by the Common English Bible. All rights reserved. Used by
permission. www.CommonEnglishBible.com.

Library of Congress Cataloging-in-Publication Data

Sowell, Lynette.
  A path made plain / Lynette Sowell.
      pages cm. — (Seasons in Pinecraft ; 2)
    ISBN 978-1-4267-5365-7 (binding: soft back,trade pbk. : alk. paper) 1. Amish—Fiction.
2. Christian fiction. 3. Love stories. I. Title.
  PS3619.O965P38 2014
  813'.6—dc23

                                                                    2014009110

Printed in the United States of America

1 2 3 4 5 6 7 8 9 10 / 19 18 17 16 15 14

For C. J., who was always born to stand out

Acknowledgments

With thanks to Sherry Gore and Katie Troyer, along with the other kind residents of Pinecraft, for making room in your community for this inquisitive writer. I will never forget my first bite of Yoder's peanut butter pie or going to a singing on one chilly winter night. I've done my best to portray things as they could or might happen in Pinecraft, thinking back to an interesting conversation Katie and I had about fiction in "real" life. The characters inside these pages are not intended to resemble one particular individual but are formed from sketches of village life and changed to suit this story.

He is a shield for those who live a blameless life.
He protects the paths of justice and guards the way of
those who are loyal to him.
Proverbs 2:7b, 8

1

*B*etsy Yoder's cheeks ached from smiling as sweat trickled down her back. She dished up yet another serving of chicken pot pie to yet another wedding guest, while her splintered heart ached far more keenly than her outer discomfort.

Amish Jacob Miller had married *Englisch* Natalie Bennett not quite a week ago, and although the current wedding celebration of a cousin here in Ohio helped buoy Betsy's spirits, she felt a throb of pain as if today she'd witnessed Jacob and Natalie's wedding all over again.

With the new union, Betsy's dream died forever. It was not fair the mercury had shot up to more than eighty degrees today, and the promised rain never fell from the clouds scudding across the sky to occasionally provide some shade. The pretty autumn weather was probably welcome to everyone in Ohio, except her.

Betsy couldn't get back to Pinecraft and Sarasota, Florida, quickly enough, and her snug room at *Aenti* Chelle's house.

"You're doing fine, Betsy, just fine," she muttered to herself.

"See? This means you are meant to stay here in Ohio," her *mamm* said. "With us." *Mamm* served up a dollop of mashed potatoes to a guest in line.

Betsy's cheeks flamed, hot as the pans holding food to feed a succession of three hundred guests—a rather small number for an Amish wedding.

A man marrying an *Englisch* wife who'd joined the Beachy Amish Mennonite church was certainly not an everyday occurrence, nor something expected nor something one necessarily wanted to see, not if you were Amish.

Which was why Jacob and his children had packed up the remainder of their belongings and moved to Florida for good. Their bishop had given his blessing for them to join the Beachy Amish Mennonite Church in Sarasota, which had become Natalie's place to fellowship. She'd passed her proving time and been baptized into the Mennonite church before driving from Florida to Ohio for the wedding. *Driving.* As in a vehicle, not a buggy. Somehow, the fact Natalie's *mammi* and *daadi* had been Amish made everything all right.

Even now, the new bride glowed in her cape dress and white head covering, but Betsy couldn't forget the first time she'd seen Natalie Bennett, clad in pink capris and a T-shirt. Betsy kept piling pot pie on brimming plates and wiping sweat from her brow. At least there was some shade with the wedding meal laid out on long tables under the trees on the Millers' property.

Her mother nudged her arm. "What, no protests? Since you aren't marrying Jacob, it's time for you to come home and stay home." Did the humid breeze whooshing through the branches above conceal her mother's words from other ears? Betsy hoped so.

Her cheeks burned. "This isn't quite home anymore, *Mamm.*"

"Nonsense. Ohio will always be your home." Her mother smiled at a guest passing by the table. "Your *daed* agreed to let you stay in Florida for a time, but now—"

"I have my housecleaning clients, and *Aenti* Chelle says I'm welcome to stay in her home."

"Your cousin Anna Mae could use some help in her quilt shop."

Betsy fell silent. Of course, *Mamm* wouldn't budge. *Daed* would have the final say, so she just needed to bide her time until she returned to Sarasota by bus. The house she'd lived in for her twenty-one years should seem familiar, and it did, along with the room she used to share with sisters Grace, Phoebe, and Emma. But during the last week or so, it seemed she saw her surroundings with fresh, grown-up eyes.

Her practical side whispered in her ear as she lifted a now-empty pan off the table.

Back here, there are more prospects, more of your friends, more of everything you've always known. Mamm is right. On a day like today, given other circumstances, it would be easy to agree to move back to Ohio, returning to Florida long enough to gather her belongings from *Aenti* Chelle's and empty her Florida bank account.

The idea made the neckline of her dress tighten. Betsy tugged at it. Constricting, limiting. She had begged *Gotte* to tell her what to do next when she learned of Jacob and Natalie's engagement. She'd taken her father's approval to stay in Florida as a sign she and Jacob would one day be together, she just needed to be patient and bide her time.

"*But living in Florida is for* old *people. You know what they say about Pinecraft. 'It's for newlyweds, half dead, and hard to get,'*" her dearest friend Lottie had told her last winter when she'd shocked everyone by asking to remain in Pinecraft and work.

Yet life in Pinecraft, while quiet and almost desolate in the summer, still held a fascination for her. The ocean, minutes away by bus ride or bicycle, if she felt especially energetic and adventurous, always pulled her in its direction. She didn't mind the occasional stares while she walked the beach barefoot, wearing her cape dress and *kapp*.

In time, she knew her heart would heal. She had to believe it. Another woman's husband shouldn't occupy her thoughts, anyway.

However, since living in Florida, she'd watched some television, ridden countless buses, shopped at *Englisch* stores like Walmart, and even had a cell phone she didn't dare tell her *mamm* about. It made it easier for her housecleaning clients to reach her.

Somehow, if she confessed the entire list to her parents and bishop, those things would pale when compared to her former thoughts about Jacob. As it was, she'd given her father an important business proposal when she arrived home one week ago, a proposal involving an outlay of money, far more money than she had saved. She'd bided her time and, a few moments ago, *daed* told her the family had come to a decision about the funding for her venture, and would let her know tonight.

"I need some volunteers for dishes," called out Esther Graber.

"I'll help," said Betsy. Scrubbing countless pots and pans would give her a way to burn off energy and perhaps by the end of the chore, she'd set her mind where it should be. She crossed the yard and headed for the Millers' house. What would become of it now that its simple rooms were swept clean and empty. Likely a cousin, or someone else in the family, would move in after marrying, and then fill it with children.

An engine's rumble at the end of the driveway made her stare in that direction. A lone figure on a motorcycle, engine idling, paused about ten yards from the edge of the road. A distant family member? Or perhaps a curious onlooker wanting to buy something? But the Millers' produce stand was closed for the season. The simple sign at the end of the driveway advertised "fresh produce, wooden furniture, homemade soap, and fried pies."

Betsy squinted at the figure on the motorcycle. She'd seen plenty of cycles around Sarasota and the idea of riding astride one of the mechanical growling beasts made her insides shake. Never, ever, would she do such a thing.

A gasoline-powered vehicle was a poor copy of the horse, although like the rider at the end of the drive, she'd enjoyed the wind on her face while sneaking a ride on Meringue across the pasture. Poor Meringue, reliable and trustworthy to ride and to drive. The mare probably wondered why Betsy had disappeared last winter and didn't return until now. Leaving her favorite horse behind again would pain her enough.

The figure—a man, judging by the broad shoulders and scruff of beard—raised a leather-clad hand and waved at her. Then with a rev of engine—too loud to be legal—the man pushed off with one foot and disappeared onto the main road.

Betsy's cheeks flamed. Of course he'd wave, her standing there staring at him like she was daft, musing about the noise and inadequacies of motorcycles. She hurried across the farmyard, pounded up the back porch steps, then entered the kitchen.

Hot air smacked her as soon as she stepped into the room, thick with humidity from the cooking going on for the last day or so. Bursts of conversation peppered the bustling atmosphere.

"Betsy, good! We need someone to dry." Her *Aenti* Chelle gestured with her head, the strings of her head covering swishing past her shoulders. "Emily's youngest just woke up, so she's off to feed him."

Betsy grabbed a dry towel from the stack on top of the pie safe. "It's been a beautiful day." She might as well start now, before anyone else tried to offer comforting, yet discreet, words of encouragement. Her friend Miriam had been right. Staying in Sarasota to be closer to Jacob hadn't worked. The bitter taste of the realization would stay with her a good long while.

What would people think, if they guessed her motivation for living in Florida? She'd long since kept going round and round with the idea of what people thought of her and refused to let this fresh thought bloom inside. Then her stomach turned over on itself as she thought of her father's ominous remark earlier. Had the family decided against her proposal?

Aenti Chelle gave her a sideways glance as she placed a clean roasting pan on the drainer. "Yes, a beautiful day. I'd almost forgotten how lovely Ohio is in the fall. The maple out front is spectacular, in all its orange glory."

Betsy nodded, grabbing a pot from the stack. She wasn't sure who this belonged to, but all pots once dried would go in the center of the family's kitchen table, and all the women would round up their cooking instruments before rounding up children to go home.

She had no children to round up, but did have four pie plates to find among the stacks of dishes. The irony almost made her laugh. At twenty-one, she wasn't quite the old maid. Not just yet.

The other ladies in the kitchen, Vera Byler and her old-maid daughter Patience, plus two of the younger girls who debated about who would be next to wed, kept the conversation going.

"Not long, and you'll be just like me," said Patience.

It took a few seconds for Betsy to realize Patience had spoken to her. The other women in the kitchen set their focus on Betsy.

"Just like you?" she asked.

"I'm an old maid and I don't mind it one bit." Patience wrapped a loaf of leftover bread for someone to take home.

"It's not so bad. I keep busy at the quilt shop and I'm happy I can be there for my parents as they grow older."

"So when does this old maidhood begin? Is there a certain age? I must be sure to mark a calendar." The whole idea was silly. Why, Esther Troyer had gotten married at thirty-two, much older than most brides, but not completely unheard of.

Aenti Chelle spoke up. "I don't think Betsy is bound for old maidhood, not just yet. And my home is always open to her in Florida, as long as she wants to live there. Business is good and I need the help."

"Humph." Vera Byler nudged her daughter's elbow. "I know my daughter is following God's path for her. It's a comfort for me to know, too, her judgment isn't being swayed by worldliness."

Betsy turned to face the stack of freshly washed pans. She'd forgotten how Vera's tongue could be, how apt the woman was at pronouncing her own judgment on how things must—and must not—be run.

"*Aenti* Chelle, thank you for your offer." She wiped a damp casserole dish with a flourish. "I'm looking forward to getting home, home to Florida."

❧

Thaddeus Zook had wasted three precious minutes by stopping at the end of his cousin Jacob's driveway. Today, his third cousin, Levi Miller, had remarried. Part of Thaddeus wanted to see the eyebrows raise, tongues wag, and spines stiffen as he came riding his Harley into the farmyard—just so he could have a slice of wedding cake.

A few might have embraced him.

"Thaddeus Zook, you're back."

Only he wasn't back. Not hardly.

He couldn't go back here, even if he wanted to. Now with no job, no apartment—he'd left in a frenzy of packing one duffel bag, along with a wad of cash he'd saved—the sooner he left the Midwest, the better.

He shouldn't have mentioned to a friend in Columbus he was ex-Amish. Someone could find him here, all because of his foolhardy openness.

He wasn't about to bring trouble to his family, even family who no longer acknowledged him or made room for him. The wheels of the Harley began doing their job of putting distance between him and Ohio.

The best thing would be for him to lie low, and the best place to catch his breath for a while would be with his grandmother. Pinecraft was more accepting, more open to the outside than places in Ohio. It wasn't one of the typical places most people expected to find an Amish community. He'd stay there until he figured out what to do next.

He set the GPS to travel interstates. He had no summer clothes, and his leathers and denim would look out of place in the balmy weather. As far as his meager household goods, he'd left those in his apartment with a note of apology to his landlord.

Thad didn't listen to the news anymore after the first report came through of a Columbus restaurateur gunned down in the kitchen of the upscale Dish and Spoon. He prayed for the family of Mitch Gabryszeski, if Mitch had one.

"I'm married to my restaurant," he'd told Thad his first day on the job. And that was it.

Something had been rotten for months at Dish and Spoon, but Thad kept looking the other way and ignored the nagging feeling in his gut that all the suits coming into the restaurant at odd hours wasn't one-hundred-percent legit. He needed a job, and pastries were all he knew.

Now with what happened to Mitch, it wasn't like Thad had a good job reference to head to New York. Also, what would prevent trouble from following him there? He'd told the police everything he knew for sure, which was little. He didn't know anything about the night of Mitch's death. He didn't see anything out of the ordinary.

Florida was the answer for now and he didn't need to pray about it.

He recalled the last civil conversation he'd had with his father.

"Why must you be a—a chef—and not something more—more—"

"More Amish, you mean?"

"This is simply not done, and I forbid it. I know the bishop will see it the same way I do."

Thad couldn't explain it to his father then, or now, but he knew in his heart he wasn't meant to build cabinets, or fix machinery, or plow the ground. Instead, from the time he'd been able to stand on a chair to see his mother cook, he'd been fascinated with the treats her hands created out of things like sugar, butter, flour, salt, fruit, yeast, eggs. He loved the chemistry of it all.

He squeezed the handlebars of the motorcycle and recalled the first time he'd rolled out his own pie dough, a little uneven and lumpy. But it was his creation, and the feeling he got inside while watching his family taste his first apple pie told him he'd found his calling.

Thad almost slowed the Harley down and turned around right there on the country road to head back to the farm. Perhaps his father had been right. The world had swayed him for a long time with its promise of fun—without consequences. Almost ten years since he'd left. Sometimes it felt like a lifetime.

It was warm enough today he'd likely take off his ·jacket once he arrived at the farm, then all could see the tattoo covering one forearm, all the way up to his shoulder. The design was a creeping vine swirling 'round his arm as if it had sprung from his skin, with both prickles and a few flowers. If he rotated his arm, you could see a pair of eyes inside the vines under his elbow.

He slowed the bike as he passed a square black box of a buggy. Now, *that* was something he didn't miss. Thad inhaled a fresh breath of air. Once you'd ridden a bike like this, you didn't want to cover the ground in anything else. The sensation of pure, open freedom was sinful.

Sin, sin, sin. It was all a sin—pride in his pie and pastries, enjoying his wonderful Harley machine, going against the family and his district's ruling concerning his chosen profession, not to mention the education he'd gained.

If he forsook it all, came home, and was baptized, all would be right again.

According to them, maybe.

But he couldn't sleep at night, forced into a cookie cutter lifestyle making him like everyone else. The same hair, the same clothes, the same—Plainness.

If it was anything Thad couldn't abide, it was being like everyone else.

"You weren't made to blend in, Thad Zook," an old girlfriend had told him. *"You were made to stand out."*

He grinned at the memory, not of the old girlfriend, but at her words, and hit the accelerator. He needed some sun, sand, and a place to start again. Or at least some breathing space to figure out what to do next.

2

*B*etsy sat beside her youngest sister Emma at the long kitchen table, built by their grandfather decades ago. The gas lamp flickered on the center of the wooden surface. The supper dishes had been cleared away. They'd consumed a light meal to follow the heavier one at the wedding earlier in the day.

After the day's unseasonable heat departed, the outside air held the bite of an early fall chill. Inside the snug home where she'd grown up, Betsy shivered. Darkness fell earlier here than in Florida and she found herself longing to see the sunset over the Gulf of Mexico.

She waited, not patiently, for her father's answer. A positive outcome held the possibility of changing Betsy's life forever. A no meant yet another disappointment. Either way, Betsy was set to depart on the next bus headed for Sarasota. Emma had tagged along tonight to the table, promising Betsy her support, although Betsy wanted to hear her father's news privately.

As usual, Betsy suspected an ulterior motive on Emma's part. As usual, Betsy was right.

Emma's skin glowed as she spoke first. "Eli asked me to marry him, and I said yes."

Betsy gripped her mug, then relaxed her hold slightly. Her fingers might leave imprints on the ceramic handle if she held on much harder.

She knew Emma and Eli Troyer had been courting. This news shouldn't surprise her. Another wedding, and another one not hers.

Daed nodded from his place at the head of the table. "I knew this was coming. He and I have been talking about house plans. Eli is set to buy some acreage with the help of his family."

"We must set a date and begin making plans." *Mamm's* face bore a similar shade to Emma's. "This is happy, happy news."

Betsy tried not to let her expression show the dismay bubbling up inside her. The effort was more challenging than keeping the lid on a pot of boiling water.

Truly, she had no inclination to think about marriage. Not after all the hoping and praying she'd done about Jacob. Her heart stung and she wondered when the sting would disappear. And now, her youngest sister, ready to wed.

Emma and Eli courted last summer, with their district abuzz at times about the young couple. No wonder Vera Byler had remarked earlier about Betsy being on her way to old maidhood.

Silly. She knew plenty of unmarried women, her *Aenti* Chelle her most favorite of all of them. *Aenti* Chelle had just turned thirty-nine and still had never married. There was some sad story behind it all, but Betsy had been too young to remember and she never dared ask her mother, let alone *Aenti* Chelle, whose parents had left the Amish and joined the Mennonite church when she was a young girl.

"You're quiet, and solemn, Elizabetts." Her *daed* used his own pronunciation of *Elizabeth*, never calling her Betsy.

"I'm just thinking." She smiled at her sister. "Emma, I'm happy for you. However I can help you, I will, even though I'll be in Florida." She glanced at *Daed*.

He nodded. "I know you want to find out the family's decision about helping you in your, ah, venture."

"Did everyone see the paperwork from the real estate agent? I have some savings of my own, like I told you." She'd asked her family to help her, to risk much, on her idea. Not just her father, but her *oncles* and *daadi*, they'd all need to help finance her dream. She needed to know soon, because the real estate agent was awaiting her word upon her return to Florida.

"Yes, everyone has had the chance to look at the terms of the lease." *Daed* fell silent.

Had the announcement of Emma's engagement taken him aback? Not judging by his calm reaction moments ago. His silence, though, troubled her.

What was so hard about leasing a building and opening a bakery? She tried not to nibble on her lip, and failed. She knew better than to pester her *daed* with questions. He'd retreat like a turtle into his shell. It had taken her years to understand his reaction, but the understanding didn't make the job of keeping her mouth closed any easier.

Tonight, however, she succeeded. Instead of opening her mouth to ask questions, she instead raised her coffee mug to her mouth and took a sip. She didn't make a face at the tepid brew.

"It's—it's in an ideal location, nestled on a side street just off Bahia Vista." She sounded like a child.

"Your *oncle* reminded me of Yoder's restaurant nearby, and Der Dutchman down the street."

Betsy nodded. "I know. Der Dutchman is large and serves all kinds of food, and Yoder's specialty for dessert is their pie. I make pie, but I also plan to serve other desserts, pastries, and doughnuts, too. And fried pies."

"Well, I don't know why you just don't open a shop here," said Emma. *Mamm* would probably say the same thing. They wanted her here, all of them. Part of her almost wanted to stay, too.

"I—I like Pinecraft. I can always come to Ohio for a visit, on the Pioneer Trails bus, or you can come visit me, and *Aenti* Chelle too. She said I can live with her as long as I want to." Betsy glanced at her father, who still said nothing.

He rose, then stepped over to the corner of the counter and picked up a folder. It was the same folder where she'd put the lease agreement, along with all her written ideas and recipes for the shop, plus a few sketches of ideas for the inside of the store. She wasn't much of an artist, but wanted the family elders to see what she had in mind.

"Here," *Daed* said as he sat down, pushing the folder in her direction. "You made a good business plan."

"You think it's good?"

"Yes, I do." *Daed* glanced at *Mamm*, who said nothing, but looked down at her folded hands. "Compared to our area in Ohio, we think you will be able to have a successful business among the *Englisch*."

Her heart leapt. "Do you mean—"

"My brothers and I, and your *daadi*, are willing to contribute the money to help you begin your shop."

"Oh, *Daed*." Her grin stretched her cheeks. She couldn't remember the last time she'd felt such joy.

He held up one finger. "There's just one, small thing."

"Small thing?"

"We think you need age and experience to be behind you."

Age? Experience?

"What do you mean?" They didn't think she could do it, that's what.

"Your *Aenti* Sarah has sent word she's willing to help you."

"Help?" She took another sip of the lukewarm coffee on reflex, then set the cup down.

"We're willing to help fund this venture. However, we think it wise you have someone to help protect the family's interests."

"Protect the family's interests?" She sounded like one of those parrots she'd seen one winter, when visiting a zoo in Florida. They repeated and squawked out words without comprehending. Oh, but she comprehended all right.

They didn't trust her. Yes, it was thousands of dollars she needed. But she was careful with money. Hadn't she shown them how, during her time in Florida, working at *Aenti* Chelle's cleaning business? She'd saved a lot of money on her own during the past ten months or so.

"You're going to have a wonderful bakery, Betsy," Emma said. "I can't wait to see it when it's finished."

Betsy nodded. "Thank you. *Daed*, please thank my *oncles*, and *daadi* too." They were investing a tremendous amount of money in her business venture.

But *Aenti* Sarah? Yes, her pies and desserts had made many a mouth water for decades. She was *daadi's* only sibling left and owned a home in Pinecraft smelling like liniment and antiseptic cleaner inside. Betsy had only been there a few times in her life, but had left with a raging headache each visit. The woman was prone to giving advice for no less than fifteen minutes at a time without taking a breath—even when said advice wasn't asked for.

Lord, this is an answer to my prayers, but I'm going to need strength with Aenti Sarah around.

Thad yawned and rotated his head from side to side, feeling like a bobblehead under his helmet. With the change in landscape, thunderclouds had rolled in as he passed through the Blue Ridge Mountains, the highway carrying him ever closer to Florida. He'd been delayed two days in Kentucky, getting a replacement part for his bike, and he gladly let the Harley Sportster eat up the miles to make up for lost time.

At dusk, with flashes of lightning and claps of thunder, the heavens opened. The rain and spray of passing vehicles doused Thad until his clothes clung to him. Thad decelerated, spotting a sign for a covered rest stop off the highway.

He found a parking spot close to a covered picnic pavilion and took shelter underneath its roof, all the while watching the rain pour down and vehicles pass on the highway nearby. A dark sedan had also exited the highway behind him. It now sat parked in the last space, closest to the highway.

Nah, he wasn't being followed. This was a highway and people took shelter at rest stops all the time. Often, if he ever took to the road on a rare day off to himself, he'd encounter the same folks mile after mile. Still, he shivered inside his wet leathers. He sank onto the stone picnic table bench. He tugged his helmet off and set it on the table.

But just in case, he'd wait until the downpour let up, then keep moving on. He needed to find a place to get a cup of coffee and a room for the night. Part of him knew it had been foolish to start out and expect to make it all the way to Florida nonstop. The weather caught up with him after all.

His cell phone buzzed. A miracle, with the way his bag was soaked. But inside, sandwiched between a few changes of clothing, maybe not. He pulled it out of the bag and looked at the number.

Stacie. He'd ended things almost a month ago, for reasons not quite clear to even him. He almost pushed the button to stop the buzzing, then thought better of it.

"Thad here."

"Thank goodness you answered. Finally."

Hello to you, too. But her tone made him pause. This wasn't the I'm-about-to-tell-you-what's-good-for-you tone. This tone had a different quality.

"Finally? Look, now's not a good time for me to talk."

"I can't talk long. In fact, I'm probably getting a new number."

"Well, good." A truck's horn blared, the sound trailing off as the vehicle disappeared into the night.

"I think you should, too."

"Why?"

"Someone came by my office today, asking about you."

"Who?"

"I don't know. I was home sick."

His pulse roared in his ears. He'd already given his statement to the police, and none of them had said anything about him not leaving town. But it didn't mean things would be safer for him if he stayed in Ohio. He couldn't call the shots. This way was better. He'd been raised to respect the authorities, yet still feared them. Power wielded by the wrong people, even for the right reasons, well, he knew what it could do to even the most well-intentioned.

"Did they leave a name or a number, or something?" If it was a cop, they'd leave a card. Or so it went on TV. Now, the men his former boss was associated with, it was rumored they left calling cards of a different, more physical kind. Even Mitch couldn't explain away the black eye he had one morning.

"No. Meg said there were two of them, in nice suits. But look, I figured I'd give you a heads-up. What's going on? Where are you?"

"I'm not in Columbus anymore." He almost told her about quitting his job, but decided against it.

"I've gotta go. Someone's at the door." The phone went silent.

He stared at it for a second, then turned it off and put it back into the mostly dry center of the duffel bag's contents. Get a new number, huh? Maybe his family had it right, shunning phones. If someone needed to see you, well, they could just stop by the house. Although, come to think of it, he'd heard a rumor about some of the family having cell phones now, discreetly hidden until the time of need.

The rain continued outside the shelter. Thad imagined palm trees, sunny skies, digging his feet in the sand. If he had to burn any bridges, he might as well enjoy the scenery and the anonymity of Pinecraft. The mainstream world had a hard time wrapping their minds around the idea of Amish and Mennonites at the beach. Some of his kind didn't talk much about what they said or did in Pinecraft, other than who they saw. If someone used a telephone, watched a bit of television, used electricity, it wasn't bragged about or discussed.

He remembered the sadness he felt as a child, leaving his *daadi* and *mammi's* house at the end of a winter vacation. Back to the cold, the constricting rules.

Thad leaned on his backpack, its softness lending some contrasting comfort to the cold stone bench and wooden tabletop under the shelter. His eyelids drooped.

He roused himself before he drifted off altogether, then stood. Time to hit the road, get coffee, and see if a warm spot for the night would present itself. As he swung his leg across the motorcycle seat, he glanced back at the sedan. A lone driver was silhouetted in the headlights of another vehicle exiting the highway.

The vehicle's lights clicked on, its engine revved to life, and the driver put the car in gear and headed past Thad in the direction of the highway ramp.

Good. Thad accelerated—carefully—and trailed the car onto the highway. The car sped off into the rain.

3

They crossed the Florida state line Thursday morning in the Pioneer Trails bus. Somewhere in its underbelly was a pair of suitcases crammed with the remainder of Betsy's belongings and a few items her mother gave her especially for her bakery kitchen. They'd both shed tears when she boarded the bus, and she watched out the window as her parents grew smaller and the distance between them increased.

Leaving Ohio by bus with *Aenti* Chelle had cut an invisible cord between her and life in Ohio. More than once she'd prayed, *Gotte, what have I done?* A cashier's check was tucked safely in an envelope pinned inside the waist of her dress. The amount made her heart pound and her stomach curl. They'd notified *Aenti* Sarah that Betsy was returning with the family's blessing. And, their money.

She shifted on her pillow and pulled the small quilt closer to her lap. *Aenti* Chelle sat across the aisle, her head bobbing gently in time with the sway of the bus.

Betsy didn't know how *Aenti* Chelle did it, sleeping peacefully as they careened along the highway, faster than any horse and buggy could take them. The first time she'd ridden the bus as an adult, she'd fought to conceal her fear as the landscape zipped by faster and faster while the vehicle picked up speed. Why she'd ever enjoyed the trip as a child, she never understood.

The murmurs and chatter grew louder as every mile they covered brought them closer to Sarasota, palm trees, sun, and sand. The peaceful side streets would be filled with bicycles and vacationers in a little more than a month. Betsy allowed herself a smile at the idea.

". . . gave her thousands of dollars, I heard," she heard a female voice say.

"You don't say?" another voice echoed.

"And her not married. It's not right. But it's their money, not ours."

"Whatever is it for?"

"A pie shop." The woman clicked her tongue.

"But we can make our own pies. I know the *Englisch* buy our pies, but a shop would be out of place in our village. And there are the other restaurants on Bahia Vista."

"Like I said, it's not our family's money being shelled out to a young girl."

"Indulgence, bad business." More tongue clicking.

"Well, I might just try one. When I'm on vacation, I sometimes want a break from baking," a third voice interjected.

Betsy sat up straighter on the cushioned seat, and grasped the armrest. She half-stood. Maybe she could catch a glimpse of the speakers. Or perhaps it wasn't the best idea. She shouldn't have expected everyone to approve of her idea of a shop, or the idea of someone her age running one. It sounded as though she did have one potential customer.

Aenti Sarah, though, was the one stipulation her father and the rest of the family had put on her shop.

"We're almost there." *Aenti* Chelle punctuated the statement with a yawn. "Ach, but I was sleepy. I should enjoy the chance to nap. Once we're back in Sarasota, it's back to the same routine."

Betsy nodded. "I expect I'll have many hours of work ahead."

"*Aenti* Sarah's meeting the bus today, so I hear." Her aunt shifted to the aisle seat.

No one had told her that. "I—I shouldn't be surprised."

"Your *daed, daadi,* and *oncles* only want you to have some guidance and help when you need it."

"I wish you could help me. You know how to run a business, after all."

"True. But baking and desserts aren't my specialty. You'll need extra hands to help bake and prep and serve, especially if you get busy." *Aenti* Chelle paused. "Also, and please don't take this the wrong way, but you're . . . young."

Betsy kept her features even, without letting a grimace appear on her face. "I know I'll need help. I don't see what my age has to do with anything. If my desserts are good, then they're good."

"Of course they are." *Aenti* Chelle shifted on the seat and faced Betsy. "But some might want to take advantage of you, assuming because you're young you're not smart. *Aenti* Sarah will be a good, ah, buffer."

"I couldn't imagine anyone in Pinecraft wanting to take advantage of my youth."

"It may be. We do look for the best in people, but we're also to be 'wise as serpents and harmless as doves.'"

Betsy nodded. Then the Sarasota city limits sign blipped past the bus. Despite Betsy's mixed emotions over the snippets of conversation she'd just heard and her aunt's words, her heart leapt. Her new home, her new venture. Even with *Aenti* Sarah and feeling everyone would be looking over her shoulder.

Then came the stop-and-go traffic until the bus swung a left onto the most familiar stretch of road for Betsy in Sarasota, Bahia Vista Avenue. A lone three-wheeled bicycle sat padlocked to a bus stop sign. The sight made her smile. Soon enough, the tricycle would be joined by others when the vacation season began.

A few more blocks, and the Tourist Church came into view, with a glimpse of Yoder's not two blocks away. The bus slowed, and Betsy braced herself with her feet as the bus turned into the parking lot.

Like the other passengers, she craned her neck to see out the window. As was the custom of many in Pinecraft, clusters of people showed up to meet the bus. It didn't matter if you were expecting anyone to arrive or not, because it was a thrill to see who—and what—would arrive on the massive travel bus.

They glided onto the surface of the parking lot at the rear of the church building. Bearded men in suspenders and dark trousers mingled with women wearing cape dresses and prayer coverings. A few people wore clothing designating they were either *Englisch*, or liberal Mennonites. Some men wore knee-length shorts, and other women wore capris.

Aenti Sarah stood with three other women, all elderly like her, all in a similar pose. They chattered and gestured as they spoke, stopping for a chuckle. She'd never seen *Aenti* Sarah laugh like that before, ever.

"We're here!" someone shouted to no one in particular as the bus ground to a stop.

Then came a flurry of gathering bags and bundles. They'd all had plenty of room on the trip, with the bus being not quite half full.

"It feels good to stretch my legs," Betsy said as she grabbed her tote bag and reached to press her hand on her waist. The envelope crackled, still there, still secure.

Inside of two minutes, they'd left the bus and the welcoming brigade surrounded them. Smiles, greetings, handshakes, and a few swift hugs.

Aenti Sarah left her group and met Betsy and *Aenti* Chelle beside the bus.

"You're here, you're here. And we have so much to do. So much to do." She tugged on Betsy's sleeve.

"Yes, *Aenti* Sarah. I want to show you my ideas."

The older woman aunt waved away Betsy's words like a swarm of mosquitoes "We'll see about that. I heard you want to bake some non-Amish recipes, like some Italian and French desserts."

"Well, yes—"

"We'll see, we'll see. I've been told to keep an eye on you."

Betsy didn't groan. Any protests, verbal or otherwise, wouldn't work. The driver opened the luggage compartment and began the process of tugging out boxes, rolling suitcases. A large box took up a good part of one of the storage compartments.

"Ah, a casket." *Aenti* Sarah nodded. "A fresh order from up north."

Betsy shivered.

"Are you chilled, child? You must be, after being in Ohio. Well, you're home now. It won't take long for you to warm up." Another pluck on Betsy's sleeve.

"Oh, there's one of my bags." Betsy pulled up the handle on the wheeled suitcase. It dawned on her she'd have to drag both of them to *Aenti* Chelle's house.

"I'll walk with you both," *Aenti* Sarah said.

❧

The office of Dish and Spoon was, for lack of a better term, a mess. And Pete Stucenski hadn't even touched it yet. He'd

spread the news that the restaurant would stay closed indef-
initely. Good thing. The last thing he needed was someone
sniffing around, wondering why Pete was rummaging through
Mitch's things.

"Mitchie, old pal, if you'd only told me where you put it."
Pete shook his head at the stacks of papers on the desk, boxes
in the corner of the room. Something smelled. Dead mouse?
He wouldn't be surprised.

Mitch, the wiseacre, was mocking him from the grave. Too
smart for his own good. Pete's throat tightened at what could
happen to his own hide if he didn't find what Mitch hid. Lives
were at stake. Shoot, an election was at stake.

The police had noted a few missing video surveillance files
over the last six months. Server error, Pete and Mitch had told
them. Mitch had made some of those "disappear" until an
opportune time.

But Mitch had to get greedy, had to open his mouth to the
wrong person at the wrong time, and nothing Pete could say
would save his friend. As soon as Pete had heard the news
about Mitch, he knew Mitch had forced their boss—and future
senator's—hand.

Pete sank onto the office chair and it groaned. "Yep, me
too."

He pulled out the top drawer of the desk. It might as well
have been someone's junk drawer, with all the doodads inside.
Rubber bands, sticks of gum, staples, pens, pencils, packets
of sugar and sweetener—no wonder the place reeked of mice.
What would he be looking for? A DVD, a digital memory card,
USB drive—what had Mitch done with the video feed from
those key nights? Pete had already made one of the files disappear—the night Mitch was gunned down.

His phone bleeped. The boss, Channing Bright.

"Well? Did you find it?"

"I just sat down. As in, just five seconds ago."

"I don't have time for this. Go through the office. Then start talking to employees."

"No problem."

"Of course, it's not a problem."

Pete pushed away a few drops of sweat beaded on his forehead. "I'll let you know what I find."

"Be quick about it. Time's ticking away. Mitch either stashed it or gave it to someone else for safekeeping. Did the police mention anything about it?"

"They asked about the missing days of security videos. But I think Mitch made some other files disappear, too."

"Just find the files."

"I won't let you down."

"Of course you won't. No one is going to be able to tie anything about this back to me." Channing Bright was used to getting his way from childhood to one of Ohio's top businesses. Now he was poised to win the biggest game of his life—a United States Senate seat.

Pete debated about sneaking to the kitchen and brewing a cup of coffee. It didn't seem right, even though the police had released the restaurant after clearing the crime scene. But if Mitch were around, he wouldn't care if Pete, his old pal, made himself a fresh cup of joe.

In a twisted way, Pete was doing Mitch a favor, ferreting out this secret. No one else needed to die because of Mitch's folly. Especially not Pete. Channing Bright had better remember the little people, after all Mitch and Pete had done to help him.

4

*T*had slowed his motorcycle down and let the vehicle glide onto Kaufman Avenue, off the bustling Bahia Vista. One sign made him pause, and it wasn't the sign for Yoder's Restaurant and Gift Shop, nor the sign for Big Olaf's Ice Cream.

Village Pizzas by Emma? Pizza. In Pinecraft? Maybe there was hope for a prodigal baker yet. The idea almost tugged a grin from his lips. Almost.

He yawned. After his night on the road, then sleeping on the lumpy mattress in a cheap motel off the interstate, he hoped his *mammmi* would welcome him. He hadn't written, hadn't called. Of course, she had no phone. But Thad knew where her home was. As soon as he'd entered the neighborhood, it all came back to him. Pinecraft had changed a little from what he remembered in childhood.

Pizza. The thought made his stomach grumble.

Arriving at *Mammi's* would wait for a few minutes. He parked in an empty parking space and noted the pizza shop was open for business now. The late morning sun felt good on his skin. He'd shed his jacket in the morning, and it was strapped to his duffel bag on the rear of his bike.

Thad entered the tiny shop behind Big Olaf's. The chilled air made the hair on his arms rise up, and he rubbed it back down.

The young lady—probably Mennonite, he judged by her hair and clothing—stared at the tattoo on his arm, then snapped her gaze to his face.

He smiled at her. "One slice of pizza, pepperoni. And a bottle of pop from the case."

"Right away."

Thad stepped over to the glass-doored cooler holding the pop. While the young lady dished up his pizza, a pair of older women entered, chattering about the bus that just arrived. They stopped short when the saw him, then continued past him to the counter.

Thad gave them a nod as he stepped up to pay for his pizza. "I can just grab the pop on the way out?"

"Right. Help yourself," the young lady replied with a smile.

He grabbed a Mountain Dew for a caffeine jolt. He'd have plenty of time to sleep. If *Mammi* let him in.

Once outside, he settled down at a table on the deck and munched on his pizza. He didn't need to gulp down the whole slice in four bites, but did anyway. The motel had promised a hot breakfast, but it included frozen waffles resembling warmed-up plastic.

Amish and Mennonites selling pizza. He shook his head over the idea, even as his taste buds soaked up the flavor of the cheese.

The two older women left the shop. One carried a pizza box, the other two small bottles of pop and a stack of plastic-wrapped sandwiches. The sight made him smile.

He took a swig of his Mountain Dew, then replaced the cap on the bottle. Time to see *Mammi*. He revved up the cycle, then passed the ladies who strolled along the street. The neighbor-hood was relatively deserted, which suited him fine for now.

One block over from Pinecraft Park, he turned onto Good Avenue and headed for *Mammi's* house. A neat little flower garden gave the simple white cottage some color. A minivan sat in the driveway, with five three-wheeled bicycles clustered around it.

So, she had company.

So, he couldn't arrive quietly.

He parked his bike in the sliver of remaining parking space, then unfastened his jacket and duffel bag from the rear of the bike. Then he slung the bag over one shoulder and stepped up to the storm door. He could see inside through its large glass pane.

A quilting frame filled the living room, and no fewer than six figures were huddled around it. One of them sat up straight and looked in his direction, then rose from her seat. She wore a cape dress of deep sapphire blue, covered by a navy blue apron. She stopped at the door and spoke through the glass.

"Thaddeus. Thaddeus Zook?"

"Yes, yes *Mammi*. It's me."

"Well, come in, come in." She opened the door and tugged him inside, probably to get the sight of him off her front step before someone happened by and saw him standing there.

Five pairs of eyes regarded him from around the quilt frame. But his attention was focused on his *mammi*. When had she grown so . . . old? Wrinkles lined her face. The fingers smooth-ing her apron had age spots. But her eyes were warm. Inside them, he saw a bit of the hurt he'd inflicted on his family by leaving the Order.

"*Danke*," he replied to her, taking care to wipe his boots on the mat just inside the door. Funny, how the language he knew and had left behind him came so readily to his lips. He let the duffel slide to the floor beside a pair of clogs.

"We're quilting today," *Mammi* said, gesturing to the work-in-progress filling most of the small front room, along with the frame, chairs, and five other women.

"I see."

No, she wasn't about to say much in front of her friends. No questions, no sermons. None of it yet.

"Would you like some orange juice, fresh squeezed this morning?"

"Yes, please."

"Come, come." She waved him along toward the kitchen, where she fetched a clean glass from the cupboard. "The juice is in the refrigerator, so help yourself."

"Thank you," he said, reaching for the glass with one hand and stifling a yawn with the other.

"You're tired." *Mammi* paused in the kitchen doorway separating it from the dining table.

"It's been a long ride."

She continued their conversation in *Dietsch*. "Well, drink your juice. You can nap in your old room. Do you remember where it is?"

"Yes, *Mammi*." He was six years old again, with newly chopped hair just above his ears, his feet dangling a few inches from the floor when he sat at her table.

"*Gut, gut.* Will you stay for a while?"

He nodded.

"*Gut.*" She headed back into the front room.

He tried not to guzzle the juice, but at first taste he remembered the freshness of real juice, straight from the orange. He emptied the glass, then set it inside the gleaming sink. A coffee pot gurgled on the counter, and the sound of laughter echoed from the other room.

Thad yawned again and left the kitchen, his boots taking him to the other side of the house where three bedrooms and the bathroom made a square, with the master bedroom getting the larger chunk of the area. Last door on the right, and he entered the room he used to pile into every winter with his brothers and sometimes a cousin or two.

The bed looked smaller. Or maybe *Mammi* had downsized to a twin bed for this room. A simple chest of drawers stood against a wall. A lamp rested on a nightstand to match the chest. A calendar, two years old, hung on the wall. The irony made him smirk. Yes, the place might as well be stuck in time. But time didn't matter if you were Amish. Which he wasn't, anymore.

He sank onto the quilt, then tugged off his boots. He stretched his aching feet and caught the pungent aroma from his socks. Yep, he'd been on the road all right. As he stretched out onto the quilt without pulling it back, he thought of his duffel bag and jacket in a heap near the front door. He'd pick them up, in just a few minutes.

Nice, soft pillows. A quiet place to close his eyes.

Someone cackled in the front room.

Well, mostly quiet.

∼∾∾

All Betsy wanted to do was curl up in bed, pull her favorite quilt over her head, and get a few hours' sleep. She found herself in Yoder's Restaurant, tucked next to *Aenti* Chelle in a booth, with *Aenti* Sarah across the table from them.

The restaurant, a fixture in Pinecraft since the 1970s, also had a gift shop nearby, which Betsy had walked through once and left before she succumbed to a sudden urge to purchase a beautiful pin. In the building on the other side of the restaurant stood a fresh market stocked with Florida produce and a shop selling various Amish items and baked goods.

With their suitcases and other luggage now back at *Aenti* Chelle's, they studied the menu. Rather, Betsy and *Aenti* Chelle studied the menu while *Aenti* Sarah studied Betsy's folder marked "Pinecraft Pies and Pastries."

"After we eat, I want to stop by the market to get some fruit, vegetables, and bread," said *Aenti* Chelle. "I'm sure my fridge is barren."

Betsy nodded. "I'm so tired."

"When I was younger, we had more stamina." *Aenti* Sarah shook her head.

Betsy ignored the remark. Thankfully, *Aenti* Chelle had driven them to the restaurant in her van.

Would it be wrong of her to order pie from the competition? The peanut butter pie was her favorite and more than once she wished she could put something like it on her menu. But she wasn't planning to copy Yoder's.

She didn't think of her business as competition. She wasn't sure if the other food service businesses nearby would think so either. Her mouth watered, and she yawned. Her two weeks away might as well have been two months.

"You have a shopping list of display cases, a cash register, a triple oven—electric?" *Aenti* Sarah shook her head. "If only we could bring in a good wood-burning stove to bake with. Using electric or gas isn't the same."

Aenti Chelle chuckled. "Imagine, a wood-burning stove, in Florida."

Betsy glanced from her Mennonite aunt to her elderly Old Order aunt. "I certainly never have."

"This is why I wanted to be part of your shop," said *Aenti* Sarah. "We need to do things the right way."

The waitress came and took their orders, but only after *Aenti* Sarah had changed her mind three times, finally settling on the chicken pot pie.

"You'll see the list I made, *Aenti* Sarah. Besides the equipment list, I mean." Betsy pointed at set of photos of the building, taken by Imogene Brubaker. "I need to get the inside painted, the electricity turned on . . ."

At the mention of the word *electricity*, *Aenti* Sarah rotated her head from side to side. "First, it's electricity. Next, you'll be bringing a television set in so customers can watch shows while they eat their desserts."

"Of course not." They'd only been discussing the plans for a few moments, and already Betsy wanted to scream. *Aenti* Sarah had electricity in her own snug little rental in the village. But *Aenti* Sarah was her elder. She could probably teach her a few things about making many pies at a time. Her hands would be a big help, too.

However, if at every turn, *Aenti* Sarah kept throwing out comments, Betsy wasn't sure what she'd do. She didn't want her reporting back to her *daed*, *daadi*, and *oncles* about her attitude, or being careless with money, or worse, losing her Plain ways.

Pinecraft was definitely a lot more relaxed than back home in Ohio. She thought of the saying, "What happens in Pinecraft, stays in Pinecraft."

Aenti Chelle smiled. "I have confidence in you, Betsy. There might be obstacles to overcome while you prepare the store, but God willing, all will come out right."

Ach, there was the rub. *Gotte* willing.

She'd thought it *Gotte's wille* she and Jacob would be together. Immediately, she chided herself for the wayward thought, even as she nodded at her *aenti's* encouragement. No more thoughts of Jacob Miller. Gideon Stoltzfus had approached her once while home in Ohio, but she wasn't interested in the least. Surely, *Gotte* had someone more suitable for both of them.

Anyway, who would go walking with a young man who told her the reason he wanted to escort her home was because of her good apple pie? His ample frame told her how much he like pie. She frowned at her glass of iced tea. Her parents, especially her mother, would have likely preferred she see what happened with Gideon, as it might bring her home to them. She'd been taught her parents knew what was best for her, what *Gotte* wanted for her.

Yes, she wanted to do *Gotte's wille* and please Him, but sometimes she wasn't sure her elders knew best. But as far as the shop was concerned she'd do her best to bend to what they wanted. Everything except for a wood-burning stove, which even *Aenti* Sarah ought to know was impractical and silly in Pinecraft.

"Thirty days," she said aloud.

"What?" asked *Aenti* Sarah, as their waitress and another server delivered their hot meals to the table.

"I want to open in thirty days. After I sign the lease at the real estate office tomorrow morning, Mr. Hostetler is meeting me at the store to go over plans."

"Henry Hostetler is an excellent contractor, even for a Mennonite." *Aenti* Chelle took a bite of her pot roast. "I know he's excited about the idea of your shop."

"*Gut.* I will call him when we get home later, to make sure he remembers he's meeting me."

More head shaking from *Aenti* Sarah. "Telephones. Personal private telephones."

Betsy opened her mouth, but *Aenti* Chelle beat her to the response. "It's a business tool, Sarah. People can reach him anytime and leave a message about work."

"A little leaven, leaveneth the whole lump." *Aenti* Sarah bowed her head to pray silently over her meal, so Betsy continued to hold her peace and did the same.

Please, Gotte, bless this meal, and bless my shop, if it be Your will. And, help me deal with Aenti *Sarah.*

Thankfully, Sarah seemed to forget about the folder on the table and ate her chicken pot pie, talking about upcoming plans to work with her friends to put in more quilts to sell at auction in January, along with the state of a yard in a nearby mobile home park. She asked if Betsy had noticed the advertisement for herbal energy pills in the latest issue of *The Budget*.

By the time they'd paid their check, which *Aenti* Chelle insisted on paying for, and making the short walk to the fresh market, Betsy's head swam like it did the day she cleaned a client's whole house when the air conditioner was broken.

"I won't be long," *Aenti* Chelle said as they entered the store, one entire side providing an open-air shopping experience. "I just need a few things for breakfast and lunch."

"I suppose I should pick up some vegetables while I'm here as well." *Aenti* Sarah picked up a plastic basket. "My garden's hit a dry spell."

Fascinated by all the products, Betsy strolled the store and wandered past displays. Homemade soup mix, pot pies to take home and bake, fresh local eggs and cheese. Even real maple syrup, apple butter, and honey.

What caught her attention, though, were the baked goods. Breads of all kinds, and whoopee pies. Although she'd just split a piece of peanut butter pie with *Aenti* Chelle, the chocolate and fluff combination made her mouth water.

Surely, there was a place for her baking in Pinecraft, too. Of course, some likely thought her prideful. No, she knew it was a certainty, not something she supposed.

But then, no one would go into business if they didn't think they could do a good job and provide something a customer wanted. Such as her *Oncle* Thomas and his cabinet shop he and her father had run for decades and employed at least twenty people from their local community.

Betsy picked up a trio of pies in a clear plastic clamshell container. No, she wasn't prideful. *Confident* would be a better word. She needed to keep it in mind and let the critics say what they may. *Aenti* Chelle, too, had said she had confidence in Betsy.

"Ready, Bets?" Her *aenti* had stopped at the register with her basket, *Aenti* Sarah behind her.

"I'm ready." She should have budgeted to bring a little extra cash with her as well, to purchase a few items for the home. Another day she'd shop, when she was less tired.

They paid for their purchases and Chelle drove them home in the van, first stopping at *Aenti* Sarah's home, part of the legacy of the Yoder family. No, they weren't related to the Yoder's restaurant folks, although if they all sat down and showed their family trees, Betsy wouldn't be surprised if there was a family connection somewhere.

"Good night, *Aenti* Sarah," Betsy said as the older woman opened the front passenger door and left the vehicle.

"I'll see you in the morning. We have much work to do. Be here by six."

"Six?" Rarely did she go to her cleaning clients' homes before eight in the morning, waiting until they were gone to their jobs. She never admitted her learned habit to sleep until the last possible moment, but it would have never happened in Ohio.

"All right, then. Eight. Bring your folder and we'll get your plans in order straightaway."

Aenti Chelle snickered from where she sat in the driver's seat.

Betsy left the middle seat of the van and wrangled herself into the passenger seat where *Aenti* Sarah had just sat.

"I don't think it's funny."

"You know, I'm going to miss having you work for me." *Aenti* Chelle pulled away from the side of the street and headed for home.

"Me, too. Working for you never involved me being anywhere at six a.m. I must admit, I'm a bit spoiled."

"You should be happy she's compromising with you to meet up at eight a.m."

"Oh, I am. Believe me."

"She does mean well."

"I know." Betsy watched the neatly trimmed yards glide slowly by as they headed in a zigzag route through the village streets. "I'm nervous about this. I don't want to let anyone down."

"You won't. It won't always be easy, but if God's hand is on this, you will do well in the end."

"I hope so." She'd thought *Gotte* was on her side before, about Jacob Miller. How could she have misunderstood? So many questions she had about where she'd misjudged things with Jacob. How could she know she wasn't making another mistake?

Others seemed so sure of what they were doing, or at least they were good at pretending. If God's will was to be done, how did she know if she was going against it?

In business, in matters of the heart, she'd try to be like *Aenti* Chelle, who seemed just fine on her own all these years. If it wasn't God's will for her to find a husband, she'd do well with the idea. Or, at least convince herself she would be. God would reward her long-suffering and patience, surely.

5

*T*had woke to a soft rap on the door. "Supper's on the stove, Thaddeus."

He gave an involuntary jerk, then remembered where he was. Pinecraft, in his *mammi's haus*. The sun had swung around to the other side of the house and light no longer blazed through the window as brightly.

"*Danke, Mammi*. I'll be right out." He yawned, stretched, and listened. No more voices from the front. The aroma of supper cooking drifted under the door and his stomach responded. What time was it?

Thad sat up on the side of the bed and stretched some more. He left his room and headed for the kitchen. Maybe his socks didn't smell as ripe as he thought they did.

Mammi would probably smile and shake her head. *Mammi*, the one who never seemed to mind when he pestered her to let him help in the kitchen when he was small. He didn't know if she'd be ashamed of his chosen profession. She likely knew about it, if his parents had told her.

He hadn't been baptized into the Order, but he'd also never been back.

Thad entered the snug kitchen to find his *mammi* at the stove in front of a pan of something frying.

"*Mammi*, I've slept too long. What time is it?"

"A little after five." She smiled at him. "You were tired."

He nodded.

"So, what brings you to my doorstep?"

"I, uh . . ." He didn't want to lie, but didn't want to tell her the truth. He thought of the simplest explanation. "I need somewhere to stay, for a little while, if you have room for me. I can help out."

"You're not in trouble with the law, are you?" Her expression narrowed for a millisecond, then she turned to pull the fillets from the hot oil.

"No, no. I'm not in trouble with the law." As far as he knew, the authorities didn't suspect him of any wrongdoing, although he couldn't say the same for anyone at Dish and Spoon.

He waited for several long, drawn-out seconds for her response.

"Well, you can stay. You'd do well to see about getting a job."

"I plan on it. My job in Ohio—well, the restaurant closed." That was true enough. "I did bring some cash with me. If you need errands run, or a hand with the lawn, I can help."

She nodded. "I'm busy, Thaddeus. There's much going on here in the village, and I'll only get busier once the snowbirds begin arriving. I do have a neighbor to help with the lawn, though."

"Do you still have your job at Yoder's?"

"One day a week. I want to keep working for as long as I can."

"*Gut, gut.*" He'd switched to *Dietsch*, the sound like foreign musical notes to his ears, words he'd thought long forgotten, now spilled from his tongue.

"You remember your speech?" She stepped over to the cabinet for some plates, but not before he saw moisture in her eyes.

"Yes, *Mammi*, I do remember."

"Do you remember *Gotte*, and your *Ordnung*?"

Thad swallowed hard. "I don't remember in the same way I do the language." He bit back more words. The constricting rules, the no questions asked, the all-knowing, all-powerful deity who must be appeased, the never knowing if he was good enough for anyone in the district, let alone *Gotte*.

He'd reached a point long ago, where he didn't care to know. Life was much easier and his way seemed to work well for the rest of the world he immersed himself in. Still, the sense of right, wrong, of looking over his shoulder never left.

"No smoking in this *haus*, no alcoholic beverages. A very few number of Plain people might imbibe, but not me."

"Yes, *Mammi*." He'd quit the cigarettes cold turkey a few months ago after he threw his back out and the doctor had given him a good lecture. And, the smokes were expensive. No drinking in the house didn't bother him, either.

"I would prefer if you went to services at a good local church."

"Prefer?"

"I cannot supervise your conscience while I listen to my own, but you need to be in fellowship."

Fellowship. Sunday had long been his sleeping-in day, when he wasn't at the restaurant before dawn, working on pastries and baking.

"To be honest, I can't promise I'll go to church. But, I'll think about it."

"Well, thank you for being honest." She dished up spoonfuls of steamed vegetables, some onto each plate.

He grabbed the chance to change the subject. "You steamed these?"

"Yes, it's healthier. I bought these fresh yesterday at the market."

"I saw the market on the way in. Is it new?"

"A few years old, and so convenient for me." She picked up a plate. "Here, time to eat. There's a singing tonight in a bit, if you want to go. At Birky Square."

"*Danke*, but no, *Mammi*." He inhaled the scent of steamed vegetables, lightly buttered, and seasoned with salt and pepper. The fish, too, smelled as delicious as anything he'd eaten prepared in a chef's kitchen. He carried his plate to the table. *Mammi* poured them some drinks. Milk.

"I would have made some pie, if I'd known you were coming," she said as she sat down across from him.

He switched to English. "It's okay. I'll make a pie for you sometime."

"I heard about your baking." She paused, taking a bite of her vegetables.

"Ah, so you did." He followed her example and ate some of his fish. Lightly breaded, lemon and pepper seasoning. Flaky, perfectly cooked. "The fish is good."

"Rochelle Keim's nephew Steven caught some and gave me a few. He's quite the young fisherman. Good Mennonite boy. Quite liberal, though."

"How old is he now? About nineteen or so?"

Mammi shook her head. "Just turned twenty-three and has his own fishing charter business already. We Plain people keep him busy."

"Twenty-three?" Yes, time had passed all right, and if he took a moment to do the math, he'd have realized it was a good twelve or thirteen years since he'd visited Pinecraft.

"Right. You won't get me out on a boat like it, but Chelle goes with him if she's not working and he has space on the boat." She fell silent again, studying his tattooed arm.

"Sounds fun to me. Maybe I'll see if he has space for me, too, sometime."

"Why ever did you do it?"

"Do what?" He guessed he knew what she meant, but didn't want to presume.

"Mark your arm up." She squinted across the table at him, taking in every detail of the ink.

"Well, I liked the design. It's interesting, not obnoxious like some tattoos."

"I still don't understand why someone would adorn themselves and carve into themselves." Her tone held more disbelief than rudeness.

He couldn't explain it himself, other than the reason he'd just given her. He liked it. He liked the free expression, and appreciated the artwork of one of the most skilled tattoo artists in the Midwest.

They finished the meal in relative silence, with *Mammi* occasionally filling him in on the status of one branch of the family or another, his cousins, and his other relatives he'd once been so close to. The thought of winter coming made him pause.

"*Mammi*, do you know yet who's coming for winter vacation?"

"Not sure. Your parents, perhaps, and your brothers and sisters if they're able to afford the trip here, not to mention time off from their jobs." *Mammi* shrugged. "They'll mostly stay here, and Edna Bontrager said she has some apartments coming open for rent during the season."

"I see." Well, maybe he'd be gone by December, or January, but probably for sure by February when Pinecraft would brim with snowbirds from parts in the north.

"Have you spoken to them recently?"

"Not since last spring, when I stopped by their *haus*." He paused. "I'm sorry about *Daadi*. I miss him. I, uh, came to the funeral." They'd buried his *daadi*, his *daed's daed*, in the spring after the ground thawed in Ohio, the last time he'd spoken to his father.

"*Ach*, well, he lived a good, long life, and his time on this earth was over. I do miss him, every day." She set down her fork. "I don't remember seeing you at the funeral. I know I would have remembered."

"I sort of stayed back, near the road." He recalled parking his motorcycle and watching from around the corner of a buggy. He didn't want anyone to see him, didn't want to be a distraction or reminder to his family of the pain he'd caused them all.

"I see."

After the meal, *Mammi* cleared the table and washed the dishes while Thad brought his duffel bag and jacket to his room. He opened up the duffel, pulling out his phone from the center of the pile, along with his knife set, each knife in its own pocket inside a long, flat, sealed leather case. He stashed the case of knives inside the closet. He wouldn't need them.

He turned on his phone. Several missed calls from Stacie, several from one number he didn't recognize. One voice mail.

"Mr. Zook, this is the Columbus, Ohio, Police Department. We need to ask you a few questions about a friend of yours, a Ms. Stacie Brenner."

Rochelle Keim, known to her nieces as *Aenti* Chelle, sighed as she sorted her laundry. Two weeks away from Pinecraft was two weeks too long. However, she'd made it a priority to return to Ohio to help her family make food for her second cousin's wedding.

She should have washed one last load before leaving, but she didn't want to use the old washing tub and wringer. She didn't think about the prospect of doing laundry and tackling her long list of to-do items concerning her cleaning clients as well as finding a replacement for Betsy once her bakery took off.

Rochelle knew Betsy's chances of success in Pinecraft were excellent. With the village nestled in a city, *Englisch* as well as Amish would flock to the store once word got around. With Sarah's guidance, Betsy would have a good adviser, despite the older woman's demeanor.

Betsy was busy writing out some recipe cards while Rochelle started the washer.

Of course, Betsy's heart probably ached after watching the man she'd dreamed of fall in love with an *Englisch* woman. The newlyweds would be home in Pinecraft soon after concluding their visit to family.

Truly, Rochelle wasn't sure how Betsy would cope once the happy couple returned to Florida. Although they attended a different church from Betsy, there was always the chance to see them at singings, in the park, at the stores, or while visiting mutual friends. However, once vacation season began, the flurry of visitors might be a welcome distraction.

Rochelle knew firsthand the value of distraction. From her own walk with heartbreak, she couldn't stay in Ohio, and had made Pinecraft her home all these years. And what a treasure, to have watched her nephew grow up into a fine young man. A more liberal Mennonite than her background, to be sure, but a young man of faith. Having her sister and family nearby had proven a balm on her own wounded heart and soul, and healing had come. She'd never had the chance to raise her own family, but she lived close enough to her sister to watch her brood grow up.

Her phone warbled on the countertop. Her sister, Jolene. What timing.

"Hello there, we're home," she said when she answered the phone.

"Good," Jolene said. "We'll be home by the weekend. It was so much nicer to take our own van and drive to Ohio. You could have come with us, you know."

"Well, I wanted to ride with Betsy. Otherwise, she'd have been alone on the bus. Not as though she'd have needed my help." She said nothing further about the state of Betsy's heart. "Besides, I needed to get back here for business."

"I'm glad we stayed a few extra days. Because something happened. If you're not sitting down, you should be."

Her pulse began to race, and she could almost hear it over the whoosh of water filling up the washing machine. "What? Did something happen?"

"Belinda Fry is dead."

"No." Belinda. Her best friend in the world, when they were both very young. A stab of sorrow struck her heart. And for the first time in well over a decade, her mind drifted to someone she'd tried to keep buried in her memories. *Silas Fry.*

6

Betsy entered the real estate office with *Aenti* Sarah in her wake. Her heart pounded. Her hands shook. But she stiffened her spine and squared her shoulders as she stepped up to the reception desk.

"Good morning," she told the receptionist, a woman with tinted blonde hair and wearing an *Englisch* pantsuit. "I'm here to see Mr. Miller."

"You must be Elizabeth Yoder. He's expecting you." The woman pointed to a short hallway with four doors, two on each side. "Last door on the right."

"This is a great deal of money you're paying them," *Aenti* Sarah whispered as she trotted behind Betsy.

Betsy slowed her stride. She hadn't been thinking of how much shorter *Aenti* Sarah was than her. Instead, she'd been thinking of the bank check written out for her lease and deposit on the bakery.

"I know, *Aenti*." Oh, but yes, she had lain awake last night for hours thinking about the amount of money she'd be spending over the next six months.

Mr. Miller, the real estate agent, looked up from his desk. "Good to see you, Miss Yoder. Are you ready to sign the paperwork?"

She glanced at *Aenti* Sarah then nodded. "Yes, sir."

They took the pair of seats across from Mr. Miller as he pulled a file from the stack on his desk.

"All right, here's your lease for a period of six months, like we discussed. Read and initial each page to verify you understand what you're signing."

Betsy skimmed the pages. Yes, the zoning was in order for the property, something she'd checked before inquiring about a lease. The lease included permission for her to have modifications performed on the building to transform it into a bakery and eat-in shop. She could alter the floors, install appliances and vents, paint the walls. She would be responsible for any building permits, exterminator costs, as well as any inspections to the property for health and safety codes.

This is a great deal of money. Aenti's words rang in her ears even as the older woman sat beside her silently. She nodded as she reread the lease.

"Do you need a pen?"

Betsy looked up to see Mr. Miller holding up a pen of iridescent plastic. "Yes. Please. Thank you." They'd had the pens personalized: Miller and Stoltzfus, real estate agents. The company had come highly recommended by several in the village. The Miller and Stoltzfus families were both Mennonite, mostly, and ran a brisk business by helping conduct some of the real estate transactions in the area.

She looked at the shiny pen and blinked. *Sign.*

Betsy initialed each page after she read it, then put her signature on the line on the last page of the lease above her name. She pushed the lease back across the desk to Mr. Miller and exhaled.

"You have yourself a bakery, Miss Yoder." The man beamed.

"It's almost a bakery. We're going to start working on it right away." She wasn't sure if she should get up now, shake hands with the man. She did want to scurry back to the kitchen and get working. But she was a business owner. There was more to her bakery than baking.

"Well, you let me know when your grand opening is, and we'll be sure to bring the office staff by for a round of pie." Mr. Miller stood. "I'll make copies of the lease agreement so you can have one for your records."

Betsy nodded. "Good."

He left the room, and Betsy glanced at *Aenti* Sarah. "It's done."

"It is." Her forehead wrinkled. "What will you do if money doesn't start coming in right away?"

"It will. It has to." She would look at the possibilities of the future, otherwise the question would follow her everywhere. Betsy pulled out the envelope containing a bank check for her deposit and first month's prorated rent.

"All right, I have your copy here. And all I need from you now is a check for your deposit. You do remember we prorated your rent for the remainder of October?"

"Yes, Mr. Miller. It's all here." She held out the envelope. He tore one side off and pulled out the check.

"Very good. On the first of November, you can make your payment here or leave it in our night depository by the front door."

Betsy stood, with *Aenti* Sarah standing as well. "Thank you." No, with amounts like this, she'd make sure someone came to the office with the money in person.

"One more thing before you leave." Mr. Miller took something from his pocket. "Your keys."

"Oh yes, I'll need those." She smiled, as he jingled the pair of keys on a ring in front of her.

She tucked the keys into her pocket and slipped the copy of her lease into her tote bag before they left.

As she entered the bright Florida morning, she felt like throwing up.

"Now, we begin work. Otherwise all the money, thrown to the wind." *Aenti* Sarah shook her head and made a soft hissing noise.

The family likely would not let her forget it if she failed. No, she couldn't have stayed home to see what happened with Gideon Stoltzfus. No, she had to be the adventurous one.

Dear Gotte, please do not let me fail.

Aloud, she said, "Henry Hostetler is meeting us at the building at nine. He's going to go over plans once more before he gets started."

"Good. It never hurts to plan well. Measure twice, cut once, I believe they say." *Aenti* Sarah looked toward the corner and the traffic light. "Oh, there's Myra Beachy. I didn't know she was here in Pinecraft already. I must stop and say hello."

They continued their walk to the corner. Betsy tried to brush the cobwebs from her mind. Oh, but she was tired again this morning. She yawned, welcoming the chance to stop for a moment while *Aenti* greeted her friend and caught up with the latest news.

A figure in black pants and short-sleeved shirt, not Amish garb but *Englisch*, caught her attention. A man, a little older than her probably, walking to Yoder's with an elderly Old Order woman. Something about his posture and his face, the thin growth of beard definitely wasn't Amish. He was the man on the loud motorcycle. Here, in Pinecraft? And what was he doing walking with the Old Order woman?

"Yoo-hoo, Betsy." A singsong voice called her attention back to the pair of women beside her.

"Oh, yes." She smiled at Mrs. Beachy.

"I was asking about your pie shop. How did you choose your recipes?"

"Most are traditional recipes from my mother and *Mammi*."

"And me!" *Aenti* Sarah interjected.

Betsy had to smile at her childlike enthusiasm before continuing. "But I'm also going to try some new flavors. Like cheesecake, tiramisu, cannoli. I'll also serve fresh doughnuts and fried pies."

"Ooh, cheesecake sounds delicious. I had it once, at a restaurant in Siesta Village." Mrs. Beachy nodded. "But tiramisu?"

"It's Italian."

"But how can you be an Amish bakery with Italian desserts and such?"

"I guess we'll just have to see how people like it," was all Betsy could say. She covered her yawn.

"You need vitamins," *Aenti* Sarah said. "I'll order a bottle of Vita-Life right away."

No need to object aloud, because that wouldn't deter *Aenti*, so Betsy nodded instead. She wanted to pull her cell phone out of her tote bag in order to check the time, but discreetly, away from Mrs. Beachy.

The light changed and the two older women finished their conversation. They hurried across busy Bahia Vista. From here, Betsy could barely see the edge of the lawn on her rental property.

Her rental. Her business. Her dream. All with her family and God's help.

"*Aenti*." She said as they paused on the other side of the street. "Thank you."

"Ah, it's nothing." But a grin tugged at the corners of the older woman's mouth.

⌘

Thad still hadn't made a return call to the Columbus police. But he worried about Stacie. Something had happened to her, something bad if the police knew she'd called him. Of course, all the way down here in Florida, he couldn't check on Ohio news, not counting *The Budget* newspaper.

He needed to find an Internet connection somewhere and borrow a computer. *Mammi* might know someone with a computer and Internet connection, but then again, maybe not. Computers were the gateway to evil, especially with the Internet. He didn't want to turn his phone on again. What if someone were tracking him?

Now he and *Mammi* stood in Yoder's market, with her selecting an item here and an item there for her basket. He was along to carry bags home, just one way he could make himself useful for her.

"You look nervous as a long-tailed cat in a room full of rocking chairs," *Mammi* observed.

"Sorry." He stepped aside for an older couple to shuffle past, the woman holding onto her husband's arm, and him looking tenderly at her. Her white hair matched his long beard that reached almost midway down his chest.

"If you have something you need to do, don't let me stop you. I can always wait for you to come back and get my bag."

"I, uh, I need to find a computer around here. For a few minutes."

"I see. Well, I'll have to think. There are a few." She pushed the cart toward the service counter. "I know Rochelle Keim has one. She has a cleaning business and advertises on the Internet."

"On the Internet. Is she Amish?" He dared himself to ask the question aloud.

"No, but her family used to be. She's Mennonite."

As if that should explain everything. Pinecraft had turned his entire experience with his people upside down. Cell phones, Internet, electricity.

When he was a child, he'd accepted the electricity and a few modern conveniences as part of "vacation," and not to be discussed upon arrival home to Ohio. But here, in the open?

"I'll give you her address and you can go by."

"Okay. Thank you."

At last, his nerves settled down for a few minutes. He tried not to fidget or start rushing on the way home. But after getting *Mammi* safely home with her groceries and getting Rochelle Keim's address, he revved up his motorcycle and headed through the neighborhoods.

The sound of the motorcycle's engine bounced off walls and made a few residents look up from their yard work, then turn their attention back to their lawns or gardens.

He found Rochelle's house on Schrock Street easily enough. A blue-gray van was parked in the driveway. It had a magnetic sign "Keim Cleaning" and a phone number.

He ambled up to the front door and knocked.

A woman with brown hair pulled back and topped by a white *kapp* met him at the door. Her cape dress matched the blue of the sky. She looked younger than his mother. Her gaze took in his clothing and his lack of shaving for three days. He'd left his helmet on the seat of his motorcycle.

"Yes?"

"Miss Keim? I'm Thaddeus Zook. My *mammi* is Esther Zook and I'm staying with her in the village. She said you have a computer and Internet?"

"Ah, I see. I know Esther. And yes, I do have Internet access."

"I, um, I was wondering if I could use it for a few moments? I need to look something up. And it's nothing bad, either, I promise." He realized he should have called ahead. But *Mammi* didn't have a phone and probably didn't think about such things.

"If you don't mind waiting here a moment, I'll be right back."

"Sure, no problem."

She nodded, then left. Through the screen door he saw into a tidy house with a ceramic tile floor. He heard her voice, murmuring something. Of course. She was calling someone who'd vouch for him. But no one knew he was here, besides *Mammi*, and maybe her quilting friends from yesterday.

Rochelle returned about thirty seconds later, her slippers making a soft scuff on the floor. "Come on in. I called a friend, who said she'd seen you at Esther's yesterday and said your *mammi* took you right in. I hope you understand. I don't usually have strangers at my door asking to use the computer."

"Yes, I don't blame you. Can't be too careful nowadays."

Rochelle unlatched the screen door and opened it for him. He stepped into the living room. A cool breeze swirled through, giving the home natural ventilation.

"My laptop's right here at the kitchen table." She motioned to a chair. "Here. Help yourself. The browser's already open." She picked up a stack of files.

"Thanks, Ms. Keim."

"You're welcome. Use it as long as you need to. Will you need to print anything out?"

"No, no. I'm just checking on news back in Ohio." This was truthful enough. He sat down at the wooden bowback chair.

"So you're just visiting Pinecraft, then?"

"I am, for a while." He typed in a search engine name. "I used to come here in the winter when I was a kid. But it's been many years."

After the website loaded, he typed in *Columbus Ohio Stacie Brenner*, and clicked enter. A list of sites popped up on the screen, mostly the ones people used to track people down. But a news page four links down from the top caught his eye.

Columbus woman attacked in home invasion.

He clicked on the link and the whole story filled the screen.

Twenty-five year old Stacie Brenner was the victim of a home invasion Monday evening in her Columbus suburb. Sometime around eight p.m., she opened the door of her apartment to a visitor, unaware of what would unfold. The intruder struck her about the face and upper body, punching and possibly kicking her stomach. There is evidence Brenner may have fought back as well.

A neighbor heard screaming and called 911. The attacker fled and left before EMS arrived, who found Brenner unconscious at the scene.

Brenner remains in a Columbus Hospital with internal injuries, a head injury, broken ribs, and a fractured jaw. Her valuables, including a television and computer system, remained untouched, although the apartment revealed signs of being searched. Her apartment complex is cooperating fully with the investigation. Anyone with information about the attack is urged to call Columbus PD.

He frowned. What was it she'd said the other night, someone was at the door?

She'd mentioned it right before they'd both gotten off the phone.

"Are you all right?" Mrs. Keim stood by the table. "You look as though you're about to be ill."

"I'm—I'm fine. I just found out some bad news about a friend back home. She's hurt, and in the hospital." He didn't want to say more.

"I'm sorry to hear it. What's her name? I can put her on my prayer list." The woman's tone was soft, caring, as though it were her own friend who lay in the hospital.

"Stacie. Thanks. It's all I wanted to find out, if she was okay." He closed the browser window. He'd been tempted to look up information about Mitch's case, and Dish and Spoon, but thought better of it. Enough digging around for today. He couldn't do anything for Stacie now, except what he'd been putting off—calling the police. He rose from the chair.

"I'm glad I was able to help."

He headed for the front door, and she followed. "Tell your *mammi* I said hello."

"I'll do that. Thank you again." He gave her a quick wave and went to his motorcycle.

His helmet was missing.

He glanced around the neighborhood, but no cars drove past. A few vehicles stood in driveways. The street appeared stretched out to take a nap in the pre-noon sun.

The helmet had cost him plenty, with its state-of-the-art safety technology and ventilation. No doubt the thief, who-ever it was, had made off with the helmet, chuckling all the way to a pawn shop or home to put it on Craigslist and sell it anonymously.

He revved the engine, the sound reflecting his anger. Normally, he didn't ride without a helmet after losing a friend several years ago to a motorcycle accident, but he wasn't about to walk his motorcycle all the way back to *Mammi's* house.

As soon as he got home, he'd call the Columbus PD and do what he could for Stacie. They needn't know he was in Florida and he wouldn't tell them unless they asked. He didn't like the feeling of looking over his shoulder.

Stacie didn't deserve what happened to her. When they were together, she was sweet, a bit clingy, and ready to drag him to the altar. And he didn't deserve her either. A woman deserved a man willing to commit to her completely.

But he couldn't, not with his old world, his old life following him at every turn. There were worse things than having an expensive helmet stolen.

⟳

Pete Stucenski crossed another employee's name off his list. The server, a college student at the university, was in tears when he left her. But not because of how he spoke to her. His mother had taught him better.

"Treat a lady like a lady, and she'll be good to you." It hadn't worked out for him in the love department, but it always helped in business.

Caitlyn, the sniveling server, had been the one to find Mitch's body in the restaurant when she went back to get her cell phone after her shift was over and the restaurant was long closed.

"I can still see him there, just lying on the floor, with blood everywhere. And his head—" She hiccuped a sob.

No, she didn't know anything. Mitch hadn't asked her for any help with office business, either. She was one of those kids focused on her education and future career. And at work, she didn't have access to anything in the back of the house. If she had, it would have already raised questions.

The restaurant employed twenty, and after this one, he had one more name. Thad Zook. Now what kind of a last name was that? Of course, his own name wasn't much better.

Thad Zook, pastry chef. Plenty of access to the back of the house, arrived early, often worked late. The dark, brooding kind of chef, and you didn't make fun of his food. Got his work done and stayed out of trouble. He had Thad's number from the employee list, so he punched it into his phone.

Straight to voice mail. "This is Thad, I can't take your call right now. Leave a message, and I'll get back to you."

"Hey, Thad, this is Pete Stucenski with Dish and Spoon. I wanted to talk to you about Mitch. It's been hard on all of us, and, uh, well, I'm hoping to reopen the restaurant as soon as possible. I just need to know how many staff I'll be able to get to come back. Anyway, call me if you get a chance."

He'd do like he did with Caitlyn and the others. If he received no answer to his call, he'd leave a message and follow up with a visit to their home. Pete entered Thad's address in his GPS and within fifteen minutes had pulled up at an apartment complex. Not ritzy, but not a complete dive, either.

Pete strolled to Thad's building and climbed the stairs to the second floor unit, apartment two. He knocked on the door, not threateningly, but boldly enough so anyone sleeping could hear it.

A young woman stuck her head out the door of the unit beside Thad's. "He's not there. Not anymore."

"What do you mean?" Pete held his balled-up hand in midair, prepared to knock again. "Is he just out?"

"No, he left. Skipped out. The manager was pretty upset. Left boxes of stuff in there. I got a nice pan set, though."

"Oh, that's too bad. I'm his boss, actually his boss's business partner. We had to close the business temporarily, but I wanted to let him know he could get his old job back." Pete smiled, lowering his hand to his side. "Did he say if he was going anywhere?"

"Nah." The blonde emerged from her apartment, a baby on her hip. "We talked every once in a while. He kept weird hours and I was always apologizing if the baby crying kept him awake. Nice guy."

"Yes, Thad's a good guy. Which is why we want him back." Pete scratched his head, then scanned the parking lot. "So, do you know anything about his family, where he's from originally?"

She shook her head. "Not a lot. They sounded super religious and he said he didn't have much to do with them anymore. Sad. We all need family."

"Yes, we certainly do." Pete's pulse raced. "Well, thanks, anyway. I guess he won't be coming back here, then."

"No, probably not." A phone warbled off in the distance somewhere. "I've got to go."

"Thanks for your help." Pete turned and descended the stairs.

Mr. Zook, where'd you skip off to? Only a matter of time, and he'd find him.

He dialed Channing's number as he crossed the parking lot. "It's me. I'm done with my list."

"Tell me you've had luck. Everyone else is coming out squeaky clean once we dig enough."

"One name on my list—Thad Zook—has skipped town it seems."

"I trust you're going to follow up."

"Of course I am."

"Find those files."

"I'm working on it. Okay? I mean, the election's coming up and you've got the lead for now."

"And that's why nothing can screw this up, before or after Election Day." The line went dead.

7

After one week of work on the building for Pinecraft Pies and Pastry, Betsy tried not to appear too giddy. She yawned and immediately felt like a lie abed. She hadn't been able to shake the sensation of exhaustion too early in the day. Of course, she had said nothing more to *Aenti* Sarah or Chelle about it. The best explanation had to be her busy-ness, the travel from Ohio, and a feeling of gloom after the wedding.

But young people weren't supposed to tire like a *mammi* or a *daadi* might.

Henry Hostetler, as old as her *daadi,* had made swift work of the demolition inside the future bakery with nary a word of feeling tired.

Small holes in the walls had been patched. Other walls framing the bedrooms had been removed to make way for a wide-open kitchen to hold the ovens and stove and commercial refrigerator and freezer. The space wasn't ready yet for the stainless steel prep table to run the length of one wall, nor the big rectangular work table to sit in the center of the kitchen.

But no one would take this for a two-bedroom box of a cinderblock home anymore. Someone had built it back in the 1940s and the structure still retained its character. An elderly neighbor had stopped by during the first day of demolition and showed her a photograph of the house from the mid-1950s. A sandy, shelled road ran in front of the building instead of the asphalt now.

Betsy tried not to sneeze at the dust. Henry Hostetler had discovered a leak in the roof and patched it. Now, he and his worker were replacing the entire ceiling with new Sheetrock.

He stood in the center of the future bakery's work area and mopped his forehead with the back of his arm. "Well, I have an idea that is a little more work, but might save you some money in the long run."

"What?" She already knew the amount of the running tab, and had hoped to order the appliances next week.

"Seeing as how the rear corner of the building is the original kitchen, I say we turn it and the rear bedroom into your work area."

"But the bathroom. It's in the middle."

"We keep the bathroom where it is, but make it a wash-room, removing the bath tub. This will let you have a work area in the kitchen, and a small walkway to the other corner of the building where you can keep your freezers and pan-try." He stepped past the current bathroom doorway. "This way you have a restroom for your customers. The front corner, just inside the front door, can be your sales area with the display cases. The opposite front end of the building, past the front door, is where you can set up your booths or tables. I'd go with tables. You can rearrange them, but you can't move booths."

She nodded. "That makes sense to me. I didn't know what we were going to do about the bathroom placement there, but I knew we had to have one for customers."

Sunlight streamed through the back door of the building. A scratching noise on the metal made Betsy stare at the door. "What could that be?" Florida had its share of lizards and other creatures, but none of them sounded like this. None she knew of.

She strode to the door and peered through the screen. A dog with fur the color of dark cinnamon and short legs, a long pointed nose, and a body as round as a stuffed sausage, stared up at her. His tongue hung out, almost in a lopsided grin. He shook his head, and his long ears flopped side to side.

"What are you doing here? We're not open yet. Perhaps you'd rather visit a butcher shop."

In response, the dog settled back on his haunches, then shifted his weight so he appeared to sit up, his paws tucked up under his chest.

"I don't have anything for you to eat, little dog."

"Who's that you're talking to?" Henry squinted at the sunlight.

"A dog. Maybe it's a stray." The Amish weren't ones to have animals for pets, not her family anyway, but maybe this was one of the few dogs in the village, out wandering for a morning stroll.

"Ah, that's a dachshund, it is. Used to be hunting dogs, they were. Nowadays, like this fellow, they're good at hunting down meals." Henry picked up a measuring tape from his worktable.

"Well, little dog, you're at the wrong door if you're looking for food. Nothing here yet."

The dog's response was an enthusiastic whip of his skinny tail, the slimmest part of his rotund body.

"Henry, do you know whose dog this might be?"

"Can't say I've seen him around the village before. Maybe he'll mosey along and find his way home." Henry pulled a notepad from his shirt pocket and headed for the nearest wall framing the bathroom.

"I suppose."

The front door opened and a voice called, "Here I am, come to see the progress."

Aenti Sarah stopped in the doorway, then sneezed. "Now, this is something else. What happened to the walls? And the ceiling?" She darted a glance above her head.

Betsy left the doorway and stepped over the wood on the floor where the wall had once stood. She explained to *Aenti* what Henry had suggested, and *Aenti* Sarah bobbed her head.

"I don't want to do more construction than necessary, but then I don't want to have to hire a plumber to move plumbing lines if we put the sink on an inner wall. Good sense."

The dog barked, the sound drowning out *Aenti* Sarah's voice.

Betsy moved back to the door. "You don't like being ignored, do you?"

"Who are you talking to?"

"A dog, *Aenti* Sarah."

She shook her head. "I must go to visit a sick friend today, but I wanted to see the progress on the bakery first."

"I think Mr. Hostetler's done a fine job so far."

"Why, thank you, Betsy." Henry let the measuring tape snap back into its roll. "I'm planning to sign off around two today."

"That's fine with me. I have some clients I must visit this afternoon, so I'll leave you to lock up."

Betsy gathered her tote bag and followed *Aenti* Sarah outside to the front lawn. "So, what do you think?"

"I'll let you know when we open and start selling pies."

Betsy unlocked her bicycle from a nearby pole. She knew better than to counter with a lengthy reply. "All right, *Aenti*."

She watched *Aenti* Sarah climb onto her three-wheeler and head off down the street. Then she allowed herself a yawn. Maybe a nap would be in order before she visited her afternoon housecleaning clients. She needed to continue earning

her own money until the bakery could pay the bills and support her.

The sound of claws clicking on the pavement made her
look down. The cinnamon-colored dog stopped by her bicycle
and sat like a lump on the asphalt.

"Go home," Betsy said. She pushed off with her foot and
began pedaling along the street. She didn't turn around, but
listened to the click-clack of claws behind her.

Maybe if she ignored the dog, it would go find its home.
She continued along, with more clickety-clack. She reached
the traffic light at Bahia Vista.

"No, go home." The four-lane road was dangerous enough
for humans, not to mention a short, chubby dog too adventurous for its own good. If she ignored him, surely he'd find
someone else to follow.

The light changed and she pedaled through the crosswalk
along with a few pedestrians and a lone cyclist like herself. Not
too much longer, and the area would swarm with Plain people
from all over the place and there'd be tricycle traffic jams.

The light turned yellow just as she reached the other side,
and she couldn't resist the urge to glance back and see if the
cinnamon dog had followed. He paced sided to side, then
darted into the street toward her as the light clicked red. A few
cars rolled forward, then stopped.

He reached her rear tire in time to escape the traffic, his tail
whipping side to side.

"Well, you certainly look proud of yourself. Don't you know
you're not supposed to be prideful? Or run across when the
light turns red?"

The dog sat, almost smiling at her. He cocked his narrow
head to one side and panted.

"Come on, then, and I'll get you some water. This must be the most you've exerted yourself in quite some time." She pedaled along the street, and the clicking of claws grew slower.

Betsy stopped again. The little fellow plopped on the side of the road beside someone's mailbox. She braked, then climbed off the bike.

"Here." She hesitated for a millisecond, then scooped the dog up in her arms. "You can ride in style." She carried him to the basket on her bike and deposited him inside. He propped his paws on the edge and looked up with brown eyes, round as marbles, and panted.

A dog. What would she do with a dog? Would *Aenti* Chelle let her keep him in the house? She'd never had a real house pet before. The family's farm had an abundance of cats, yet none of them stayed in anyone's house.

She coasted up the driveway and glided along the sidewalk to the front door. The storm door was open to let fresh air inside.

"*Aenti?*" She popped the kickstand down, then slung her tote bag over her shoulder, and scooped up the dog. She entered the cool house.

"In the kitchen."

"Um, I found a dog at the shop today. Or, he found me." She entered the kitchen and set the dachshund on the tiles. He waddled over to *Aenti*, his tail wagging.

"He seems like a friendly little guy." *Aenti* Chelle crouched down to pet him, upon which he flopped down and rolled to the side.

"I'm going to give him some water, if you don't mind."

"Of course." Her *aenti* rubbed the dog's belly.

Betsy found a plastic bowl and filled it, then placed it on the floor by the wall. The dog rolled, ungracefully, to his feet and shot over to the bowl, where he began lapping up the water.

"Thirsty critter," *Aenti* Chelle commented. "Well, I'm off to a client's this afternoon. Do you have your appointments squared away?"

"Yes, ma'am. I have two homes over on Beneva, and one on Fruitland Road."

"Should I wait for you, or will you take your bicycle?"

"I'll take my bicycle."

Aenti Chelle grabbed her keys from the kitchen island. "Be safe, and I'll see you at supper. If you want, you can leave your dog on the lanai until we get home. He should be fine out there."

"Okay. I'll start asking in the village if anyone has lost a dog."

"Or ask Imogene. She might get the word around."

Her *aenti* left them to themselves, and Betsy's stomach growled. The clock said 11:45, so she had just enough time to eat a sandwich before leaving to do her work.

Betsy scrubbed her hands at the faucet. Once she dried her hands, she reached up to remove her head covering so she could smooth her wisps of hair. When she removed the covering, a handful of hair came off along with it.

Her heart pounded. This was more than the usual hair that came off during a brushing.

Gotte, what is wrong with me? Aside from feeling more tired than usual, everything else seemed fine. Maybe *Aenti* Sarah was right. Vitamins should take care of the problem.

⸱⸱⸱

Thad had talked to the Columbus Police Department about a week ago, but the memory of the conversation followed him throughout the following days. Poor Stacie.

He'd made himself useful for *Mammi*, trying to distract himself by sprucing up *Mammi's* yard, front and back.

Yes, she had someone mow the lawn, but there were little things to tend, like tightening the drain spouts and restringing her clothesline. Thad knew how to use a screwdriver, swing a hammer, and do passable construction on small projects, although it wasn't his favorite thing to do. The house's slate blue trim needed scraping and painting, its surface peeled by the Florida sun. *Mammi* had selected a similar shade for the trim. The house would look fresh by the time he was finished with today's project. Today, Thad kept busy by taking care of the trim, letting his mind wander while he scraped and *Mammi* fussed over her tropical hibiscus plants. He'd already scaled the ladder to trim dry leaves from the palm tree in one corner of the yard.

His mind again took him back to the talk he'd had with the police. They didn't seem to consider him a suspect, especially since he was on the phone when Stacie's intruders arrived, and his location didn't place him at the scene of the home invasion. When they asked where he was at the time they spoke, he confirmed he was at an out-of-state rest stop in the pouring rain. He didn't know if they had the GPS tracking availability, but knew someone could probably place him there at the rest stop beside the highway.

No, he didn't know if anyone had been following Stacie. Yes, they had dated for a time, but he'd broken things off with her because he wasn't ready for the altar, and she was. They'd parted as friends.

Not being a suspect relieved him.

But a voice mail from Pete Stucenski, Mitch's business partner? Now it jangled his nerves a bit. The guy used to wander in and out of the restaurant, checking on his investment, occasionally chatting with the suits who frequented Dish and Spoon for a late supper, usually the last sitting of the evening.

Those suppers meant discreet conversations lasting until after closing. Thad was usually cleaning up and leaving so he could get a good night's rest before coming back early the next morning.

Stucenski reminded him of a used-car salesman, slick and chatty, but all the while making you wonder what he really wanted. Thad was glad to have given up on cars and switched to a cycle. Motorcycle salesman, now they could sell to you, but you were happy about it the entire time.

"And so that's the reason why we're having a benefit haystack supper Saturday night," *Mammi* was saying.

A haystack supper in Pinecraft? Now, something like a haystack supper would be a good thing and another welcome diversion. He'd missed the reason she gave for the fundraiser, but the food likely wouldn't be beat.

The sound of an approaching vehicle made Thad glance past *Mammi* to the street. A minivan rolled up to the mailbox and parked. Its side bore a magnetic sign: Hostetler Handyman.

An elderly man, not as old as *Mammi* but older than his *daed*, passed the front of the van and strolled into their yard.

"How-do, Mrs. Zook?"

"Hello, Henry, I'm doing well, especially with my grandson Thaddeus visiting."

The man craned a look up at Thad, still keeping his balance on the ladder, and holding a scraper in one hand. "Nice to meet you. I'm Henry Hostetler."

"I've heard of you, Mr. Hostetler."

"All lies, except for the good parts. But you can just call me Henry." He grinned and his face crinkled into a smile framed by wrinkles from the sun. "Mrs. Zook, I wanted to see if you would donate some desserts for the haystack supper on Saturday. My sister-in-law Melba's feeling poorly and can't make her part of the desserts."

"Why, I most certainly can."

Thad climbed down from the ladder and joined the pair on ground level. "So who's the haystack supper for again?"

"For the flood victims in Mississippi," *Mammi* said, giving him a scolding look. "I told you not five minutes ago, and you said you would be willing to help, too."

"Uh . . ."

"When I asked if you'd help me, you nodded yes."

He had. He'd nodded to something. Now Henry and *Mammi* both stared at him. "I'm—I'm sorry. My mind was somewhere else."

"Well, make your mind come back here," *Mammi* chided.

"Yes, ma'am." He felt repentant for not listening to his elder, but her mock outrage, he knew, held a warmth behind it.

"So how long you here for, Thaddeus?" Henry asked.

"Uh, I'm not sure."

"This place is not quite as dead as a ghost town, but just you wait. The season will come roaring in on the Pioneer Trails buses, and you'll run out of time before you run out of things to do and people to visit."

No awkward questions from this man, thankfully.

"I don't mind the quiet," Thad said aloud. Not too much. The evenings were quiet as all get-out. He missed the news, keeping up with local events, more than *The Budget* newspaper each week. He wasn't much on small talk or visiting for hours, either.

"You looking for work while you're here?"

"Maybe." Thad glanced at *Mammi*, who'd turned to face her plants and pick at wilted flowers. "Not sure how long I'll be here. I'm a pastry chef by trade."

"Huh. You don't say. Looking for a cooking job?"

"I'm not sure." He hesitated. He longed to be back in the kitchen, but if anyone did look for him, an upscale restaurant was likely the first place they'd go. As long as no one knew he was in Florida . . .

"Fair enough answer." Henry looked at *Mammi.* "So, can you make some pie or cobbler? Because it's what Melba signed up for."

"I can make both," *Mammi* said.

"Well, I should finish scraping. The trim's not going to paint itself, either." Thad headed for the ladder and scaled it once more, then picked the scraper from the rain gutter. He continued peeling off the old paint, preparing for the new.

He wished he could shed *his* old life so easily. But here he was, his childhood past in his face yet again. He didn't get the intonations of disapproval as much as he would back in Ohio among his family there. *Mammi* had been nothing less than loving and kind, letting him stay in her home and helping her. There wasn't much to do to make it look better, and he didn't want to rattle around doing nothing.

With Henry's reminder of the winter season coming with all its visitors, Thad wondered if any of his friends from the old days would come. He'd be a misfit again, like he was now, only be reminded of it more so. Their opinion shouldn't matter, but still . . .

Murmuring voices drifted his way as Henry walked back to his minivan, *Mammi* chatting away as she walked with him.

"Doesn't say much, does he?" Henry asked.

"He always was the quiet one. But he takes it all in, you can tell. Pray for him, Henry."

"I will, Mrs. Zook. I will."

Thad didn't miss the glance Henry sent his way. A fatherly glance, more than he'd ever seen from his own *daed.*

A lump swelled in his throat, and he kept scraping old paint from the house.

8

Aenti Sarah arrived at *Aenti* Chelle's promptly at noon on Saturday. The afternoon would be spent preparing cupcakes for the haystack supper that night at Pinecraft Park. Winston, as Betsy had dubbed the dog, announced Sarah's presence with a furious bark.

"What is this beast?" *Aenti* Sarah asked when Betsy opened the door for her, nudging Winston out of the way with her foot.

"This is Winston. He's visiting for a while. I'm trying to find his owner." Betsy glared at the dog. "Hush. This is *Aenti* Sarah. She's family."

"I've brought something for you," *Aenti* announced as she followed Betsy into the kitchen. "Applebaum's Energy Elixir, in gel tablets."

"Applebaum's Energy Elixir?"

"Yes. I saw it in *The Budget* and ordered a box for you. I only brought one bottle to begin with. There's a money-back guarantee if it doesn't work."

"What's in it?"

"Herbs, all kinds of healthy things supposed to help give you more energy. Two pills a day per bottle, so you should have enough for a month."

Betsy accepted the bottle from *Aenti* Sarah. "Well, thank you." She would take a moment later to read the label before she tried the pills. She and her friends enjoy a good laugh over some of the ads for nontraditional remedies promising all kinds of things for good health.

She hadn't told anyone about some of her hair falling out, not even Miriam back in Ohio. And it hadn't seemed to happen again after the one incident the other day. And she'd seemed to have a little bit more energy. Likely, the concern was all in her head. Or on it. She set the bottle on the counter, in the corner away from all the baking supplies spread out everywhere.

Then the three of them began the work of baking cupcakes, no fewer than two hundred forty. Betsy prepared the fillings, some whipped cream filling, others cream cheese and chocolate chips, but all would be graced with her homemade buttercream icing. If she didn't think so herself, she'd have said it was the best buttercream anyone could want: sweet, with real butter, yet not too sweet. The chocolate icing was fudgy and rich.

She might add cupcakes to her menu. This would be ideal for older people who lived alone or a couple who didn't have children around to eat sweets. However, her *daadi* always managed to sneak another slice of the whole pie when someone wasn't looking.

Part of her wanted to spend the afternoon at the shop, watching Henry and his helper making progress on the renovations. A day of rain had hampered some of their efforts on Thursday, but Henry had brought a pop-up canopy and set it up over the uncovered patio out back.

She'd stayed up late last night, writing press releases for the shop. Several local newspapers would run a simple brief no-cost community announcement. The same newspapers also offered to run a paid advertisement complete with a graphic, but she had nothing designed and no pictures of the finished building yet.

In the morning, *Aenti* Chelle had helped e-mail the press releases. Betsy had tried using the computer a few times, but the idea of the world at her fingertips almost tied her fingers in knots. Plus, would her parents approve? She didn't really need a computer for "work," as a few Amish managed to justify some computer use for their jobs at factories and such.

Her mixer whirred the softened cream cheese in the bowl, and Betsy added powdered sugar to the mix to create a sweet, yet tangy filling. She stopped the mixer for a moment, scraped the sides of the bowl, and restarted it. Before she whipped the cheese too much, she sprinkled in chocolate chips.

"I can't say as I've ever had cupcakes with filling like this before," *Aenti* Sarah said above the dull roar of the mixers. She slowed her mixer, then increased the speed again. "Using this mixer gives my wrist a break, but I don't think it makes the baking any easier. Why do we have to rush? I can mix just fine by hand." She shook her head.

"Why, *Aenti* Sarah, it's all right if you want to mix by hand. I guess I've gotten used to using the electric mixer."

The admission didn't bother her. Certainly, a year ago she would have never imagined saying such a thing. Trying the electric appliance, yes. It was oh, so nice to let the mixer do the hard work while she read the recipe or washed a dish or two.

Winston, in the meantime, watched them from his favorite spot by the wall. In the course of a few days, he'd grown to be part of the household. No one in the village recognized the dog. A Mennonite neighbor suggested they bring him to the vet for a checkup and to see if he had a microchip implanted. The appointment was set for Monday, and Betsy dreaded it.

Aenti Chelle looked up from where she stood, filling the cupcake tin with batter. "You look worried, Betsy."

"It's nothing. I'm borrowing trouble, as my *maam* would say." She grabbed a teaspoon and took a bite of the sweet cupcake filling. Her taste buds rejoiced, but the flavor did little to quell her swirling thoughts.

Aenti Sarah turned off her mixer. "Today has enough troubles of its own. We need to get these cupcakes finished on time and delivered to the park on time. It's plenty to worry about right now."

The next two hours passed in a blur of batter, cupcake papers, and sticky fingers from cake and filling. Betsy's worries left her alone while she busied herself in the baking. In a few weeks, at the grand opening, she'd be doing much the same. Perhaps *daed* and the family were right in assigning *Aenti* Sarah to help. True, the older woman's demeanor was a bit prickly at times, but she was a hard worker and had the best of intentions.

At last, they stowed the cupcakes in foil-lined cardboard box lids and had all twenty dozen loaded into the back of *Aenti* Chelle's van. Betsy wanted to wander off for a nap, with Winston flopped on the foot of her bed, but knew the option was unrealistic. Instead, she read the label of Applebaum's elixir, then poured a glass of water and downed one of the gel caps.

She did take a moment to change her dress before leaving as well as brush her hair and put it back up under a fresh covering.

"Elizabeth? We're ready to go." Betsy didn't miss the note of urgency in *Aenti* Sarah's voice.

"Coming!" She glanced to the floor. "Come, Winston, you need to stay on the lanai while we're gone." He scampered past her as she walked the hallway to the kitchen.

She opened the sliding glass door and Winston trotted out into the screened area.

"You be good and watch the house while we're gone." There was no real concern for safety; however, she reminded herself Pinecraft was in the middle of a city and anyone could wander through the neighborhood.

After checking to be sure the makeshift cupcake carriers weren't off balance in the rear of the van, Betsy buckled her seatbelt and they pulled out for the short journey to Pinecraft Park. Riding in a motored vehicle had become a natural part of living in the village, but part of her missed the soft sway of a buggy and the view of the countryside drifting past as the horses pulled them along.

Within three minutes, they'd navigated the quiet streets to arrive at Pinecraft Park. Someone had set up tables under the pavilion for serving food. White tablecloths, held down by containers of food, flapped in the light breeze.

A modest-size crowd, especially for mid-fall, had gathered. Some wore the traditional clothing of the Plain people, as Betsy did. Others worse simple skirts and blouses. Still others wore typical *Englisch*-style clothing of denim jeans or slacks for men, while some ladies wore capris. She'd heard someone call Pinecraft a "kaleidoscope," and after she found out what a kaleidoscope was, she had to agree. All different types of Amish and Mennonites, tumbled together in a group. Somehow, particularly on nights like tonight, the blend worked well.

Betsy caught a whiff of the food when she slid open the van door.

"Great, you're here!" called out a woman in plaid capris and a white cotton T-shirt. She marched to the back of the van. "Desserts, right?"

"Right. Cupcakes, three kinds, some filled and some plain inside." Betsy touched the edge of her covering, which felt ready to slip from her head. "I can help you serve them if you'd like."

"Of course, come on over to the table."

Betsy pulled a tray of cupcakes from the rear of the van, then followed the woman in capris to the pavilion, with the *aentis* following behind her. This was her recipe, her way to change a simple cupcake into something a little different.

The crowd milled about, transforming itself into a line. Someone whistled, and the group fell silent.

"Thank you all for coming," said a bearded man at the head of the first table, where someone had placed a stack of plates. "I'd like to ask a word of prayer before we pass through the line. Make sure you have a meal ticket purchased from Edna Troyer at the small table in the corner, and turn your ticket in to the first person at the serving line."

Betsy scanned the crowd as they bowed their heads. A figure midway down the line caught her attention. A man, wearing all black, a faint shadow of beard on his face. Today he wasn't astride a motorcycle or walking with a *mammi* in the village. Whoever he was, he had sat at the end of the Millers' driveway in Ohio not two weeks ago.

Although she'd pondered the idea of Pinecraft being a kaleidoscope, this man definitely stood out from the rest of the group, as varied as they all looked.

He, in turn, scanned the crowd as well, his gaze falling on the desserts.

Bishop Smucker began to pray aloud over the food before the supper began.

The man in black's focus drifted upwards and met Betsy's stare.

He winked at her before bowing his head.

Her cheeks burned as she shot a look down at her cupcakes, then closed her eyes. Served her right for gawking. Before she'd ripped away from the force of his stare, she caught something in his own expression.

Sorrow, regret, and something like longing.

❧

Thad passed through the line, piling his plate with the makings of a fine supper. Earlier, he'd balked at the idea of going to the haystack fundraiser.

"I'll send a donation and you can bring me a plate."

"No, if you're helping me take the food, you ought to stay." No arguing with *Mammi*.

So there he stood in the line, listening to the chatter of people around him. He couldn't believe his nerve, winking at the tall Amish young woman on the serving line. She looked vaguely familiar, which surprised him. Maybe she was someone he'd known growing up, or maybe not.

She moved with a certain grace, with her capable hands passing out cupcakes to those here for supper. She smiled at one older woman, and a dimple appeared on one cheek. She laughed, then quieted her expression, glancing around.

Their eyes met again and she snapped hers to the person beside him, namely *Mammi*, then back down to the cupcakes.

A grin tugged at one side of his mouth. His knew his appearance definitely didn't match the Plain people surrounding him, or even their more liberal counterparts, friends, and relatives. Yet, he couldn't see himself going to a local department store to find a T-shirt, khaki shorts, and flip-flops to look more like a tourist.

Because he wasn't a tourist. *Vagabond* seemed to fit better at this point. Maybe one day he'd get the flip-flops and khakis, but not today.

A few more steps, and he'd be directly in front of the blonde. She had full cheeks and although her cape dress did its modest job, Thad ventured a guess curves lurked beneath its full and proper fit.

Goodness, man. You don't even know if she's married or not. But he was not looking to meet anyone at this point in his life. However, he normally didn't wonder about married women or admire them too much. Enough of his upbringing had stayed with him. He had enough respect for marriage not to tread where he shouldn't as a single man.

"Cupcake?" she asked when he stepped up across from her.

"What kind are they?" he countered.

"These are chocolate, filled with a mix of cream cheese and chocolate chips. The others are vanilla, with a white chocolate filling."

"White chocolate? Is it a pudding, or more of a ganache?" He couldn't resist giving her a little culinary banter.

"Ganache?" She blinked at him. "I—I'm not quite sure what it is."

"It's a blend of chocolate and cream."

"Oh, I see." Two bright pink spots appeared on her cheeks. "Well, which one do you want?"

"One of each, please."

"Um, all right." She slid a pair of cupcakes onto the paper dessert plate he balanced on his right palm.

"Thank you, Miss, or Mrs. . . . ?"

"Miss Yoder." She spoke her name to the cupcakes in front of her and didn't look up at him through her pretty eyelashes.

He moved on, but only so he wouldn't see her dive underneath the table, something he was afraid she'd do if he continued to speak to her so boldly.

Nope, not married and yet quite young. The difference between the older Amish women was they were friendlier to him, for sure. Anyone under forty, or even younger, didn't talk to him. Which was fine with him, anyway.

Thad reached the end of the line and the beverage table, but his hands had enough to carry. He'd come back for a cup of pop once he found a seat. Some people carried their plates home, but, of course *Mammi* took a place at a picnic table. She tapped the empty spot beside her when she caught him looking.

"Here, sit." *Mammi* shifted and made room for him. He was the sole male at a table of biddies in bonnets. Their heads bobbed as they chatted and talked, wondering about who would arrive on the next bus and if anyone had any rentals in the village immediately available.

He started on the contents of his "haystack" piled on his plate. Layer after delicious layer danced on his taste buds. The food might have been prepared in humble kitchens throughout the village, but the flavors rang true and the quality of food, while simple, rivaled a gourmet. Love, the best ingredient of all, permeated each bite.

Some might call it silly, but Thad knew the passion he carried for food was shared by many present today. How else could people from such varied backgrounds come together here in one place? As a child, when visiting Pinecraft he'd taken the relative harmony for granted. Now as an adult, after seeing the ugly parts of his *Ordnung*, he'd kept his distance with good reason.

Here, though, in Florida with hundreds of miles between him and Ohio, he reminded himself that Pinecraft's standards were different. People did things here they'd never imagine doing back home.

Thad saw the blonde Amish woman, Miss Yoder, step away from the dessert table, then go through the line with the other servers to make their owns stacks of what remained. She nodded and said something to a familiar-looking woman—Rochelle Keim—the same woman who'd let him use her computer the other day.

Rochelle slipped her arm around Miss Yoder in a slight hug. Miss Yoder's expression held admiration for Rochelle Keim. No, not sisters. Cousins, maybe? Although Rochelle Keim was closer to his mother's age than Miss Yoder's youth.

"What's caught your attention, Thaddeus?" *Mammi* asked, a lull in conversation making her voice ring out across the tables.

"Oh, I saw Mrs. Keim, the woman who let me use her computer."

"Miss Keim, she is." Another woman at the table said. "Never been married. She's one of the old maids of Pinecraft."

"Ah, I see." He took another bite of his food.

"Her great-niece is following right behind her, from the looks of things," someone else said. "She turned her nose up at Gideon Stoltzfus, but then Jacob Miller married another."

It sounded like a reality TV show Stacie liked to watch. So, he took it Miss Yoder was the niece.

Nah, her marital state didn't matter to him.

But he did like teasing her about ganache.

⟡

"Stop hedging me, Thomas." Pete Stucenski had the young pastry chef right where he wanted him: sweating, and literally in the corner. The young man across from him in the booth almost shuddered. *Good.* "I promise, I'll make a few phone calls and you'll find it hard to get work. Maybe as a busboy, or maybe a waiter. But kiss the culinary scene good-bye."

Thomas, twenty-one years old if he was a day, cracked his knuckles. "Look, I want to keep my job. I told you. Thad told me once he used to be Amish. Used to live in the something-burg area. Wait. Millersburg. I started laughing because we were drinking Miller Lite and the name Miller is Amish. He didn't think it was too funny."

"Good. See, I'm trying to get the staff back together, and I realize people have to live, to make money. Dish and Spoon hit a rough spot financially, especially after what happened to Mitch."

The young man's posture relaxed, almost wilting. "Yeah, money comes in handy. I'm interested, if you need me back."

"Out of curiosity, did you see anything out of the ordinary at the restaurant? I know the police talked to you, but you know they still haven't found who killed Mitch." Pete took a sip of his Merlot.

"No, not really. People came and went all the time, having meetings and stuff. But you did, too. I was too busy carving up dough most of the time. Some of us gotta help make the money around here." Thomas grinned at him with the cheeky confidence of youth.

"That's the spirit, son. If your number's the same, I'll give you a heads-up on a reopening date. We're going to have a media event, invite all the local bigwigs. The future Senator Bright is talking about making it his election night headquarters, if we open in time."

"Wow, we'll have to open soon."

"Right. We're talking with his PR reps now. So keep your phone handy. We're going to need a good cake from a good head pastry chef." Pete slapped a ten-dollar bill on the table. "See you around."

He left Thomas grinning in the booth. Millersburg, Ohio, huh? Time for a road trip. It would be easy enough to take a day trip with his girlfriend to see some quilts and cheese and furniture. And, hunt down the elusive Thaddeus Zook.

9

*B*etsy hoped the Applebaum's elixir gel tabs would start to work soon. Nine days after taking them twice a day as instructed, and she still had to drag herself out of bed. Worse, more strands of hair fell out in the shower this morning.

Her hair now dry, she pinned it up and set a fresh head covering over the twisted bun. She used a few extra hairpins, to keep any stray hairs from flying away and to secure the *kapp*.

If not for her tiredness and the hair issue, she almost wanted to skip out to her bicycle. The Pinecraft Pies and Pastry building looked more like a shop every day, with the plumbing updated and the electrical work inspected and passed. Today, Henry and his small crew would lay tile for the kitchen floor. The older, what some called "vintage," linoleum would be too slick for the kitchen, but would give a charm to the front of the store.

Aenti Sarah, true to form, would meet her there to help "supervise." Likely, she'd bring a basket of sandwiches and fixings for the workers' lunch.

Winston sat by the front door, his head hung low. She guessed he was pouting because she'd been leaving him home whenever she went to check on progress at the store. After his visit to the vet, he'd been found free of any microchip.

"All right, come on." She scooped him up. "Just don't jump out of the basket." She went to the garage where her bike sat until she needed it. Soon they were off, cycling toward the shop and squinting from the Florida sunshine.

Word had started to get around about the bakery, with a few interested individuals stopping by to see progress. Betsy didn't want anyone to see the inside until everything looked fresh and new, and the scent of baking pie hung in the air.

Ganache . . . *Aenti* Chelle had even helped her look up a recipe. The idea of the concoction made her mouth water. The memory of the exchange with the mysterious stranger made her heart beat just a little faster.

Warning signs screamed at her. He wasn't Amish. Even if he used to be, it didn't count. Clearly, he knew something about baking, making him extremely interesting. What man liked to bake? And clearly the man had nothing else in common with her. He'd covered one entire arm in a tattoo. The others didn't seem to stare much at him during the haystack supper. The year-round residents saw enough of the *Englisch* every day.

But for an Amish man to leave, and do such things to himself? Yes, people left, all the time. People were shunned, and the degree and manner of shunning depended on their district and family. Even *Aenti* Chelle had been shunned, to a point, by the family, and her parents had been the ones to leave.

They ate together, but at separate tables—although those tables were put together to form one long eating space. A technicality, but still shunning. Sometimes the idea seemed silly to Betsy. How could someone exclude a person as loving and Christlike as *Aenti* Chelle?

There was a family story behind it all that no one would tell her.

She pondered the man in black and *Aenti* Chelle all the way to the shop. Part of her wanted to ask and discover the man's identity. And there was something about his eyes, a loneliness there, a restlessness.

She understood both feelings. Both had brought her here.

Winston barked as they pulled up to the shop. She couldn't wait to see the sign, which would be ready to install in one more week. With renovations drawing to a close, Betsy knew she needed to prepare a shopping list for the menu, another area where *Aenti* Sarah's expertise would come in handy.

She would call her father at the phone shanty tonight, and let him know about the shop, and how helpful *Aenti* Sarah had been.

"Good morning," Betsy called out as she freed Winston from the basket's confines. She stepped partway into the shop.

"Morning, Betsy." Henry stood at his worktable, covered with boxes of tile. Today, he wore a pair of dark trousers, stained by paint and held up with suspenders, topped by a faded tropical print shirt. "Thaddeus and I are about ready to start tearing up the kitchen floor. He's getting the rest of the tile from the van."

"These are the last two boxes." The man in black stood behind her in the doorway. His strong arms held two boxes of ceramic tile.

"Oh, excuse me." She stepped out of his way. *So his name is Thaddeus.*

He entered the shop and placed the boxes on the worktable. "Just tell me what to do, Henry."

"You know I will." The older man picked up a tool resembling a garden hoe. "Grab the other one, and we'll see about getting this floor covering peeled up, then see what we've got underneath."

Thaddeus flicked a curious glance in Betsy's direction. "So, Miss Yoder, have you worked on a ganache filling?"

Henry darted a look between them. "Oh, so you've met. I should have introduced you."

"We've not exactly met," Betsy hurriedly explained. She studied the box of tiles. He'd told her he'd pick up something with texture, that wouldn't grow slick with spills yet be easy to clean.

Winston skittered over in Thaddeus's direction. The man sank down onto one knee. "Hey there, little guy."

Winston licked his hands, then did his submissive flop onto his back for a belly rub. Betsy tried not to roll her eyes.

"This is Thaddeus Zook, from Ohio. He's here in the village with his *Mammi* for a bit. I picked him up for some work in the meantime. I've got several projects going, as you know, so I have workers at each one."

Betsy nodded. "I'm Betsy Yoder, and this is my bakery."

Thaddeus nodded in return. "I knew the Yoder part, and Henry told me all about your shop. I think it's a good idea. If the rest of your baking is like those cupcakes, you'll have people lining up at the door on the first day."

Her cheeks flamed and she looked away. "I'm thankful you're here. I mean, here to help. Once the floors go in and the painting's done, I can get appliances ordered."

"I'm a pastry chef by trade. So if you need any tips, just ask."

"Thank you." A male pastry chef? Maybe it wasn't strange in the *Englisch* world, but she could see how the oddity might be perceived in Ohio. Some men knew how to cook a few dishes, even do simple sewing repairs or darning, but generally anything home-related the women saw to.

Likely his district—hers, too—might not smile upon such a twist of occupation. Or maybe it was his family's disapproval? She'd had a few friends who left the Order or at the least had never been baptized into the church, all because they wanted to further their education in something besides basic medicine.

Henry interrupted her musings as she let herself stare at Thaddeus, who picked up the tool. "It'll take us a few days to get the kitchen finished. Rather than tile over the old lino-leum, I thought we'd try pulling it up and checking the sub-floor, just in case there's any hidden water damage. Will save us headaches later."

"Thank you. It's a good idea. Please, let me know if you need anything. *Aenti* Sarah said she'd bring some sandwiches for lunch." She snapped her fingers. "Winston, come. Let the men work. You're too small to help and you don't have thumbs."

"He can be moral support." Thaddeus grinned at her.

Neither Jacob Miller nor even Gideon Stoltzfus had ever grinned at her like that.

❧

Rochelle Keim sat at her computer, grateful for an after-noon of quiet. No client appointments, yet she spent her time online, editing her business web page. She knew the dangers of the Internet, and kept herself accountable. Accountability meant safety, protection, for her and those she loved.

Yet she decided to read the story again about her former best friend from childhood, Belinda Fry, who'd been the one to marry Silas. Part of her mourned not just Belinda's passing, but for the friendship lost many years before.

She picked up a recent copy of *The Budget* newspaper, the national edition. Jolene had dropped off the issue and tucked it into the screen door while Rochelle had been out seeing to clients.

Rochelle opened the newspaper and paged to the section for her home district. Or former district.

> Mrs. Silas Fry, age thirty-eight, succumbed to injuries received in a van rollover accident outside Millersburg. Mrs. Fry was returning home from a trip to visit cousins in Sugarcreek when the rented van she traveled in was struck by an eighteen-wheeler on the highway. Her husband of eighteen years and two children mourn her loss but are thankful for the support shown them by the community.

Two children? Silas had two children. Those poor young ones must be devastated.

Married eighteen years. Had it been so long? Were Rochelle to look in the mirror, she'd see the confirmation in her eyes. A lifetime.

Betsy had been not quite a toddler when things fell apart for Rochelle, and she'd consoled herself by spoiling her eldest sister's first great-niece via marriage, the granddaughter of her husband's Amish brother, whenever her brother-in-law's extended family visited Pinecraft. They'd maintained a special friendship over the years as Betsy grew, in spite of the wide branches of the grafted family tree.

When Betsy had come to live with her last winter, Rochelle wanted to warn her young great-niece with everything inside her being not to pin her hopes on Jacob Miller. She'd seen the signs herself as the relationship between Jacob and Natalie had grown from a small seed, then blossomed.

In fact, during her conversation with Jolene the other day at church, she'd mentioned the newlyweds were due back in Sarasota any day. The children from Jacob's first marriage, Rebecca and Ezekiel, had already returned and were staying with Jacob's *mammi* and were already back into their school routine.

Meanwhile, Rochelle knew Betsy's heart still bore a healing wound, not inflicted merely by Jacob's marriage to Natalie, but by her own dream of what couldn't be.

Nobody else heard the soft sobs from under Betsy's door in the evenings all those months ago, when she realized Jacob was lost to her forever. Afterward, Betsy had squared her shoulders and dove headfirst into planning her bakery.

Rochelle understood because the same pain had chased her away from Ohio and caused her to set roots in Pinecraft. She touched the newspaper, the black-and-white evidence of grief. Although she'd left Ohio not long after Silas made his choice, she hadn't left her faith and she still considered herself Plain.

She closed the newspaper, bowed her head, and said a prayer for Silas, for Betsy, and for herself. *Please, Gotte, a new beginning for all of us.*

❧

Thad reminded himself that his work for Henry Hostetler was temporary, only until he knew what to do next. He mopped his damp brow with a clean rag Henry lent him. He'd been tempted to apply at one of the restaurants near Siesta Key Beach, but thought better of it. The feeling of needing to look over his shoulder was fading the longer he remained in Florida, but still . . . The culinary world was wide and vast, and although his work could speak for itself, a reference check would alert some people to his location.

He'd called Pete Stucenski back last night and the call went to voice mail. He left his own message: He'd received Pete's message, had considered the possibility of returning to Dish and Spoon, but he wasn't interested at this time. He hoped the message would satisfy Pete's curiosity, if Mitch's business partner were truly interested in reopening the restaurant.

"You about ready to call it quits for the day?" Henry leaned on the scraping tool as they stood in the middle of the future kitchen, its sub-floor now revealed.

"I think so." No, he would have been useless on the farm or in the cabinet shop, or swinging a hammer as a contractor. "Good thing you decided to rip up the linoleum. Looks like there was a leak around the sink at one time."

"Right. We can get the rotten wood pulled up first thing in the morning, then get the barrier laid down, and the tile put in place."

"All in one day?" Thad couldn't believe it.

"All in one day. Call me a little ambitious."

"Okay, a little ambitious." Thad grinned at Henry. Who didn't like the amiable Mennonite with his tropical shirt and suspenders? Thad had never met anyone like him. He'd have remembered meeting the man years ago. At least he thought he would.

Henry tilted his head back and let loose with a laugh. "C'mon. Let's get the rest of this cracked excuse of a linoleum floor into the dumpster and shut down for the night."

Thad helped lug the rest of the broken-up flooring to the Dumpster now parked in the driveway. A trio of Old Order men stood by the edge of the lawn, chatting and watching the activity. One of them waved Thaddeus over in their direction.

He hesitated, then headed toward them. "Hello."

"Hello, young man," said the one with the longest beard. "I understand this is to be a bakery?"

"Yes, sir, it is." Thad glanced over his shoulder. "I heard it might open around November tenth."

"Ah, good, very good," said the shortest man. He rubbed his chin. "It'll be nice to have another place to visit when we want conversation, a good cup of coffee, and dessert."

"I'm sure Miss Yoder will appreciate it." Thad nodded. "I'll let her know, when I see her."

"Young man." Long-beard addressed him again. "Are you familiar with the Anabaptist faith?"

"Uh, why, yes I am." *All too familiar.*

"It's never too late to return to your roots. God always accepts a repentant one back into the fold."

"So I've heard." The men were kind and well-intentioned, but right now Thad's body cried out for a shower, a couple pain relievers, and some quiet. Not a theology discussion. And how did they know he used to be Amish, anyway? He could be just some Joe off the street.

"I once had many questions, and I found answers," said the shortest man. "I traveled the world far and wide, and I could find no peace for my soul, until I found rest in the Lord, in hard work much like you're doing, and the refuge of community."

"I'm . . . I'm happy for you, then." Thad glanced over his shoulder again. "Well, uh, thank you for stopping by today."

"Of course," Long-beard said. "We'll be praying for you, young man."

"Thanks." *Sort of.*

Thad waved as the men continued along the street, and then he met Henry at the van. "Anything else?"

Henry shook his head. "This will do it for today. I see Peter, James, and John talked to you."

"Peter, James, and John?"

"They're three brothers from Indiana who spend the winter here. This year, they're here early." Henry shut the door to the bakery, and locked it. He shot Thad a look. "So, they try to convert you?"

"Uh, sort of." Thad didn't flinch under Henry's scrutiny. He had nothing to hide.

"They backed off pretty quickly."

"Maybe they realized I was being polite, but not interested."

Henry opened the driver's door to the van, and climbed behind the wheel. Thad took his place in the passenger seat. "Not interested, huh?"

"No, not really. If I was interested, I would've 'come back,' as they put it, a long time ago."

They pulled away from the front of the shop and headed toward *Mammi's haus*. Henry slowed as he drove around an Old Order couple on a pair of three-wheeled bicycles.

"You're not in any trouble or anything, are you?"

"Like with the law? Of course not." Thad inhaled the fresh air as they drove along. The days had grown shorter since he'd come to Florida, night falling faster. He exhaled sharply.

"I'm sure your *mammi* asked you, too."

"She did. But no, not in trouble with the law. The restaurant I worked at in Columbus closed, temporarily. I'm not quite sure when it's reopening, so . . ." He gestured feebly.

"So, why not stay in Ohio and see what else you can do? I watch Food TV. I know chefs can work in different restaurants. Columbus is called the 'new foodie mecca.' So why here?"

Thad tried not to squirm in his seat. "Look, I just needed a change. For now. I don't plan on making this a permanent stay."

"Okay, okay, fair enough. I won't pry anymore." Henry shook his head. "Forget I asked. I just don't want anyone to show up and make trouble. Some people think they can hide out among the Plain people, and get an easy ride of it."

"I'm not doing that. I could have gone anywhere else—"

"Yes, you could have. But why here?" Henry stopped at a stop sign. "Okay, I won't say anything more. You ever want to talk, I'm all ears. If I can help, I will."

"Thank you." Thad felt his hackles lowering. He took another deep breath. "So, you really watch Food TV?"

"Yup. I like to watch the recipes."

"But do you cook?"

"Naw, I only like to imagine how it all tastes."

At that, Thad had to laugh.

10

*B*etsy didn't know what made her more giddy, the sight of her new floor or the fact she'd seen Thaddeus Zook every day while he installed the new floor with Henry. The younger man had no clue about what he was doing, following Henry's instructions and sometimes having to redo a tile.

Thaddeus intrigued her, the way he quietly attacked the job in front of him, despite his lack of experience. While she and Winston lurked in the background and she studied paint swatches in a variety of lighting, every so often he'd glance her way.

Yesterday, Thaddeus had spread the tile adhesive on the prepared sub-floor with the flourish of a pastry chef icing a cake, then set the tile in place. He eyed the gap between its neighboring tile and put the spacer between them. Henry showed him how to use the wet saw, and thankfully, Thaddeus had a good eye for measuring, like any good baker.

"Oh, Henry . . . Thaddeus . . . it's beautiful." She stood in the kitchen doorway, surveying the floor while the grout cured. Not long now, and the appliances would arrive. Today, supposedly, so she found herself, not unwillingly, waiting at the bakery for the delivery truck.

Did she see a red flush creep into Thaddeus's neck? She tore her gaze from him and Henry, and studied the floor. By Monday, one week before grand opening, the sign company would deliver the brand-new sign *Aenti* Chelle had helped her draw.

Gotte, this is really going to happen.

Daed had sounded pleased with the progress the last time she'd spoken to him on the telephone. Despite the fact the business he ran had telephones, he still refused to let one into the house. He never asked about the phone she used to call him with, and she never volunteered it was a cell phone she kept tucked inside her tote bag.

"Very *gut*," he'd said.

Yes, it was all very good. She wasn't so presumptuous to know how God felt when He looked at His creation and deemed it all "good," but looking at her bakery, maybe it felt a little similar. Her dream, now within reach, would come true in one more week.

A large truck came roaring from the direction of Bahia Vista, with the name of an appliance company covering the side of the trailer. Her stove and oven, refrigerator and large freezer.

The vehicle ground to a halt, belching smoke from its tailpipe. The smell made Betsy grimace, as the delivery driver opened the door and climbed down. He approached the building and carried a clipboard.

"Delivery for Yoder?" The man clomped past her in work boots, like she was invisible.

"I'm Betsy Yoder." She followed him into the bakery.

"She's right behind you," Henry said from the kitchen entryway. Thaddeus was on his knees, applying grout to the tile in the corner. He paused, looking up at them as they stood in the entryway.

"Oh." The man turned around. "See, Honey, this is your order form." He spoke slowly to her, as if she were slow of mind. She had a second cousin who was born slow and was now almost fifty years old, but still had the mind of a child. This was exactly how the deliveryman spoke to her now.

"Thank you." She received the clipboard from him. "There should be the stove, and separate freezer and refrigerator."

"Right, right." He extended a pen in her direction. "Sign please."

"May I see them before I sign?" Her *daed* had warned her of making sure everything she ordered was accurate.

He snatched the clipboard from her. "Whatever."

Thaddeus stood, hands on his hips. The skin of his neck now flamed red, probably the same shade as her face right now. Why was the delivery man treating her so rudely? She had treated him only with respect. A low rumble sounded in Winston's throat.

"Hush, Winston, or I'll put you in the bathroom until he's gone." Betsy followed the deliveryman into the sunlight.

He opened the rear of the truck, sliding a large single door up into the roof of the trailer. Then he tossed the clipboard onto the bed of the truck so he could tug a ramp down to the street level.

Within fifteen minutes, they'd unloaded the refrigerator, freezer, and the stove.

Immediately, Betsy knew the stove now sitting on the sales floor of the bakery wasn't the correct model. She'd ordered the expanded stove, with a double oven and eight burners. This had a single oven with a warming compartment on the side, and only six burners.

"Um, sir, I don't believe this is the correct stove. The one I ordered has eight burners, this one has six."

He glanced at the clipboard in his hand, and the stove. "Just sign it. I've made the delivery."

"But this isn't the right stove." She remembered seeing both of them when she'd been to the restaurant supply store in Tampa, and she and the *aentis* had all agreed the double oven would work best.

"Look, I don't have time for this."

In a flash, Thaddeus sprang between her and the delivery-man. "No, you look. She ordered the stove she wanted, and it's your job to deliver it to her. If it's not the right one, it's not the right one." He poked the man in the chest with his index finger.

"Don't touch me."

"Don't harass the lady and treat her like an imbecile."

"Now, you two, let's calm down," Henry was saying.

"Shut up, old man." The deliveryman took a step back just as Thad took a step forward. "What, you coming after me?"

"Stop it, Thaddeus," Betsy heard herself saying. "Just stop. Please."

"Aw, you people." The deliveryman waved them off. "C'mon Stu, let's get the stinkin' stove back on the truck."

Betsy's knees shook beneath her skirt. She'd never seen anything like this, not firsthand. She wrapped her arms around her waist. Why some people were rude, she never understood. But this man—he'd been outright hateful, treating her, yes, like an "imbecile," as Thaddeus had said.

"Sign for the two items I did deliver." The deliveryman shoved the clipboard in her direction while Thaddeus stood close by, looking like a thundercloud ready to burst.

"All right." Her hand shook as she grasped the pen. "I'll call the store and let them know they put the wrong item on the truck."

"Whatever." He stomped off, climbed back in the truck, and disappeared in a cloud of fumes.

Betsy sank against the refrigerator. "What was wrong with him?"

"He's a pig, is what he is." Thaddeus glared out the door, then he turned to her. "Are you okay?"

He reached for her arms, his touch so gentle, when moments before he'd looked like a dog defending its brood.

She nodded, biting back the hot tears stinging her eyes. "I'd heard about people like him. They think because I'm female and I'm Amish, I'm stupid. Not even any of my *Englisch* house-cleaning clients have ever treated me in such a way."

"Well, you're not stupid."

A tear escaped and before she could swipe it away, Thaddeus reached up and used his thumb to brush it away. The simple gesture touched something inside her, something Jacob never had. The idea of someone like Thaddeus paying such close attention to her, to her feelings, supporting her dream—even though he was a paid worker—well, she'd never imagined it.

"Thank you." She swallowed hard and brushed the remainder of the tears away. "But please, don't ever do it again."

"Do what?"

"Don't fight the man, or anyone like him. It's not right."

Thaddeus took a half step back. "I can't promise you. No, I don't like to fight. I'd rather not. But I'm not going to stand by while you, or any woman, is insulted."

Henry cleared his throat. "I understand the feeling, Thaddeus. But like Betsy says, you're better off not fighting. I won't tolerate it with my workers. I have a name to uphold around here, and I won't do it, even if the other fellow might deserve any knocks he gets."

"Ah, okay then." Thaddeus headed toward the door. "If you don't mind, I'm going to take a break. I'll be back. Give me about thirty minutes and I'll help you set these up."

He left them, Betsy not knowing what to say. Instead, she sighed. "I should call the supply store."

"Be careful, Betsy."

She nodded, not quite knowing what Henry meant, but thinking she knew what he meant. Especially by the way her heart raced when Thaddeus touched her.

"Hellooo," *Aenti* Sarah's voice rang out, "Is anyone ready for a snack? And why is Thaddeus Zook storming down the street?"

◆

It took a lot for Thaddeus to blow a gasket, but when scumbags like the delivery driver acted like they did, he couldn't help himself. Any pacifist Anabaptist notions were forgotten. It was one of the other things he wished people in the *Ordnung* understood. Sometimes, there came a time to fight for something. Not often, but he wanted to keep the option on the table.

No, he wasn't a big or overly muscular man, but he had enough wiry strength in his limbs, especially when he'd been working out at the gym. He'd long ago resolved to never become a squishy pastry chef.

He followed the street around until he hit Fry, then hooked a right and took the street until he arrived at Pinecraft Park. The smack of shuffleboard paddles striking pucks rang out through the neighborhood.

A few diehard players must be brushing up on their skills before the winter crowds descended and the park became a round-the-clock circus of activities.

Thad's anger burned off the closer he got to the edge of Phillippi Creek. Now this was a Pinecraft memory of happier days of childhood, throwing rocks in the water, watching the fish jump, and asking dozens of questions to fishermen trying to reel in a catch. Best of all, they might catch a glimpse of an alligator, which by the time they got home to Ohio, the telling of its size might have grown to dinosaur proportions.

A heron stood on its long legs on the opposite bank of the creek. It spread its wide wings and lifted off the ground, soaring away over the city.

Not many more days and the park would fill up, the older men playing bocce, men and women honing their shuffleboard skills, the youth playing volleyball, young parents chasing toddlers through the playground equipment.

For now, though, the park was how he liked it best, empty except for the two shuffleboard players, an old *Englisch* woman wearing a large floppy hat fishing at the creek, and a man, sitting alone at one of the picnic tables under the long pavilion in part of the park.

And Thad.

The ashes of his anger blew away on the light breeze. Thad closed his eyes and let the sun soak in.

Don't fight the man, or anyone like him. It's not right, Betsy had said.

Even Henry had tried to calm them both down.

They'd been right. If he'd landed a punch and the police were called, the deliveryman could have pressed charges. He would cause fresh shame to his family in Ohio, should they learn of the news, and shame his family and friends here. His rash actions would have served no purpose, aside from feeling a sense of justice at hurting a man.

Clearly, though, Betsy had been humiliated and belittled. Like most of her Amish contemporaries, she'd finished her formal academic studies at eighth grade and had gone no further in the classroom. However, it didn't mean she lacked in life experience or common sense.

He'd checked into her family back home—the same Yoders who owned and operated Yoder Woodworking & Custom Cabinets—and they had a mini-empire. No relation to the Yoders who owned the Sarasota restaurant, market, and gift shop, though.

Even if he were Amish again, there was little chance her father would have found him suitable for one of his daughters. A pastry chef for a son-in-law.

Someone like Betsy, though, reminded him of all he'd left behind. All the good parts, anyway.

He found a piece of shell and flung it into the rippling creek. As the waters closed over the shell, Thad determined never again to do something to bring such a look of hurt and distress to Betsy's face.

Thad turned his back on the creek and decided to cut through the pavilion on the way back to the shop. He'd left Henry in the lurch and they had to check the grout on the floor before moving the appliances into the kitchen.

"How's it going?" The man sitting at the picnic table nodded at him. A five o' clock shadow darkened his face. A canvas duffel bag, overflowing with clothing, sat on the concrete slab floor of the pavilion. Another bag, this one of clear plastic and stuffed with aluminum cans, rested beside the other bag.

"I can't complain," Thad replied.

"You got any smokes on ya?"

Thad tapped his pocket. "No, sir. I'm afraid I don't. I quit a while back."

"Good for you." The man glanced toward the creek, then back at Thad. "The stuff's bad for ya. I've tried to cut back, but it's not easy. Cans are slim pickings today. You got a buck or two to spare?"

Thad did have a few dollars, so he gave them to the man. He didn't do things like this in Columbus, but here, even in a much smaller city like Sarasota, he realized that people still found themselves in hard times.

"Thanks. God bless you, young man."

"You're welcome." He nodded at the man and headed back to the bakery. He'd been gone less than twenty minutes, and had promised to be back within thirty. Funny thing, he never remembered there being homeless people drifting through the park years ago. Or maybe he just hadn't noticed.

Children lived in blissful ignorance of many things until they grew up. He'd realized that all too well once he'd left home and, going against his father's wishes, he'd earned his GED. To go to culinary school then was the ultimate slap against the traditional roles of the Amish men.

You were made to stand out. Stacie had been the one who told him this; now he remembered. He wondered about trying to call her, to see if her condition was any better. He prayed so.

⁂

Pete's cooler was stocked with plenty of cheese, and the back seat of his car held shopping bags of preserves, pot holders, handmade soap, wooden birdhouses, and one special bag held a quilt.

Ginger, his girlfriend, agreed happily when he proposed taking a weekend trip through the Amish country in the Millersburg area. Of course, she wanted to stop at every farm with a sign posted with items for sale. He cut her off at stopping at a furniture store.

At one farm, however, he did discover a Zook family—several generations—in one row of farms. At a simple roadside stand, selling the last few jars of preserves, he asked about Thaddeus.

"I'm looking for a family named Zook." He posed the question to a salt-and-pepper-haired matriarch who glanced at her husband.

"We are the Zooks," the husband said, his voice having an almost singsong tone. "Why do you ask?"

"I have a friend in Columbus named Thad Zook, and he told me he had family in this area." Pete mopped his forehead with a handkerchief. The humidity today was uncommon for late fall.

"Ah, I see." The man fell silent, but he continued placing carved wooden paper towel holders on a table.

"I have a son named Thaddeus Zook." So, the matriarch had found her voice. "But he doesn't live here anymore."

"Oh, all right. If it's the same Thaddeus, I've actually lost touch with him," Pete explained. "I heard he might be looking for a job and I wanted to see if he'd come work for me."

The woman frowned. "We haven't heard from him in months. I'm sorry we can't help you more."

"Thank you, thank you, anyway." He paid for the preserves and turned to leave. "Say, do you have family anywhere else, besides here?" It was a long shot, but he glanced from the wife to her husband.

The man spoke first. "My mother lives down south year-round."

His wife glanced at him with worried eyes. "He would never go there."

"Where?" Pete ventured to ask.

"Florida." The woman's frown deepened. "Thank you for stopping by today."

Pete nodded. "Thanks again. God bless."

The couple watched him and Ginger head for the car, Ginger jubilant over her latest purchase.

"Honey, I think I've got all my Christmas shopping done and it's only November."

"Good for you, Babe." Pete unlocked the car. Time to head for home and see what he could learn about the Zooks in Florida.

As they headed along a back road toward the interstate, his phone rang. He saw the number. Just a little insistent. He promised them answers, but a man had plenty of business to conduct. After all, their issue wasn't his difficulty. He was only doing them a favor.

"Yes?" He answered with his Bluetooth.

"Did you find anything out? Because tomorrow's Election Day."

"Of course, it is. I haven't forgotten. I need to check something out before I let you know. If it's nothing, I don't want it to waste anyone's time."

"You've already wasted enough time."

"Not fair. Hey, I'm letting the future United States Senator from Ohio use Dish and Spoon as his election night headquarters. Isn't it enough?"

"For now. But get us what we need. And while you're at it, get rid of this phone and get another number."

Pete rolled his eyes. Ginger mouthed: *What's wrong?* He shook his head.

"Sure, no problem." Never mind, he'd have to change his old contacts. No wonder Mitch had two phone lines.

11

*B*etsy snuck a look out the front window of Pinecraft Pies and Pastry on Monday morning. A small cluster of villagers of varying ages gathered near the sign. Nerves jangled inside her, not borne out of pride, but of not disappointing her family. They'd invested in her, and she knew they had given her an opportunity not many young women her age could experience.

Both she and *Aenti* Sarah had arrived at the shop no later than five in the morning, turned on the ovens, and began prepping and filling pies. *Aenti* Sarah made batches of her flaky crust, while Betsy stirred up pie fillings.

Word had spread through the village, thanks to the signs posted on telephone poles. The signs gave the hours and days of operation, along with a short list of pies and pastries. By eight a.m., the curious, and hungry, Betsy hoped, waited for her to unlock the door.

She had the *aentis* and Henry to thank for their help. And Thad, who'd apologized for the incident with the delivery driver. The appliance store had sent a replacement stove right away—and with a different driver, although Betsy had said nothing against the man.

"You should unlock the door. I'll pour the water into the coffeemaker," *Aenti* Sarah announced. She loved the instant pour-through feature of the large commercial coffeemaker, where customers could help themselves to a cup of the hot brew. Betsy had also set up a hot water dispenser for tea beside it with a variety of herbal tea bags.

She glanced around the room before she unlocked the door. Black-and-white checked tile floor, with six square tables with red laminate tops, with four chairs for each table. The display case held an assortment of pies, still warm from the oven, along with trays of fried pies, and even some sugar-glazed and cake doughnuts.

The supply made a good start for her first day in business.

Betsy unlocked the door and flung it open. "Good morning, everyone. Please, come in." She stepped aside to let her first customers through the door.

Aenti Sarah set the coffee to brewing and the aroma filled the room, along with customers.

"The coffee is free this morning . . ." Betsy announced, then paused. "Along with doughnuts."

Aenti Sarah darted a look in her direction. "Elizabeth . . ."

Sometimes it was best to give. She smiled as she pointed out the menu on the wall. The first flurry of customers soon came and went, and after the first hour both she and *Aenti* Sarah perched on stools behind the display case.

"Ach, quite a busy start to the morning." *Aenti* Sarah fanned herself with a dish towel.

"Ya." Betsy smiled at the nearly empty case, where not long ago the pies and pastries had waited for customers. She'd resisted the urge to start counting her cash just yet.

She hoped for a good turnout the first day and so far the foot traffic had not disappointed. What did disappoint her was the glaring absence of Thaddeus Zook. Maybe he was too tired, or had slept in, as he called it. Betsy ignored the disappointment and thought ahead to her supply of merchandise.

"So, how much should we bake for the afternoon?"

Aenti Sarah, asking her a question, instead of giving an order or making a pointed suggestion.

Betsy glanced at the wall clock with a simple white face and black numbers. "I think we should wait and see who comes in the next hour."

"I'll go start some fresh dishwater."

"I'll help you."

"No, no." *Aenti* Sarah waved her off. "You need to wait for your customers to come. They want to see you and buy pie and pastry."

"Okay." She watched her great-aunt slip softly from the stool and step carefully into the kitchen. Then she studied the street outside the front window. An older couple, strolling past, eyed her shop, glanced up at the sign, and kept going.

Well, it was only the first day. Her *daadi* and his two brothers had started their woodworking shop inside a shed on her *daadi*'s farm. Now the operation filled a 10,000-square-foot warehouse, workshop, and showroom on one of the main highways near town. They'd had a small start, too.

Maybe one day, she could pay *Aenti* Sarah for her hard work instead of feeling as though her *Aenti* was the boss.

A figure approached the shop on foot. Whoever it was carried a plant inside a pot. Its green leaves partly blocked the person's face. It was a man, judging by the shoulders, T-shirt, and tan shorts with lots of pockets ending at the knee.

The man stopped at the front door, and shifted the potted plant to the side. Thaddeus? But the familiar shadow of beard on his face was gone. His smooth face made him look younger.

He entered the shop, the flip-flops on his feet making a smack-smack on the tile floor. She tried not to giggle. His jeans and dark T-shirt had disappeared somewhere along with the *Englisch*-looking beard.

"Why are you laughing at me?" he asked, setting down the plant on the countertop.

"Your clothes. You look *Englisch* now, ready for the beach." She glanced at the plant, a potted hibiscus with a few buds that would soon open into wide orange flowers. "Oh, it's so beautiful."

"It's for you, to congratulate you on opening the bakery." He studied the pies in the case and leftover pastries and doughnuts. "Wow, what to choose? I already know it'll be delicious."

"Thank you, and thank you for the plant." She checked behind her. *Aenti* Sarah hadn't seen him come in with the plant. She would not hide anything from her aunt, but if everyone had known how she felt about Jacob, what would they say when they saw how Thaddeus Zook made her feel?

"Free coffee today, huh?" Thaddeus stepped away from the counter and over to the refreshment area.

"That's right. I might make the coffee free every day. I'm not sure yet." She tried not to touch her hair or her covering or the apron.

He poured a cup, skipped adding cream or sugar, and rejoined her at the counter. "So, your menu . . . anything with ganache on there?" He lifted his gaze and scanned the hand-lettered menu board, which resembled a chalkboard from school, with the items listed in different colors of chalk.

"No." He was teasing her again. She quirked half a grin at him. "I'm still perfecting my other desserts, like cannolis. Eventually I want to try making flan."

"Have you had flan before?" He raised one eyebrow as he looked at her.

"Yes, I have. At a Spanish restaurant here in Sarasota. I'd never tasted anything quite like it before." *Aenti* Chelle had taken Betsy there for her birthday this year, to her great delight.

"When it's cooked properly, you won't." He took a sip of his coffee. "Good coffee."

"*Aenti* Sarah always makes good coffee. Me? Not so much." She wanted to ask him so many questions, but held back. Clearly, he'd forsaken his Anabaptist faith. Clearly, too, he had burdens, which she didn't have the right to know or the responsibility to help carry.

"What is it?" He studied her face and she tried not to break away from her gaze, but didn't succeed. Instead, she let her eyes take in the sight of the pies in the clear case below her fingertips. *Aenti* Sarah had carved a dotted "A" for apple and "C" for cherry in the various pie crusts, and so forth.

"I shouldn't ask, but, I wonder why you're here. In Pinecraft." There. She'd said it. A clattering in the kitchen, of metal against tile, made both of them jump. Betsy swung around. *Aenti* Sarah had dropped a large metal sheet pan on the tile floor. Maybe she should have Henry install a swinging door, or a Dutch door, between the display area and the kitchen.

"Ah. Visiting my *mammi*."

She shook her head. "But it's not quite winter yet. Not much goes on around here until winter. It's quiet."

"I like the quiet." He shifted from foot to foot. "But I could ask you the same thing. Why would someone your age live here year-round? Why open a pie and pastry shop here? Why not back in Ohio? Your family is there, and Pinecraft is for, well, mostly elderly people."

She couldn't answer, at first. She almost added the typical, "And newlyweds," phrase some used when describing Pinecraft. Oh, what it must be like to be a newlywed, basking in the perpetual sun and occasional thunderstorm, with miles of sand minutes away.

"Because . . . because . . ." True, she could have opened a store near her family's home. She could be in her own bed every night, getting up in the morning to her *mamm's* cooking before she started out the day.

"Never mind." Thaddeus shook his head. She rather liked his jawline, now that it was smooth.

The bell jangled over the front door, and in came a familiar face, one she hadn't expected to see in Pinecraft at all.

Gideon Stoltzfus.

He closed the door behind him, stood in the center of the shop, and stared at them both.

✺

The man who'd just entered the bakery had shoulders nearly as wide as the door, and he'd had to duck his head a tad when he crossed the threshold.

The guy looked vaguely familiar, probably an acquaintance from years past. Now he remembered. Gideon Stoltzfus. Rumor had it he could lift a buggy with one hand and had even lifted one off the victim in a buggy crash, saving his life and pulling him out of the way of traffic. Gideon had accomplished that feat at the age of sixteen.

The same man stared at Betsy now like a prize he'd been seeking, treasure at the end of a pirate's map.

"Elizabeth."

"Gideon." Thad had never seen Betsy stiffen like this before. "You're in Pinecraft?"

"I have taken leave from my job. I used my vacation savings to come early, before it is too busy. I go back after Christmas."

He turned as he spoke, taking in the sight of the shop. "This is your shop."

Thad wanted to interject, "No, it belongs to a family down the street," but thought better of the smart-aleck remark. Nothing set his teeth on edge like people stating the obvious.

"Gideon Stoltzfus." Thad stood his ground at the counter. "I've heard of you before. Thaddeus Zook."

Gideon stared at him as though he'd just sprouted a set of horns from his forehead. "But I don't know you."

Of course, Thad leaving the district had a lot to do with it. He might have known Betsy, too, had he stayed. The thought prickled his mind.

"No. I've been . . . away from the district for a long time."

"I see." Gideon now stared at Thad's flip-flops. Yes, his toe-nails needed trimming. He hadn't gotten so far yet, but he had other things to do on his first day off, besides Sunday, since working on the bakery project for Henry.

"Well, I'll let you two catch up, then." Thad glanced Betsy's way. Her face bore a tint of light pink, as if she'd been pulling weeds outside for an hour.

"Do you want some pie? Or a doughnut? Or a fried pie?" She gestured to the case. "And, you should sit and finish your coffee."

She wanted him to stay.

"I would love a fried pie, Miss Betsy." He leaned over the glass. "Cherry, if you have it."

"Yes, I do." She touched the strings of her head covering. "Would you like it warmed up?"

He wanted to give her a cheesy line like, "Just give my pie the warmth of your smile," just to see what Gideon would say, but decided against it. This time.

"Okay, one cherry fried pie." She reached for a paper plate, then put on a sheer plastic glove and pulled a pie from the display, popped it on the plate, then put it in the microwave for a few seconds. "There. I decided to warm it up another way." She took the plate out and placed it in front of Thad, then smiled.

"How much?" He glanced at the menu and reached for his wallet.

"Nothing."

"I couldn't—"

"Yes, you can. You and Henry helped make this place a reality for me, and I'm thankful." She did the downward glance thing she did the first day, with those feathery eyelashes of hers. She probably had no clue how it affected him, or Gideon, for that matter.

He cleared his throat and reached for the plate. Their fingers touched. He cleared his throat again. "I think I'll go over in the corner and eat this while I finish my coffee."

Gideon held him in his gaze as Thad took the half a dozen steps to a table closest to the coffee pot. Hey, he had as much right to be here as anyone else.

The brick wall of a man turned his back on Thad, which was fine with him. The man wanted him to leave? Well, he'd stay for a while, just because of it. And, he had the distinct impression Betsy didn't want the man in her shop.

Thad took a bite of pie. Yes, the young lady could cook. The cherries tasted sweet, yet not too sweet with a hint of tartness, the crust crisp and flaky. He washed the bite down with a sip of coffee. Life was good, very good right now. Thank *Gotte*. And yes, at moments like this, he did thank *Gotte*, if He were listening.

He knew eavesdropping was considered impolite, but he strained his ears anyway. His ears, unaccustomed to the *Dietsch*, took a few seconds to translate.

When was she going back to Ohio?

No, she wasn't going back to Ohio.

How did she get the money to do this?
Her family had helped invest in the bakery.
Did she remember the promise they'd made to each other?
She didn't know what he was talking about.
All those nights, walking home from the singing together?
We weren't together. We were in groups and you walked beside me, but I didn't walk beside you.
I believe Gotte wants us to be together.
He hasn't told me.

The girl had a backbone about her, despite the soft and sweet exterior. A strand of her long hair, golden with light amber tones, had come free from its constraints.

Betsy looked behind her, into the kitchen, then glanced at Thad. It was a silent cry for help, or seemed like it, to him.

Just then the bell over the front door clanged and in came an Amish family, a husband and wife with a daughter about nine and a son about seven. Jacob Miller, with his new wife. Would Jacob remember him, and if so, would he talk to him? Thaddeus sat back and watched, taking another sip of coffee.

"Betsy, you have a lovely shop." Jacob's wife, a slim brunette with dark hair, blue cape dress, and spangled flip-flops, scanned the room until her focus stopped on the pies.

"Thank you." Betsy gripped the counter with both hands.

Gideon stepped aside and let the family place an order, after much back and forth and deliberation about flavors versus pie versus purchasing four fried pies. He then moved to the nearest table and took a seat. Clearly, the man wasn't going anywhere.

Thad polished off the last of his fried pie. Nope, he decided as the bell clanged over the door once again, Betsy didn't need rescuing. And he wasn't about to stay and face off with Gideon anymore, and scratch the tiles like a banty rooster. Time to go.

He didn't look back as he left the bakery.

12

Betsy arrived home before supper and not even Winston's wagging tail and happy licks to her hands could make her smile. *Aenti* Chelle had started a slow-cooker lasagna in the afternoon and delightful smells of sauce and Italian sausage filled the kitchen.

Gideon Stoltzfus had shown up at the bakery with the happy Miller family literally almost on his heels. All the while, Thaddeus Zook had sat in the corner, taking it all in as he drank three cups of coffee. Then, he'd left and the afternoon passed in a blur of customers, with Gideon finishing off nearly one whole pie the entire time and countless cups of coffee.

Long ago, she'd considered encouraging Gideon's interest. Last year, her last summer and fall in Ohio, maybe she'd been unfair to him by giving him her attention. Then around the same time, Jacob had caught her interest and she'd abandoned any real thoughts of Gideon as a possible husband.

Now, here she was a year later, with no Gideon, no Jacob, and with a jumble of feelings and thoughts about Thaddeus Zook she dared not share with anyone.

"Supper's ready when you are," *Aenti* Chelle called down the hallway to Betsy's room.

"I'll be right there," she replied. "I'm going to shower first, though. It's been a long day."

Betsy opened her bedroom door, with her robe over her arm. She paused at the linen closet long enough to pick up a fresh towel.

"Supper will keep. You freshen up," *Aenti* Chelle called from the kitchen area.

Betsy glanced around the corner as she headed toward the bathroom. *Aenti* Chelle sat at the table, her face lit by the glow of her computer screen.

Betsy's muscles welcomed the hot water washing away the tiredness of the day. Truthfully, after the shower, she wanted to slide beneath the covers and do nothing but sleep. Four a.m. would come early, the time she knew she had to get up and prepare to face the next day's customers.

She rinsed her hair while leaning her head against the tile and crying as the water poured over her. Seeing Jacob and Natalie had ripped off a painful scab on her heart. Yes, she was healing, but it had taken longer than she'd thought. Then there was Gideon, showing up in Pinecraft.

Enough. She needed to count her blessings, of which she had many. A family who loved her, a roof over her head, plenty to eat, good health (except for the tiredness), and her new bakery. And those were the first to come to mind.

She turned off the faucet and the rest of the water swirled down the drain. Soon she'd bundled herself in her soft robe and left her hair down to air dry. The weight of her hair felt strange as it hung to her waist.

"You look comfortable," *Aenti* Chelle said as Betsy entered the kitchen.

"The shower helped." She yawned as she put a small slab of lasagna on her plate along with a tong's worth of salad. "I'm going to sleep well tonight."

She sat down at the chair across from her aunt, then bowed her head over her meal silently to ask the blessing. When she looked up, *Aenti* Chelle was studying her face.

"Betsy, what's wrong? Your eyes look red."

She wanted to give the excuses of hot water or her tiredness. Instead, everything came tumbling out along with the tears, Gideon showing up, along with Jacob and Natalie, and the way she felt drawn to Thaddeus Zook, something she'd told no one.

The forbidden tears continued as she spoke. "Oh, *Aenti* . . . I'm so . . . overwhelmed, and I'm so tired."

"I know it was hard for you, with Jacob. But I didn't know about Gideon."

Betsy picked up her paper napkin and blew her nose. "What's the phrase the *Englisch* girls use? 'Led him on?' Part of me feels like I did. I was just being nice, I thought, and, well, some of the other girls were getting married. But we never courted. We only walked home, in groups, after church."

"It doesn't seem to me like you would do so, not deliberately. But he's here in Pinecraft?"

"Yes. He said he's taken a leave from his job, and he'll go back after Christmas. He's very clear about why he's here. To court me. Or, convince me to agree."

"What a fine kettle of fish. Did you tell him specifically you're not interested?"

"Yes, I tried. He said he believes *Gotte* wants us to be together."

"What do you think?"

"I told him *Gotte* hadn't told me we should be together. He almost laughed at me, that I would presume to know what *Gotte* wants, and it be different than what Gideon knew." She crumpled up the napkin and set it beside her untouched supper plate. "But *Aenti*, how do we know *Gotte's* will? I don't know if *Gotte* would tell me what to do, like Gideon claims he knows."

Truthfully, she wasn't sure about knowing *Gotte*. She knew the rules, but as far as the all-powerful *Gotte*, the king of heaven and earth, taking time to let her know what to do, she didn't think He would have the time, with all the billions of people in the planet and the entire universe to keep in order.

"Oh, people have asked the same question for centuries, I'm sure." *Aenti* Chelle closed her laptop computer. "What I have learned is God can speak to us a number of ways, through the Bible, through others who believe in Him, through circumstances in our lives, and through prayer."

"I didn't know. I was hoping for a voice, or something." Betsy felt rather foolish. She'd heard Bible stories of *Gotte* speaking to people and didn't think He did it nowadays, not with a voice or any other way. Somehow, though, through some mystery she couldn't understand, *Gotte's wille* would reveal itself. Or so she'd always believed. And after her hoping and praying for an answer about Jacob didn't come, well, she'd been hoping against hope for her bakery.

The uncertainty of it all—the bakery, Gideon, her healing wounds over Jacob, her new feelings and interest in Thaddeus, piled on top of her exhaustion, almost took her breath away. She remembered the one time she'd ridden on a Ferris wheel at a Sarasota fair last winter, when she crested the top of the wheel and came down on the other side—terrifying, stomach-dropping, holding on for her life to the bar. Yes, that was the feeling.

"You're not alone in feeling that way. Did you know, though, the Bible says we can boldly approach what's called God's throne of grace, to obtain mercy, and find grace in our time of need?"

Nobody had ever talked to her this way before. All her life, she'd grown up and accepted what she was told. "No."

Mercy, grace, help in her time of need. Outwardly, she needed nothing. Inwardly, she needed rest, peace, and calm assurance. She touched her still-damp hair, and a generous clump of strands came loose, stuck to her hand.

"Oh, Betsy." *Aenti* Chelle stood, then rounded the edge of the table to join her on the other side. "I know your soul and spirit hurt right now, and I'll pray for you. But your hair, and this fatigue? How long has it been going on?"

"I don't know. For a while now . . ." She studied her crumpled, used napkin. She felt rather crumpled herself. "*Aenti* Sarah gave me some Applebaum's Energy Elixir gel tablets to take. They help a little bit. I think."

"Huh." *Aenti* Chelle reached out and touched Betsy's hair. Betsy had a vague memory, of her *mamm* brushing her hair when she was young. "We need to make an appointment for you to see the doctor. And soon."

Betsy nodded. "All right." She'd never been to an *Englisch* doctor before.

"Meanwhile, let's pray." *Aenti* Chelle touched Betsy's arm. "Heavenly Father, we come to You today on behalf of Your beloved child, Elizabeth. I ask You to grant her strength, wisdom, peace, and clarity, in matters concerning her business, her life, and her heart. Also, for this ailment, whatever it is, I ask You to help make it clear as well. Amen."

The simple prayer touched the tender ache in Betsy's heart, like a soothing balm poured over the places hurting the most.

"Amen." Betsy looked up. "Thank you, *Aenti* Chelle." She'd never heard anyone pray quite like this before.

Thaddeus pulled the wet laundry from the washing machine. *Mammi* allowed herself the luxury of an electric washer, but still kept a clothesline in the backyard to let the sun do the work of drying clothes.

A sunny day ahead, again. With winter trying to reach farther south, Ohio had already had its first snowfall. Not in sunny Sarasota, though, where winter would only nip and not bite.

So far, he'd been here almost a month. He'd found a tenuous peace after leaving Columbus and the state of Ohio, but the niggling feeling of someone catching up with him hadn't left. It came when he was idle, so he tried to keep busy in the village, helping Henry when he could and his *mammi* as well. Thad lugged his basket of damp clothes outside. *Mammi* had offered to help him with laundry, but he politely refused. There were some things your *mammi* could see when you were a kid, and it didn't matter, but Thad would rather take care of things himself now.

He stopped at the clothesline. He couldn't remember the last time he'd hung clothes outside. Maybe as a little tyke, chasing his *mamm* and insisting he could help and do it too.

Always running after her, he knew it had broken her heart when he ran the other direction. At the time, he didn't have a choice. The constricting feeling of the sameness, same clothes, same hair, and the same expectations of his *daed* and family. It was leave or let a big part of himself die.

He still felt the ache and throb of his fingers when he'd missed his mark with a hammer swing. Yes, he'd helped Henry with Betsy's shop, but it was different. Maybe, just maybe, he'd keep up the contracting work with Henry, if the older man needed him. He'd enjoyed the tile work, the precision of cuts and the artistry of the patterns.

But no, he couldn't go home again. He kept pulling his clothing from the basket and clipping it to the line.

The back door banged, and Thaddeus turned. *Mammi* headed toward him, her face glowing. "Thaddeus." She waved a small piece of paper. "I heard from your *mamm*. She told me they'll be here soon for vacation. She and your *daed* both. I believe some *oncles*, *aentis*, and cousins are coming, but I haven't heard just when."

Great. The quiet would end. His actions when he was eighteen had turned into a double-edged sword of emotion: elation he'd found freedom to get his education and pursue a culinary dream, and yet sorrow for the damage to relationships his actions would incur. He'd stuffed the sorrow aside and embraced his new life for ten years now.

Thad clipped the last damp T-shirt to the clothesline.

His father had told him once, when Thaddeus had informed them of his graduation from culinary school and employment as a pastry assistant, all would be forgiven, should he come home and be baptized.

No, they hadn't shunned him, not exactly. He never intended to be baptized if he didn't intend to join the *Ordnung* wholeheartedly. Which was as things should be. No one should commit their lives to something as serious as an Amish Order, not if they weren't prepared for what such a commitment meant. He didn't know that he ever would be.

"You're not saying anything." *Mammi* stopped beside the basket. "Won't you be happy to see your family again? Especially your *mamm*?"

"It'll be nice to see some of them." He picked up the basket. "Will they all stay here?"

They walked to the back door together. "Your parents will, and maybe one of your *oncles* and his family. I have plenty of room."

Maybe he had better find another place to stay. But he didn't say this out loud. His *Mammi's* face glowed a happy shade of pink, in contrast to her white hair and head covering.

"Well, I know you'll enjoy having a houseful again. I always looked forward to coming here when I was small." He entered the house first, with *Mammi* behind him. He stopped long enough to put the empty basket on the washing machine.

"You will always have a place here, Thaddeus."

"Thank you."

She patted his hand. The simple gesture of affection made his eyes burn. *Mammi* had always accepted him, loved him, never spoke her opinion on him pursuing a life in the *Englisch* world.

"I must leave now," she said. "I'm meeting the group at Edna Grabill's for quilting and then lunch."

"I'll see you later, then."

Mammi left and Thad sighed. She was probably giddy inside about the family coming and ready to tell all her friends.

No matter how much he'd pulled his feet from the Amish world, it seemed as though one foot remained behind, his other foot planted in the *Englisch* world. What the family tried to call his *Rumspringa*, he called independence. This wasn't a phase. This was him, Thaddeus Zook.

Not Amish. Not even Plain. Not blending in.

Thad left the laundry area as soon as he heard the front door close behind *Mammi*. Ever since he'd come to stay with her, this was the first time she'd brought up his family.

However, once they arrived, it might be fun to see some of his cousins who had children. He knew Jacob was here in the village, living with his *mammi*, who married Thad's *mammi's* brother-in-law. The branches of the family trees, connected and grafted by marriage, made for some curious relatives, making Jacob Thad's second cousin by marriage.

The idea of so much family should feel suffocating, except for Pinecraft. The place gave Thaddeus a sense of refuge at the moment, reminding him of what he'd left behind, yet not pushing too hard into his own life. No one seemed to stare at his tattoo quite as much anymore.

Now the idea of his family encroaching on his little island of peace? It almost made Thad want to hop on his motorcycle again and hit the open road. But he had no idea where he would go. For now, he'd make do with the bit of foundation he still had left here. He went to the fridge for a glass of orange juice.

༺ঔ༻

"Did you ever find it?" the voice on the phone asked Pete.

"No, I didn't. I've scoured the restaurant. The employees I trust most are looking for it too. I told them I'd make it worth their while if they found what I was looking for. You should have seen them start turning over pans and digging through cabinets."

"What did you tell them it contained?"

"Vital records for the restaurant Mitch left somewhere and I need them bad."

"Mr. Bright wants all loose ends tied up in a nice little bow, meaning this potential problem goes away."

"Wasn't he happy with the election night party here, especially since he won?"

"Ecstatic. The new senator from Ohio especially liked the *fois gras* on crostini."

"Good."

"But he doesn't want anything Mitchell did to come back and haunt you, if *you* get my meaning. If you think you've accounted for everyone, think again."

Pete wanted to tell him Thad Zook left the state, and he was the only one unaccounted for. Thad was a nice kid, caught in the middle like him.

"I even went back and talked to everyone, asking them about Mitch and if he'd given them anything to hold for him, or if he'd acted strangely. Just like the police did. And nothin'."

"I don't want to hear it. No loose ends. If you know of any, tie them up."

"I'll let you know what I find. I—I might have to leave town for a while."

"Mitch told us the same thing. Do you know something you're not telling us?"

"Not exactly. Well, uh, one of the pastry chefs isn't around here anymore. I mean, I talked to him on the phone, but I found out he moved a few weeks ago."

"You're just now telling me this?"

"You told me to handle it, and I am."

"Handle it faster."

"Got it." He hung up the phone to give him what little upper hand he had. A man couldn't do it all. He had a business to run, a restaurant to officially reopen, not to mention publicity and a worried staff to soothe. A new manager to hire. He wasn't responsible for whatever Mitch had done.

Florida, it is. Ohio's getting a little chilly, anyway.

13

*B*etsy's life was an exhausted blur until she saw an *Englisch* nurse practitioner and had blood drawn for some lab work. Thanks to *Aenti* Chelle, she secured an appointment via another patient's cancellation. Within one week, the blood work was back.

Hypothyroidism. Betsy had never heard of the word, nor did she know much about the thyroid gland and its function. Hers definitely had been underactive, the nurse's attending physician told her, with her thyroid hormone level too high as her thyroid tried to keep up and couldn't. He put her on a pill she had to take once a day for the rest of her life, and she'd have to go back to have her blood drawn from time to time. An ultrasound of her thyroid revealed no other problems, for which she was thankful.

So while this was life-altering news, it wasn't something completely tragic. One day her hair would grow back again. In the early morning light, she brushed her hair and was reminded of her vanity. Oh, she so loved her hair. Sometimes she wished she could be more like the *Englisch* girls, who did such fun things with their tresses, especially when at the beach.

However, she wanted a man to love her not just for her hair, but for more. Gideon had somehow managed to catch her eye during church meeting last Sunday. However, he kept his distance when she surrounded herself with several ladies after the meeting concluded.

Betsy twisted the length of her hair into a knot and fastened it with hairpins. She frowned. Had she done the same to poor Jacob? Continually made her presence known to him? Tried to catch his eye?

Oh yes, she had. She recalled last winter, especially after little Rebecca Miller was gravely injured after being struck by a car while crossing Bahia Vista. Jacob and his children remained in Pinecraft through early spring. Not long after Rebecca's injury, Betsy had made her decision to stay in Florida and work for *Aenti* Chelle's cleaning business. Good housekeepers in Sarasota earned a respectable wage, far more than Betsy could earn in Ohio.

Now here she was, on the receiving end of someone whose attention she didn't want. No wonder Jacob had looked perplexed so many times last winter. No matter what she had done, short of stooping to something underhanded, nothing would change Jacob's mind about her.

Aenti Chelle, still in her robe, appeared in her doorway. "Do you want me to drop you off at the shop? I don't mind."

"No, I'm going to take my bicycle. It's light enough outside and I'll take Winston with me. He'll enjoy the ride." She reached for her head covering and used the few remaining hairpins to fasten it onto her hair. In response to his name, Winston wiggled himself at the foot of her bed.

"All right." Her aunt yawned. "I'll head back to bed, then."

"Thank you, anyway." She smiled as her aunt went back into the hall. If she didn't get a move on, *Aenti* Sarah would let her hear about it once she arrived at the shop.

Soon she was out the door and zipping along the vacant streets of Pinecraft, Winston sitting in the basket, his ears drifting back on the light air. He sneezed.

Lights glowed in a few homes as Betsy passed through the neighborhood. She could walk these streets blindfolded, and would probably know the streets she passed by name. Fry, Kaufman, Graber, Miller, all names of her people. The sweet taste of freedom here, she'd never felt anywhere else. Yet with the freedom came security. In spite of the city and all the distractions it offered, these snug streets made her feel protected and sheltered.

She didn't wonder what would have become of her if she'd stayed in Ohio, yet breathed a silent prayer of thanks. On days like today, she could see the hand of God working in spite of her questioning. Yes, she had chosen to stay here, mostly because of Jacob. But many months ago, as she'd become convinced of the harsh truth Jacob would never love her, not as she deserved, he'd said, she realized she had to choose. Stay here, or return to Ohio?

Betsy took the curve around the corner of Graber and saw the kitchen lights on inside Pinecraft Pies and Pastry. *Aenti* Sarah was already there, mixing up fresh pie crust and lighting the ovens. She cut across the pair of parking places beside the bakery and glided to a stop outside its back door. Winston put his paws on the edge of the basket.

"Be careful, I don't want you tumbling out." She took him from the basket and set him down inside a little pen Thaddeus had somehow constructed out of wooden scraps and painted white. It resembled a short picket fence, enough to keep Winston inside and out of trouble.

"No dogs in the kitchen," she warned Winston, before turning her back on him and entering the back door. She left the storm door open so the morning breeze could help cool the kitchen. And so Winston wouldn't feel quite so left out.

"I've lit the stove already." No "good morning" from *Aenti* Sarah, who already had four pie crusts rolled out, and now cut shortening into the flour mixture for more crust.

Betsy smiled at the phrase "lit the stove." No wood or propane stoves here to cook on, mostly electric. The allowance was made for vacationers who probably either rejoiced at the convenience or lamented the quality of cooking with electricity. An electric stove in some ways didn't bake the same as an open flame-heated stove. She'd learned to manage, like they all did, and the elders let small conveniences slide. There were far, far worse compromises people could make than using an electric stove.

She entered the sales floor and stepped around the display case. On went the coffee pot so the water in the brewing tank could heat. They'd already moved the microwave into the kitchen after the first morning, after *Aenti* Sarah pointed out customers might not like seeing the appliance prominently displayed in an Amish-owned and operated business.

Betsy didn't argue. Some visitors might be easily offended. Maybe it was her youth, but she didn't see what the problem was in using a tool to help her in her job. Still, she complied and now the microwave sat just inside the door to the kitchen on a work table, in easy reach to help customers wishing a warmed-up slice of pie.

"We should make homemade ice cream, too," *Aenti* Sarah announced as she formed a section of pie dough into a rounded shape before rolling it out. "People like ice cream on their pie."

"Or, we could buy some from Big Olaf's. Just vanilla. They're already doing the hard work for us." Big Olaf's ice cream shop lay but a block or so away, and Betsy couldn't recall the last time she'd passed through its doors to enjoy a sundae made with her favorite flavor, maple walnut, drizzled with chocolate sauce, and topped with whipped cream and a cherry.

"Hmm, I suppose we could."

Betsy had quickly learned that one of her own ideas had surpassed her *aenti's*, when she replied, "I suppose," to whatever Betsy had said. She smiled at the response.

"Good. I'll pay them a visit and see if it's possible. But only vanilla."

Betsy checked the apple slices she'd prepared the evening before, still basking in their juices and coated with cinnamon and sugar. Along with the apple mix, she stirred the other flavors she'd prepared, blueberry, cherry, and blackberry.

The next two hours passed with much rolling, cutting, and shaping of crusts. Then came the doughnut mix and dough for fried pies. Betsy turned the sign to "open" promptly at seven a.m. and flipped the switch for the lights.

Henry had suggested some pot lights, or recessed lights, in the ceiling, along with small electric lamps hanging over each table along the wall. The effect gave a peaceful atmosphere instead of the harshness of fluorescent light. The kitchen, however, glowed with the help of bright-white fluorescent bulbs, all the better to work by.

Within five minutes, the brothers Peter, James, and John arrived for their "morning cuppa" and fresh doughnuts.

"This are *gut*, very *gut*, Elizabeth," James said around a mouthful of glazed doughnut.

"Thank you, thank you very much." Betsy gestured to the coffee pot. "Help yourselves to coffee refills." She'd decided to keep the same policy as opening day: free coffee for all. However, she put a glass jar beside the pot for donations. Any donations, she'd give to the Haiti relief fund. The idea warmed her heart to help collect for a good cause. It was worth forgoing whatever funds a ninety-nine-cent cup of coffee might earn her.

After one week of trying the idea, the money in the donation jar amounted to nearly fifty dollars, and no one complained when they saw the jar. Or, if they couldn't pay, it was all right, too.

An unfamiliar man entered the shop and stepped up to the counter. He yawned, the expression almost comical as his face stretched. He removed his straw hat and rubbed his forehead, then stroked his beard.

"New shop, I hear."

"Yes, Mr. . . .?"

"Troyer. Daniel Troyer." He scanned the menu, then glanced her way. "I'll have a slice of apple pie, please."

"Certainly. The coffee's free, so help yourself."

He nodded, then headed over to the pot. He inhaled the brew as it streamed into his cup. "Smells good. I always welcome a strong cup of coffee. After all, it's the best part of waking up."

Daniel Troyer returned to the counter. "How much do I owe you?"

"Three-seventy-five."

He pulled out his wallet and gave her a five-dollar bill. "There you are. You can keep the change."

"Why . . . why thank you. If you'd like, you can go ahead and put it in the donation jar by the coffee pot."

"I'll do that."

"Would you like your pie warmed up?"

"Yes, it would be nice."

She slipped into the kitchen, grateful for the Dutch door she'd had Henry install. A few seconds in the microwave, the pie warmed up, then she pulled out the plate of pie. The bell over the door made its bright jingle. Another customer. This made her smile as she pushed through the door.

Gideon Stoltzfus. She kept her smile in place and nodded to him. He grinned and helped himself to a cup of coffee.

"Here you are, Mr. Troyer."

Gideon swung around. "Ah, my new next-door neighbor. I didn't get to greet you when I saw you arrive last evening."

Daniel Troyer nodded. "It's all right."

"How long you here for?"

"The winter. I find the weather is much better here. Truth be told, I resisted coming to Pinecraft. But here I am. I fell ill and couldn't work for a time. I'm getting to the age now where I'm not quite as fond of the Indiana winters."

"Ah, so you're from Indiana."

The two men kept chatting, Gideon and Daniel comparing places they knew, and finding mutual friends and a possible distant cousin relating them both. Such was the case in Pinecraft. If you spent a little time with a presumed stranger, you might find a connection you never imagined.

Good. Betsy smiled as she placed the serving pie back into the case. Daniel Troyer kept Gideon from peppering her with questions and bestowing too much attention on her. Part of her wished, though, that Thaddeus would pay her a little mind. Part of her, too, wished to learn more about Thaddeus and his journey outside the *Ordnung*. She banished those thoughts from her head and instead planned some possible adjustments to her pie and pastry menu.

A crash and shriek from the kitchen made them all look toward the kitchen door.

Aenti Sarah! Betsy pushed through the Dutch door with such force it smashed open against the stainless steel worktable.

Thaddeus whistled a long-forgotten tune as he strolled the street from Yoder's fresh market. He held a bag of vegetables for *Mammi*—fresh beans, some snap peas, and sweet corn. On her last trip to the store, she'd forgotten them, and she planned to bring marinated vegetables as a side dish to the potluck and singing tonight at Birky Square.

She'd invited him to come with her, and, of course, he'd turned her down. Although she'd extended an invitation to similar activities, this was the first time a disappointed expression had crossed her face. He tried not to let it niggle at him. Maybe him fetching the vegetables for her would ease some of her disappointment.

He approached Pinecraft Pies and Pastry and saw a small group clustered in front of the building. An ambulance, lights flashing and engine running, blocked part of his view. What on earth? Had something happened to Betsy? Or her *aenti*?

Thad stepped to the rear side of the ambulance just in time to see the small group part. *Aenti* Sarah, her face ashen and wearing an oxygen mask, was the one strapped to a gurney and covered with a blanket.

Betsy followed the EMTs, her own face pale. "I can't ride with her?"

"No, but you can meet us at the ER," said one EMT, a bulky fellow who looked like he could carry *Aenti* Sarah under one arm without much difficulty, if he had to.

Rochelle Keim's van rolled up a safe distance from the ambulance. She shot out from behind the driver's seat. "What happened?" She glanced Thatddeus's way as she reached the others.

Betsy met her *aenti* at the edge of the grass. "She fell, somehow, in the kitchen. And she couldn't get up. I didn't know what to do, so I called the ambulance. She got a little angry at me, said I was making a fuss over nothing."

"Ach, you did the right thing." Rochelle hugged her great-niece. "I'll drive you to the hospital."

"I'll close the shop. It'll only take a moment."

"Betsy," Thad spoke up. "I can take care of the shop for you. Show me what you have, and I'll run it until closing, or until you get back, whichever comes first."

"I can help, too," said another voice beside him. A woman, not quite Plain yet not quite *Englisch*, stood by his right elbow. She wore a kerchief on her head, not a bandana, and looked almost old enough to be a *mammi* herself. A Nikon digital camera hung from a strap around her neck.

"Thank you, thank you both." Betsy glanced from Thad to the other woman, then turned her focus to the ambulance.

The EMT worker slid the gurney into the back of the ambulance, and two EMTs climbed inside to join Sarah. The driver trotted around toward the front of the vehicle, and it pulled away from the edge of the street, lights flashing. The siren's wail began as they reached the edge of the block and bustling Bahia Vista.

The crowd dispersed, some of the people offering Betsy words of comfort and promises of prayer. She nodded, then entered the bakery, with Thad and the photographer behind her. Betsy continued into the kitchen where she faced them both.

"Thaddeus, have you met Imogene Brubaker yet? She's a fixture here in Pinecraft."

"No, I haven't." Thaddeus set the bag of vegetables on the stainless steel work table in the center of the kitchen. Its surface was crowded with pie pans filled with crusts, the crusts' edges neatly crimped.

"Imogene Brubaker, part of the woodwork," the woman said, offering her hand, which Thaddeus shook. She shook his hand like working a water pump. "Nice to meet you, Thaddeus . . ."

"Zook. Thaddeus Zook."

"Ah, of the Zooks. Where are you from?"

"My family's not too far from Millersburg."

"Here for the winter, then?"

"Here for now, anyway."

They stopped the small talk and pleasantries so Betsy could prepare to leave for the hospital.

"Well, Thaddeus, you know the menu," Betsy said. "I do have a few pies, ready to bake in case you need one. I have some doughnut mix prepared too. Those are in the freezer. If you need to cook a few more doughnuts, or fried pies, the cooking oil is in the cast-iron Dutch oven on the stove." Her words had the tempo of a woodpecker's peck.

"Betsy, *Aenti* Sarah is going to be all right." Rochelle held the Dutch door open to the kitchen. "Thaddeus and Imogene will keep things in hand here for you as well. Come, let's see to *Aenti*."

Betsy stopped in front of Thaddeus before leaving the kitchen. "Thank you. I know you'll take good care of things here."

"You know I will." He reached out and squeezed her hand. "Let us know how she is."

At his touch, she colored, but didn't pull away. "Thank you. I will."

He released her hand, and then she and Rochelle left. As they passed through the front of the bakery, a few customers who had entered gave their messages of encouragement to both of them.

Thad glanced at Imogene. "Time to get busy."

"Hold on just a second. We ought to talk for a minute." She stepped into the front of the bakery, and her voice rang out clear enough for Thad to hear through the Dutch door. "Hi, everyone. Thaddeus Zook and I'll be keeping an eye on the shop for Elizabeth. If anyone wants coffee, get some coffee and we'll be right out in a moment if you want pie or anything."

Imogene came back into the kitchen. "So, like I said, we should talk." She took the camera from around her neck and set it on top of the microwave oven.

Thad squared his shoulders. "Okay."

"What's with you and Betsy? I know you're a Zook, and you're obviously not part of your *Ordnung*. She is." Imogene crossed her arms over her chest.

"Are you part of your *Ordnung*?"

"No. But I'm not taking someone by the hand and looking at them with a certain look in my eye." The lady didn't seem angry. More protective, if anything. "I've seen young women led away from their Order with visions of romance with a handsome *Englisch* stranger dancing in their heads, and the idea all the things forbidden to them are now within reach."

"I'm not *Englisch*."

"But you are handsome. And you've had years of unbridled freedom, I'm sure."

Thad almost chuckled. *Unbridled freedom?* "Miss Brubaker, I care about Betsy. I'm not going to hurt her. It would be the last thing I'd want to do. I'm fully confident she'll soon meet a suitable man from her district who's devout, plain as pepper flakes, and they'll marry and she'll go on to have a wonderful family."

"Well," she said, her demeanor softening, shoulders lowering. "Okay. You keep it in mind."

"Oh, I do. Probably more than most people know."

"All right, then, Mr. Zook. You're the pastry chef. Show me what to do. I've been meaning to stop by here for some pictures, but I wasn't planning on running the place. But I don't mind at all."

"How about you take orders and run the register, and I'll be your gofer." He liked this lady and her feistiness.

"As long as you're not a weasel, it's fine by me." Imogene grinned. "Get it? Gofer? Weasel?"

"I got it." He laughed.

The morning clicked by with a steady stream of customers, some of them wanting to know what had happened to Sarah, and when Betsy would return. Most had a cup of coffee or tea, and some selected a slice of pie or doughnut.

Thad kept to the kitchen as much as possible, not wanting to create more curiosity than already existed about who was running Pinecraft Pies and Pastry while Betsy and Sarah were absent. His hands knew exactly what to do in the kitchen, popping pies into the oven, frying fresh doughnuts. Betsy and her *aenti* had done the hard work. Even with what little he did, being back in a kitchen again felt great. He fulfilled his real purpose, not fumbling with tiles and carpentry work.

A lull in traffic left the bakery empty, with Imogene humming behind the counter. Thad joined her at the counter but didn't hum. Instead, he wiped his hands on a black canvas apron he'd found hanging on a peg by the back door.

"Well, I say we did a good job." Imogene, her camera back in her hands, surveyed the supply of pies and pastries in the case. Then she glanced at the wall clock. "No wonder the place is empty now. The Pioneer Trails bus is arriving soon. I bet it's pretty full."

"Why?"

She half-squatted, then zoomed in on a trio of pies in the case. "There. I need to write about Betsy's pies on my blog . . . Thanksgiving's coming."

Ah, right. Next week. He hadn't thought much about the date. Back in Columbus, he'd only thought if it in terms of pastries and desserts at Dish and Spoon, and if he would have the next day off to sleep.

"I wonder if we'll get any more customers once the bus arrives." Which included his family, although *Mammi* said they wouldn't arrive until the first part of December.

"We'll wait and see. We can always close shop and then reopen after dinner. Last time I talked to Betsy, she said afternoons were the slowest. And you have some vegetables in the bag on the counter."

He touched his forehead. "Ah, *Mammi's* probably wondering what happened." As if she'd heard his thoughts, Thad looked through the front window of the bakery to see his *mammi* bicycling up the sidewalk.

Thad went out the front door. "*Mammi*, I'm sorry. I saw Betsy's *aenti* being taken to the hospital, and then I offered to help at the bakery."

She nodded as she parked her three-wheeler, then latched it to the bicycle rack with her padlock. "I know. I figured as much. I was out weeding a moment ago when someone stopped by and told me. I decided not to go to quilting anyway. But I thought I would come pick up the vegetables so I can get them marinated for tonight."

He reentered the bakery. "I'll get the bag and bring it right out."

"Thank you."

"Do you need me to carry it home for you?"

Mammi shook her head. "No, it's only two blocks and the bag is light enough."

"All right." He headed for the kitchen, snagged *Mammi's* bag of vegetables, then joined her at the counter.

"Don't forget, the singing is tonight," she said as he handed her the bag.

"I haven't forgotten," which didn't at all mean he'd attend.

After *Mammi* left the bakery, Imogene said, "Your *mammi* is kindness personified. I always feel so warm after a conversation with her. She's one of the reasons Pinecraft is such a good place all year-round."

"She'd be embarrassed to hear you say so."

"Probably." She studied his arm, the one with the vines reaching from his wrist and disappearing under his T-shirt sleeve. Then she held up her camera.

"Ah, I don't think anyone's taken a photo of it before, not counting the artist." He extended his arm forward, then twisted it. The design had become a part of him and he hardly took notice anymore. It had become part of him, like his hair color or eye color.

"May I?" Imogene reached out her hand.

"Sure."

It felt strange, to have someone touch his arm.

"Did it hurt much?"

"It hurt, but the artist didn't do it all at once. They did it in stages, with the outline, then color, and finally details." The process took a while, but at the time, he thought it was worth it.

"So why'd you do it?"

"Do what?"

"Get a tattoo at all."

"Well, I like art and interesting designs. I liked this one a lot. I figured if I got one, it had better be something good because it's permanent."

"Huh. Okay. But couldn't you put a picture of it on a wall somewhere and enjoy it just the same?"

Boy, this lady didn't quit. But he liked her, even when she zoomed in with her camera on the detail in the green vines. The camera's shutter clicked.

"I always have it with me. It's hard to explain." No, he didn't get it because "all the other guys were." He just plain liked it.

"All righty, then." She released her camera, letting it dangle by its strap. "Thaddeus Zook, even without the tattoo, you would still stand out in a crowd."

"I didn't get it to stand out."

The bell over the door clanged, providing a welcome pause to the subject. An older couple entered, dragging rolling suitcases behind them.

The man was Old Order, from the top of his straw hat to the sensible black shoes he wore, his wife with a navy blue dress and apron a shade lighter. They stopped in the center of the bakery.

"Where is Elizabeth Yoder?" the older man demanded as he eyeballed Thad's tattoo and took in the sight of Thad's apron. "And who are *you*, working in her bakery?"

❧

Rochelle sighed as she leaned back on the cushioned chair in the emergency room. Poor Sarah and Betsy. Sarah, typically the picture of health and fiercely independent, could run circles around people decades younger than her eighty-five years. Except not now, not for a long while. Betsy, so full of energy yet needing Sarah's persistent guidance to help her in her venture.

Rochelle would help her young great-niece more, if not for her own business. And now, who knew what had happened to *Aenti* Sarah? She prayed it wasn't serious, a simple slip and fall on the kitchen floor.

"Cup of coffee?" a gentleman asked, holding a steaming cup. Daniel Troyer. She had run into him first thing that morning, while chatting with friends at the market. The Amish man, perhaps five or so years older than her, wore a beard, which signaled "married" to her. However, his eyes held a warmth and kindness in them that she found appealing.

Almost like Silas Fry.

But Silas Fry in her life might as well have been a million years ago.

"Oh, thank you." She took the toasty warm cup from him.

"I'm staying catty-corner across the street from Mrs. Yoder. Such a kind woman." He took a seat, keeping one empty chair between them. "I came when I heard."

"You didn't have to come."

"I wanted to see if I could help at all."

"What about your wife?" Rochelle had to ask.

"I have no wife." He looked down at his hands. Smooth hands, for an Amish man. "I'm here for the winter. It's been many years since I ventured south to Pinecraft."

"Ah, I see." She sipped the coffee. Cream and sugar. She preferred cream only, but the sweetness helped soothe her nerves while she waited. Betsy had come out not five minutes ago to let them know the doctors were sending *Aenti* Sarah for a CAT scan.

"So, what line of business are you in, back in Indiana, Mr. Troyer?"

"I managed the billing for a cabinet shop until I fell ill and had to stop work for a while earlier this year." Daniel stroked his beard. "Last winter, the weather was too much for me in Indiana, so I decided to come to Pinecraft and see how this winter goes for me."

"And, how's it going so far?"

"The best winter yet, if I count the last thirty minutes or so."

She felt his warm smile from two seats away, and her own face flamed. Then she inwardly chided herself. Entertaining such conversation, in a hospital waiting room, when she should be thinking of and praying for *Aenti* Sarah.

Rochelle kept silent and drank her sweet coffee. She hadn't truly noticed a man, not like this, since Silas. It was both silly and childish. She'd only just met Daniel Troyer. And he didn't know her, either.

14

*B*etsy pulled her phone partway out of her tote bag and glanced at the time. Not quite two o'clock. *Aenti* Sarah had at last been whisked back for blood tests, X-rays, and another scan more than an hour before. The *Englisch* hospital had almost immediately set to work in assessing *Aenti's* physical condition.

Aenti had been wheeled to the radiology department, cheerful yet in pain. *"Gotte's wille* be done," she said.

A lump made Betsy's throat ache. Not good, to have *Aenti*, one of her biggest allies in the village, laid up with an injury. Not now, or any time.

Aenti Chelle had gone to the cafeteria to see about bringing back some sort of a snack. Their new friend, Daniel Troyer, accompanied her. Everyone's stomachs grumbled. The energy from a slice of buttered toast Betsy had eaten in the early morning hours had long since worn off.

Betsy thanked *Gotte* many times *Aenti* Chelle had taken her to the hospital. Her *aenti* moved freely, confidently in the *Englisch* world. Betsy didn't know if she could, even after nearly one year in Florida.

A man and a woman in Plain clothing entered the waiting room area. Betsy sprang to her feet.

"*Mamm—Daed.*" She went to them and surprised herself, and probably them, too, by giving them a hug. "You're here early."

"We arrived just in time," *Mamm* said. "We left our bags at the house, and found a driver to take us straight here."

Daed nodded. "The bishop will be here soon to pray with all of us."

"Good. I wasn't sure if *Aenti* Chelle was able to notify anyone yet."

"Word travels fast in the village." *Mammi* took a seat on the nearest cushioned chair.

"We stopped at the bakery first." *Daed* gave her a pointed look. So they'd seen it. She couldn't quite read her *daed's* expression.

"I—I was hoping to show it to you myself. *Aenti* Sarah fell in the kitchen, and I was so scared. I called an ambulance right away."

"You did the right thing. But, you left the bakery in someone's hands we don't know." Her father frowned. "An *Englisch* man, with a tattoo. Imogene Brubaker is one thing. She'll do right by you. But the man?"

"Thaddeus Zook isn't *Englisch.*"

"Well, he doesn't look Amish."

No, Thaddeus wasn't. She remembered the strength in his hand as he squeezed hers, the warmth and kindness there. Maybe something more, too. She pushed the thought out of her head. Times were, when she was younger, she believed her parents knew what she was thinking. This made her fearful then, and not a little nervous now.

"You're right. But he's a good pastry chef, from what I understand. He worked in a fine restaurant in Ohio."

Her *daed* shook his head. "We will talk about this later. We should gather to pray for *Aenti* Sarah."

"Of course, yes, *Daed.*"

Here came *Aenti* Chelle and Daniel Troyer, along with the bishop from Pinecraft and his wife. Betsy immediately sat up a little straighter and smoothed an unseen wrinkle. Was her head covering straight? As though *Mamm* knew, she reached over and patted down a wayward hair on Betsy's head.

But the smile the bishop had for all of them was warm and comforting. His wife greeted *Mamm* softly, then did the same with Betsy.

"We were so sorry to hear the news. Sarah is one of our faithful, and we will pray for *Gotte's* will to be done." She touched *Mamm's* arm.

"I'm thankful we arrived today." *Mamm* nodded.

"And Betsy, I've heard of your bakery, and your *aenti* has been helping you."

"Yes, she has been a big help to me." Betsy looked down at her lap. She tried not to think of the cell phone in her tote bag. She didn't know if anyone else in the group had one, besides *Aenti* Chelle. Well, maybe Mr. Troyer.

They sat in a corner of the waiting room and bowed their heads as the bishop prayed. He prayed in their language, with a strong, yet subdued voice. Betsy found the language and his words comforting.

"*Grant Thy mercy and grace to our sister, Sarah Yoder . . . We thank Thee for the many years Thou has bestowed upon her . . . We ask for Thy guidance and strength for those who minister to her . . .*"

A sudden ringing noise interrupted the bishop's words, and the noise came from the tote bag at Betsy's feet.

The phone!

Peter Stucenski had his head bowed in prayer and desperately prayed to Anyone who might be listening for no one to call on him to pray. He didn't know any German, Dutch, or whatever language the preacher now spoke.

Then the young Amish woman's phone started going berserk in her bag. Pete squinted in her direction. She turned a shade of chili pepper red as she snatched the bag from her feet. She jammed her hand inside, fumbled around, then scrounged for the phone. Successful, she discreetly held it inside the bag and pushed some buttons.

"I am *so* sorry," was all she said. The kid looked ready to melt into the cushions.

Pete knew the squeamish look. He'd been there before, his phone interrupting an important meeting with clients.

Thankfully, the minister said a few more words before the "amen," and no one had asked Peter to pray.

His head perspired and his faced itched, the more he sat there in the waiting room. All because Rochelle Keim had caught his eye. Something about her sweet smile and secrets in her hazel eyes drew him to her. He hadn't counted on this. Now here he was, in a prayer circle of some kind.

The idea had been simple at first. Get to Florida, make sure Thad Zook wouldn't recognize him if they saw each other in the "Amish land" of Sarasota, then find what Thad had brought with him to the Sunshine State. It shouldn't be too difficult to lie low; Thad had only seen him once or twice, face-to-face at the restaurant.

His wove a generic story ahead of time, of being attached to the Troyer family, seemingly a common enough name in the Amish world. Concocted with the help of the Internet, he finalized the story and after a few phone calls secured paid accommodations for four weeks in the village at a much better price than a hotel. Now, with a few discreet questions and showing up around the village, he'd homed in on Thaddeus Zook.

Others back in Ohio probably wanted him to go in, with proverbial guns blazing, and demand Thad turn over what he had to ensure his overall health and well-being. But Pete wanted to find his way more subtly, get in, get out, and then let Thad go on his merry way, none the wiser, if possible.

Someone like Thad, if he knew what he had, would undoubtedly go to the authorities. Pete wouldn't find it so easy to disavow his own knowledge of what Thad possessed, what all of them knew. With Pete's softer approach, he could make the little problem go away, and no one got hurt.

Then he had to run into Rochelle Keim. The chance encounter in a little market in the village seemed innocent enough. However, after the uproar at the bakery and at seeing Rochelle's distress, Pete had stepped up to help her. Or, Daniel Troyer had.

She glanced at him now that the prayer was done. "Mr. Troyer?"

"Yes, Miss Keim?"

"Do you have plans for Thanksgiving dinner? I know the church has its meal on Sunday. But next Thursday, what about you?"

"Ah, no, I have no plans."

"Well, then, if you would like to join my family for supper, you will be most welcome."

"Thanks. I'd like to very much."

A man approached them, a stethoscope around his neck. "Yoder family? I'm Dr. Plank. I'm an orthopedic specialist. Mrs. Yoder is stabilized, but we must perform surgery tomorrow morning to put a pin in her hip."

Rochelle turned her attention then to the physician, but Pete swallowed hard. Sometimes, a man just couldn't help himself.

༚

Thad stretched and yawned after he returned home. He and Imogene had closed the shop for the afternoon, not long after three.

"People will understand. They'll be expecting Betsy to be with her family," Imogene had said.

True, but Thad thought of her bottom line. Every hour not open for business would cost Betsy money.

"If you meet me back here in the morning so I can get into the shop, I'll bake a few items fresh before we open." Betsy hadn't asked him to do it, but a setback like a medical emergency this early in her venture wouldn't help her business, not if she didn't have someone capable to run it.

"Here. Keep the key." Imogene had pressed it into his hand. "I won't be up stirring before eight a.m. Too early for my blood."

He twirled the key between his fingers. *Mammi* puttered around the house, sweeping and mopping. Her humming drifted back to his room. No matter that the family's arrival was weeks away, the news of their visit was incentive enough to send *Mammi* into a cleaning frenzy of the already-spotless home.

He wanted to laugh at the idea of *Mammi* cleaning in fast-forward, but thoughts of his family kept the laughter in check. They might ignore his presence at *Mammi's*, or worse, ask him to leave the house. But it was *Mammi's* home and she would have the final say. Or would she? If *Daadi* were still alive, he wondered if they'd have welcomed him into their home at all.

The sight of Betsy's father looking like a stern thundercloud reminded him of his own father. The man had shown up at the bakery, of course expecting to see his daughter, not Thad and Imogene, a mismatched odd couple of sorts, trying to run the shop and Betsy gone.

Thad had stood his ground as he explained, listing his resumé, but not going so far as to state his reasons for being in Pinecraft. Nobody needed to know. At this point, he still wasn't sure what had brought him here other than self-preservation and something else, something he couldn't put a name to just yet.

A soft knock sounded at the door. "Thaddeus?"

"Come in, *Mammi*."

She pushed open the door as he sat up on the bed. "Were you sleeping?"

He shook his head, then set the bakery key on his dresser. "Just stretching. It was a long day and I've been out of practice in the kitchen."

"It's almost time for the potluck and singing. Would you . . . would you please come with me tonight? The Bontragers will welcome you, I know. They welcome everyone." She sounded infinitely weary, despite her high energy at cleaning mere moments ago.

He thought of Betsy's *Aenti* Sarah, of the fragility of the elderly. What if something happened to *Mammi*, and he'd refused to accompany her? "All right, I'll go with you."

"*Danke*, Thaddeus."

"You're welcome." She smiled at him, then closed the door.

Thad rummaged in the dresser and found one of his thermal shirts, dark gray. Now, *this* was something he wouldn't have much use for in Florida. He eyed the sleeves. Too warm, and the material clung to his skin.

He took the shirt with him into the hallway, then headed for the kitchen. "*Mammi*, do you have a pair of scissors handy?"

"In the drawer beside the stove." She opened the refrigerator and took out a large plastic bowl. "What are you going to do?"

"A little something to this shirt." He found the green-handled scissors, then cut one of the sleeves off with a flourish. "There." He set the shirt and scissors on the counter, then slid the lone sleeve up over his tattooed arm.

"Well, you're resourceful." *Mammi* stared at his arm, covered from the edge of his T-shirt sleeve to the wrist.

"I thought so." He couldn't help it if people didn't know his insides and misunderstood him. But his outsides? Those, he could control. The reflex to be on the defensive about his tattoo remained close to the surface, but he didn't want to reflect badly on Betsy. She'd trusted him with her bakery, and he didn't want to disappoint her.

He and *Mammi* left shortly after five, walking along Kaufman and heading toward Bahia Vista, with Thad carrying the container of marinated vegetables and *Mammi* tugging her sweater around her.

"I'm so glad you said you'd come with me."

"I don't mind." The Thaddeus Zook he used to know loved going to singings, hearing the harmonies, the tones blending together. Tonight, he didn't know what he'd hear. He didn't recall much about Pinecraft singings. Sitting up late, falling asleep on his *Mamm's* lap, listening to the sound of a guitar, banjo, or both. The soft wail of someone's harmonica.

They had to step around a cluster of bicycles parked along the Bontragers' driveway, and not a few parked on the front sidewalk. An older man, slightly balding and wearing a Cardinals baseball cap, was setting up metal folding chairs in the side yard. A trio of men stood in front of a storage shed as they tuned a pair of guitars and a banjo.

Phillip Bontrager, the man in the Cardinals cap, greeted him like a relative, telling him *Mammi* had only good things to say about her grandson. Thad didn't quip back a response saying not all his family would have such glowing words about him.

"I hear you're a pastry chef," Phil said as they shook hands while standing on the carport. His wife Myra smiled and waved as she bustled in and out the side door of their home.

"Yes, I am. Or was." Thad tugged on the makeshift sleeve he'd fashioned less than an hour before.

"So, you're here on vacation, then."

"Sort of. I'm, uh, going to look for work around here. I like the climate much better." The admission startled him. The longer he'd been in Florida, the more he saw the benefit of not being faced with digging out after winter storms, dealing with ice and slush, and everything else about a Midwestern winter.

"It is nice. Sarasota has a number of excellent restaurants. Unless you're thinking of heading somewhere like Miami?"

"No, I hadn't thought of it." Thad glanced at the table filling the length of the carport. As more friends and neighbors arrived, more dishes covered the table. One thing always made him homesick for the old days—the food—delectably simple, made with love, unpretentious. Generous.

"It looks like we're all set." Myra surveyed the table as she set a basket of plastic of forks, knives, and spoons at the end. "Phil?"

"Let us bow our heads and pray over the meal." Phil removed his baseball cap, and the men followed suit, some like Thad who wore no hat, a few with traditional straw hats, and others with caps like Phil's.

Thad closed his eyes.

"Heavenly Father, we thank You for Your rich blessings upon us. Bless the hands of those who prepared this food, bless our lives to Your service, and let us have good fellowship to honor You tonight. Amen." Phil's voice echoed off the nearby wall, and off a shed a few footsteps from the carport.

"Amen," chorused some voices.

"Let's eat!" Phil motioned to the table.

Just as with the haystack supper, Thad found himself in a food line, but this one shorter. Friends chatted, their conversations punctuated with chuckles. A few spoke in lower tones, their glances darting around the open yard and courtyard area where the musicians rested their instruments.

A few voices caught his attention.

"Tattoo . . ."

"One of *those* people, come to stir up trouble among us."

Thad glanced around the assembled group, where people dined on their meals while sitting on folding chairs, lawn chairs, and such. Nobody else looked as though they'd have a tattoo. While his was covered tonight, he knew word had already gotten around the village.

Stirring up trouble? Him? Not at all. Far from it. His mission the entire time in Florida had been to lie low.

"Don't pay them any mind," *Mammi* murmured beside him. "They don't know you, and I do. Come, Phillip has a spot for us at the picnic table in the backyard."

"What are they talking about, besides my tattoo?" He tried to keep his voice low as he followed *Mammi* around the side of the house.

"*Englisch*, filming in the village a while back for a television show, with some young people who used to be Amish, pretending they just left their Orders, or something like that." *Mammi* shook her head. "People want to be left alone. Anyone can visit Pinecraft. But trying to start trouble and get people angry at each other, and them, too? It is wrong."

Now it was Thad's turn to shake his head. He settled onto the bench, placing his plate on the table. "I didn't know. I didn't watch much TV back . . . back in Columbus. Other than the news."

"Sometimes I wonder if it's a good thing to live here." *Mammi* sighed.

"I like it here." Another admission, this time after swallowing a bite of someone's broccoli casserole, with rice and cheese. Part of him did truly like Pinecraft.

"Well, as I said, don't pay them any mind."

"Don't pay who any mind?" Phil took a seat directly across from Thad.

"Oh, never mind, Phillip. Some people, muttering about Thaddeus."

"Why would they?"

"I never joined my Order. I left . . . the Amish to go to culinary school." He didn't regret his choice, not completely. He glanced at *Mammi* to see if she reacted at all to his words. He knew it pained many members of his family. Some, it goaded into anger. Some, like *Mammi* and his own *mamm*, it caused sorrow.

"Ah, so you were never baptized?"

"No." Thad wanted to change the conversation to something else. Food, music, alligator hunting in Florida, the everescalating price of gasoline. He knew what the others would expect of him, in order to return to the Order—go before everyone, confess his sin and wrongdoing, forsake everything, and ask for forgiveness. He couldn't do it, especially if he wasn't sorry for any of it.

15

The shadows grew longer and the temperature dropped, reminding Thad of winter's approach, even here in Florida. After the meal had been cleared away (he'd stuffed himself with homemade chocolate chip cookies and a slice of pie), they all tugged chairs and benches to form a semicircle in the courtyard that made up part of the Bontragers' side yard.

Thad positioned himself against a pole supporting the carport, leaving his open seat for someone else. As the darkness fell, more neighbors showed up on tricycles. The low light provided an ample cover for Thad's presence.

Of course, he was out of place. He didn't look much different than some of the *Englisch* youths who would sometimes commandeer the basketball court in the park.

"Good evening, everyone," Phil said from where he stood at the edge of the group. "Thanks for coming. We're going to enjoy some good music together. Myra's started the coffee pot perking and some hot water for hot chocolate or tea, so if anyone gets a might chilly, we'll have beverages to warm you up."

Then the music started. The atmosphere lifted as much as it could with an assembled group that included a few Old Order folks. Thad grinned at the sight of some of the more "liberal" ones keeping the beat by tapping their knees, nodding their heads.

The first of several rousing Southern Gospel tunes rang out. One of the men, a guy he'd seen around the village a few times, was really getting down playing his acoustic guitar. Thad had forgotten how much fun people watching could be. Around here, you never knew who or what you'd see. Tonight was no different.

And thankfully, no more personal questions came from anyone while the music was playing. The muscles in his shoulders unknotted themselves. Coming tonight hadn't been so bad. *Mammi* smiled up at him from the folding chair someone had lent her.

After four songs the pace slowed, and the fervent guitar player now plucked a soft melody. The banjo player's technique mirrored his friends'.

"Amazing grace, how sweet the sound that saved a wretch like me! I once was lost, but now am found; was blind, but now I see . . ."

The harmonies struck an inner chord with Thad as the guitars and banjo music ceased, and there was nothing left but the chorusing voices.

" 'Twas grace that taught my heart to fear, and grace my fears relieved; how precious did that grace appear the hour I first believed."

Fears relieved? He didn't have fears, not anymore. He'd resigned himself to the fact he was likely bound for hell, whatever it was. He'd thought long and hard as any young adult could before leaving his family. They thought it had been easy for him to leave, he was sure. In the end, it had been the only way for him to keep breathing. Grace was for other people, not him.

Thad reached up. He brushed away two wet patches, one on each cheek.

No matter what he did here, no matter how many sleeves he put on his arm, he was an outsider. No matter how much he helped *Mammi*, or Betsy. Maybe it was safe to return to Columbus again, get his old job back. Or else head someplace else like Miami, as Phil mentioned earlier.

"You okay?" a voice said at his elbow.

Imogene, with her bandana-covered hair and peasant skirt. Her expression was filled with concern.

He shrugged. "Yeah. The song just gets to me. Been a long time since I heard it."

"Ah, so I see."

He faced forward again as the voices continued through the verses. It was just a song. It couldn't change reality.

"Well, I'll come by the shop in the morning before it opens."

"I've got the key, remember? I'll be fine."

"I thought you might want to talk."

"No." He liked the older woman with her quirky demeanor.

"I'll come anyway."

"Suit yourself." He hoped he didn't sound brusque, but a guy could only take so much verbal poking.

"I always do."

Imogene's remark made him chuckle.

※

This morning Betsy felt all of fourteen again, too old for school and yet not truly accepted as one of the adults. She took a sip of orange juice and kept listening for a knock at the front door. They were set to go to the bakery first, then to the hospital to wait while *Aenti* had her hip pinned.

No one had scolded Betsy for the phone in her bag ringing during prayer, but her *daed's* expression had told her plenty. Not a good impression, especially not with her shop just opening and her wanting to prove to him, and all of them, that investing in her venture had been wise. And, the thing had to ring while the bishop was there, of all people.

The phone call had come from Imogene, letting Betsy know she and Thaddeus had the store in hand, they would lock up around three or so if it was okay, and they were praying for *Aenti* Sarah.

Last night Betsy had thanked God in prayer for friends like Imogene and Thaddeus, who willingly stepped in after *Aenti's* fall. She had no idea of what to do, especially now *Aenti* Sarah would be unable to help in the bakery. It didn't matter just now, of course.

Seven a.m. and a knock sounded at the door. *Aenti* Chelle had already departed for her first housecleaning clients of the day. Winston skittered ahead of Betsy. His bark echoed off the tiles in canine outrage.

Daed stood at the door. "You are ready to go, Elizabetts?" He stared down at Winston from the other side of the screen.

"Yes, *Daed*. I'm going to put Winston on the lanai and make sure he has some water and food." She paused. She hadn't told them about the dog. She hadn't hidden him, and it wouldn't truly matter.

She left Winston pouting on the lanai but already sniffing at the air drifting in through the screens. She didn't think he would make any puddles in the house, but she still didn't want to chance it.

Within a few minutes, she'd climbed into the back seat of the car, driven by a distant cousin of her mother's. Ironic. This cousin had been shunned, yet her family depended on the cousin for a ride to the hospital.

"We will stop at the bakery for a moment," *Daed* announced. "Your *aenti* doesn't go in for surgery until nine, so we have plenty of time."

Plenty of time for what? Betsy nibbled her lower lip. Not good, not good.

A few early birds were up and about, some toting laundry to the Pinecraft Laundromat, others strolling to the market. The cousin pulled up in front of the bakery, where a light glowed from the rear of the store. The sign still read "closed," but Betsy led them around to the rear of the shop.

Thaddeus stood at the work table. He held a rolling pin above a lump of dough and paused with his hands in midair above the pie crust. "Oh. Good morning."

"Good morning." She noticed his arm, the one with the tattoo, had some kind of a dark gray sleeve over it, his other arm bare. "Is Imogene coming?"

"I believe she is. I gather she's not a morning person?"

Betsy shook her head. "She's not one to rise early." *Daed* stood beside her, glancing from her to Thaddeus, then back to her again.

"How's your *aenti*?" Thaddeus asked.

She liked the sound of the *Dietsch* coming from him. She opened her mouth to reply.

"She is having surgery this morning to repair her broken hip," *Daed* announced. "I've been thinking, Elizabeth, you will still require help in the bakery, but you need an expert. I've spoken with Vera Byler."

"Vera?" Betsy was going to be sick, and it wouldn't do to heave all the orange juice she'd just drank onto the work table.

"Vera is a good baker and respected member of the community. In fact, Vera will be arriving in about thirty minutes."

Betsy glanced at Thaddeus. "*Daed*, Thaddeus is an excellent baker."

"I'll work for free," Thaddeus said. "I know you're just getting the business off the ground."

"It simply won't do." *Daed* shook his head. "We can't have you on the sales floor in the front."

Thaddeus's jaw twitched. The expression in his dark eyes crackled, but the pies lined up on the table received the heat of his glare. Betsy stared at the pies, too. Their edges, neatly crimped. Designs carved in the crust tops with the tip of a knife. One pie with the cut-out shape of an apple on the top, complete with a pair of dough leaves. Elegant. Beautiful.

"*Daed*—"

"I can do prep work overnight, Mr. Yoder. If Betsy and Vera leave me a list of what they need done, I can get the prep done so they can bake first thing with fresh ingredients."

Betsy studied her *daed's* face. She could scarcely breathe. The idea of giving Thaddeus a chance meant something to her. To him, too. Although she couldn't understand why he didn't want to be paid.

"All right." Her *daed* let out a breath. "We'll try it for a week."

"Thank you, *Daed*." Betsy felt the grin on her face as she looked at Thaddeus.

"We must get to the hospital."

"Yes," Betsy said as they turned to leave. "Thank you, Thaddeus."

"Of course." Then he winked at her while her father's back was turned. Her cheeks flush, she hurried after her father.

❧

Rochelle wanted to kick the flat tire. Her van had limped to the side of the street moments before, the right front tire making a pathetic *wubb-wubb-wubb* as the vehicle ground to a halt. Just what she didn't need. She had not quite two hours before she had to see to her afternoon client, a particularly fussy and picky socialite with a beachfront home. If she didn't have any clients, she could have walked the mile back to Pinecraft.

No, kicking the flat tire wouldn't solve her problem.

She touched the button on her phone. Henry Hostetler wasn't answering, and she wasn't sure who else to call about changing a flat tire. Calling a tow truck would be expensive, and pointless, for just a flat tire. She had a perfectly good spare in the rear compartment of the van.

She strode to the back of the van and popped open the door. She could do this. Surely she could get the old tire pulled off, and put the spare on.

Rochelle pulled out her plastic bin of cleaning supplies and set it on the ground beside her, then pulled the flat cover off the wheel well where the spare tire rested.

"Need a hand?"

Rochelle started, knocking the top of her head on the open van door above her. "Ow!"

Daniel Troyer stood a few paces behind her, a sheepish grin on his face. He darted forward. "I'm *so* sorry. I didn't mean to scare you."

Tears in her eyes, Rochelle rubbed the top of her head. Her covering managed to stay in place, and she moved it more securely into position.

"It's okay. I'm not scared of you."

"Good." Daniel stepped closer. The man's eyes were gray, not blue.

She swallowed hard. "Do you happen to know how to change a tire?"

"Of course." He motioned toward the curb. "Step aside, Miss Rochelle."

Daniel pulled the tire from the storage spot without any effort. Such strong, capable hands and muscular arms. So much like Silas. "You have tools, a jack and iron?"

"Oh, uh, yes. They should be right under the tire." She glanced into the compartment and picked up the canvas bag containing the jack and iron. "Here."

"All righty, we'll get you back on the road in no time." He squatted beside the van and removed the hubcap. The lug nuts wouldn't cooperate with the tire iron. He grunted and fought, trying to loosen the nuts. The expression on his face made a laugh bubble up inside Rochelle, tired as she was.

"What's so funny?"

"The look on your face while you wrestle with the flat."

He smiled up at her, and the smile made her heart leap inside her. What was it about this man? She felt her phone buzz. She didn't recognize the number. She'd call them back.

At last, the nuts loosened and Daniel removed the flat tire, then settled the spare in its place. "See? Nothing to it. Now I just need to get these tightened up so you can get on the road."

Five more minutes, and Daniel was standing, stretching, then carrying the flat tire to the rear of the van. "There." He set it inside the back of the van.

She'd finished her clients for the morning and her stomach grumbled for lunch. The noise made her clamp her hand over her waist.

"Hungry, huh?" Daniel said as he stepped around her to remove the jack from under the van.

"It's been a while since breakfast and I had a busy morning."

"Let me take you to Yoder's for lunch."

Rochelle considered the offer. This man caught her attention and she hadn't been prepared for this. Not in the least. "Um. . ."

"When was the last time you went out for lunch with a friend?"

She pondered his question. "With my niece, when I got back to Sarasota about a month or so ago."

Daniel cranked the jack's handle and the van's right front end lowered to the ground. "Too long." He pulled the jack from under the van, then stood.

"I have an afternoon client at two."

He glanced at his watch. "It's a little after twelve now. We can get a table if we hurry."

"All—all right." It was only lunch, she kept telling herself, even as Daniel put the tools into the rear of the van, followed by her cleaning supplies.

"Don't be nervous. I'll follow you on my bicycle, and you can get us a spot in line."

Rochelle nodded. Her heart beat faster. "I'll see you there in a few minutes."

16

Aenti Chelle had been acting strangely, ever since the day of *Aenti* Sarah's surgery. At first, Betsy paid the change little mind, but after a week, she stopped holding her silence when on her *aenti's* day off, she entered Pinecraft Pies and Pastry along with Daniel Troyer.

Daniel stood at the coffee station, pouring two cups of coffee while *Aenti* Chelle studied the fresh pastries and pies in the case.

"I don't know what to choose. I know everything's delicious. Daniel, what do you want?" She glanced over at him, her cheeks flushed.

"Surprise me," the man said with a grin.

Aenti Chelle turned her attention back to the glass display case. "I'll have a glazed doughnut and a chocolate fried pie, please."

"Right away." Betsy pulled one of each from the case and placed them on small paper plates. She leaned across the counter and whispered to her *aenti*. "So, you like this Daniel Troyer?"

"I do. I do." *Aenti* Chelle's gaze slid sideways. "Careful, or he'll hear you."

Betsy nodded, sliding the plates toward her aunt. "No charge for you today."

"Oh, Betsy, I couldn't."

"You've been such a help and an encouragement to me, and I'm grateful."

"Well, thank you." Her blush deepened, the closer Daniel came.

With steaming cups of coffee in both hands, Daniel joined *Aenti* Chelle at the case. "So what did you choose?"

"Glazed doughnut for me, a chocolate fried pie for you. They're still warm."

"Wonderful." A shiny flash at his wrist caught Betsy's attention.

"That's some watch, Mr. Troyer."

"Ah, my watch." He touched his wrist with his right hand. "It was a gift. I know it's a little flashy, but it does its job well. Of keeping time."

Was it her imagination, or did her observation of the watch make him nervous? Betsy tried not to frown as the couple walked to a small table by the front window. Daniel Troyer claimed to be a distant relative. But something didn't sit right about him. She dared not ask her family, not now. But maybe Thaddeus would help her. He could use a computer and she trusted him. She sighed as she entered the kitchen to see if Vera's pies were ready. From the delightful smell in the kitchen, she guessed they were.

Aenti Chelle was, as the *Englisch* said, smitten. All the more reason to see if Daniel Troyer had any secrets. But Betsy almost envied her *aenti*. She knew the feeling well, had felt her heart pound raucously in her chest when saying good-bye to Thaddeus this morning, him leaving the bakery as she arrived.

Vera Byler, though, put a damper on any dizziness Betsy might have had while watching Thaddeus depart shortly before dawn.

"Pies are almost done," Vera said now, looking up from rolling out more dough. "I'm not surprised we're not busier."

"Why do you say that?"

"Thanksgiving's tomorrow and everyone is picking up their pies from Yoder's instead." She frowned as she rolled out one more crust for pumpkin.

"I'm not surprised either, but it's all right. I make more than pie here." She gritted her teeth. *Aenti* Sarah had been far more easy to deal with.

"I can't see this place lasting longer than your lease. I hear most businesses close within the first year. How long is your lease, anyway?"

"Six months." She wanted to add, "Not as though that's any of your business," but said nothing more. Vera had been the one to remark about Betsy joining the ranks of the old maids before too long.

"How late do you plan to stay open today?"

"Until six o' clock. I hope some people will stop by the bakery on their way home from work. I ran ads in the Sarasota newspaper." Betsy glanced at the clock. Eight more hours, then they'd close and go to their homes to help their families continue Thanksgiving dinner preparations.

"I certainly do hope you're not wasting your family's money." Vera picked up a bowl of pumpkin pie filling, ready to pour into the crusts.

"Mrs. Byler, it's been my fervent prayer for a long time now." She felt her hackles rising, like one of the yard dogs back home. Vera giving voice to Betsy's fears almost made her shudder. Her irritation cooled a bit. Vera wasn't trying to hurt. In her own negative way, she was trying to help.

The bell to the door outside clanged, and Betsy scurried out to the sales floor.

Gideon Stoltzfus, again. She then remembered how she'd treated Jacob, and gave Gideon a sympathetic smile.

"Good morning, Gideon."

"Betsy. I'll have the usual. I'd also like to purchase a whole pie, please." He grinned at her, then stepped over to the coffee pot. "Ah, I see your coffee is running low. I can refill the tank for you."

"No, thank you, but if you bring me the reservoir I can refill it. What kind of pie would you like?"

"Strawberry rhubarb. I'm taking it to my grandparents' for dessert tomorrow." He returned, holding the empty water reservoir for the coffee maker.

"Thank you." Betsy pulled out a paper plate and also Gideon's usual, a sticky bun covered with nuts and raisins. She took the plastic container from him, then entered the kitchen.

How could she let him down easy? She'd done it before. Or so she'd thought. She'd even tried the direct approach the first day he marched into the bakery. However, every morning since he'd been in Pinecraft, he came to the bakery and purchased a sticky bun and helped himself to a cup of coffee before leaving to go off and do who knew what.

Now wasn't the time for crushing his hopes, however. She filled the water tank for the coffee, then reentered the sales floor. Gideon waited at the counter, still grinning. He'd already taken a bite of the sticky bun.

"A group of us are going to the beach on Sunday. Maybe you could come with us."

She hesitated while passing the edge of the counter on her way to the coffeemaker. He knew her weak spot, the beach. She hadn't taken the time since she'd returned to Pinecraft to make the twenty-minute trip to Siesta Key Beach, to kick off her flip-flops and wiggle her toes in the sand.

As she reconnected the water reservoir to the coffeemaker, she considered his offer. Going as a group. Maybe, if she were clear about things, she would go. A few of her friends had arrived in Pinecraft for winter vacation, and she had yet to see them.

Betsy turned to face Gideon. "I'm not sure." The sales floor was empty, save *Aenti* Chelle and Daniel. "I've been busy with the bakery, and now with *Aenti* Sarah having surgery."

"Surely you don't have to stay in the village on Sunday. You can visit your *aenti* and then go to the beach."

"I suppose I could." At that, his face brightened. "But, Gideon, please understand. You are my friend, and only a friend. I've known you my entire life, and I don't see you as anything more. I'm sorry if, before, you might have had, um, ideas about us."

Now, his expression sank a little. "I do understand. It's why I mentioned all of us going, in a group."

She imagined the sand, white as cake flour, under her feet. The call of the birds, the sight of the blue waters, and scent of salt.

"All right. I'll go. What time were you all thinking?"

"About five or so." Gideon grinned widely. "Now, my pie?"

"Oh, yes. Strawberry rhubarb. I'll go fetch a box for it." Betsy scurried from the bakery sales floor.

❧

Thad listened to the voices drifting from the house, but maintained his spot outside on the back patio. He occupied one of a pair of chairs facing the yard. The last time he'd had a Thanksgiving meal like this and had the chance to kick back was the last November he'd lived at home. Since then, Thanksgiving meant another day to work and feed hungry crowds who would rather go out to eat than stay home. This meant a succession of upscale desserts ranging from pumpkin flan to a chocolate mousse with an accompanying cranberry foam.

He rubbed his stomach. He'd pay for this tomorrow, he was sure. *Mammi* had put out two tables for the meal, butted up against each other, with the family occupying one table, and him seated at the end at the smaller table, along with the few extra dishes not on the main table.

Their version of shunning, by not "eating with him" at the same table. The awkward table setup was covered with a voluminous white tablecloth covering both tables. Thad knew, though, where one table stopped and the other began.

At first, conversation had been strained, halting after *Daed's* prayer over their supper. *Daed* had said nothing to him as they ate, but his gaze kept wandering in Thad's direction.

The last long conversation he'd had with his father had been seared into his memory. Pleading, outrage, preaching, Scriptures, condemnation, concluding with exasperation. Thad's resolve to leave and further his education in a nontraditional field grew with each approach *Daed* had taken.

At tonight's meal, none of that had happened, thankfully. Perhaps *Daed* had decided today wasn't the time or the place.

When someone did talk to Thad, it was about the bakery as well as his work with Henry Hostetler, which had tapered off for the time being with Thad helping at Pinecraft Pies and Pastry. Thad gave answers readily enough, all the while allowing his taste buds to rejoice at his family's cooking.

The back screen door banged.

"There you are," his *mamm* said as she stepped off the patio. "Did you get enough to eat?"

"More than enough." Thad patted his stomach again.

She wiped her hands on her apron before she sat down. "Good. It's good to see you at our table again." She switched from English to *Dietsch*.

Thad braced himself mentally. He noted a few more wrinkles in *Mamm's* face, on her hands. "The food is as good as I remembered, probably better."

"Your *mammi* didn't say you were here, visiting, in her last letter to us."

"I wondered if she would."

"You know you can always come home again. Your *daed* says Henry Hostetler spoke highly of your work. You're quite good at tiling. I'm sure your *daed* can help find a job for you somewhere."

Thad frowned. *Mamm's* voice held soft, tender tones.

"I can't go back. I'm sorry." Henry was probably trying to smooth things over between Thad and his *daed* by complimenting Thad's skills, but consigning a family member to hell couldn't be fixed by a mere career change.

Her face crestfallen, she glanced toward the house. "Truthfully, I never minded you wanting to be a baker or chef. But your *daed*, and the bishop, and the others . . ."

"It's okay, *Mamm*. I made my decision a long time ago. I'm fine."

"No, you're not. You're unsettled, like—like a boat without an oar." She waved her hand to create a breeze. "Being among the *Englisch* hasn't been good for you."

He didn't care to argue with his *mamm*, not only because of lack of respect, but because he half-agreed with her. A boat without an oar. Drifting through life, unable to steer or find direction.

"If I don't have an oar, maybe I can find a sail." He smiled, hoping his *mamm* would as well. "*Mamm*, it could have happened even with me not being among the *Englisch*."

"You need us, and we need you, too. All of us." Her voice caught.

You weren't made to blend in; you were made to stand out.

"I—I'm sorry." What else could he say? The old smothering feeling was coming back. He sucked in a breath.

"I pray one day you are sorry enough." *Mamm* frowned, then got up from the chair and strode to the house.

Thad released the breath, then sighed. Laughter and chatter inside, without him. Someone said something about breaking out the dominoes or the corn hole set. Thad almost wished he could join them. If he couldn't be accepted as he was, he couldn't be a part at all. Sure, Pinecraft was a good place to pretend he fit. However, face-to-face with his family again, his pretending wore thin.

He stood. Should he go inside, to have a cup of coffee and more dessert, or sit at the edge of the group and be a reminder of the pain he'd caused?

No, a walk through the village. Thad trudged around to the front of the house and glanced at his neglected motorcycle. He'd ordered a new helmet online and it was due to arrive soon. If he was going to start anywhere again, he at least needed it to get around.

His footsteps carried him away from *Mammi's* house and in the direction of the park. He could sit in a corner of the pavilion at a picnic table, or keep walking. If the homeless man could hang out in the park, so could he.

Another figure approached the park, too, causing Thad to smile again. Betsy, walking along with a dachshund resembling a short, round sausage more than a hot dog.

Betsy glanced up and saw him, and a shy grin flickered across her face. She murmured something at the dog waddling along on four paws, then glanced Thad's way again.

"Happy Thanksgiving," he said as they drew closer to each other.

"Happy Thanksgiving to you," she replied, then cast another glance at the dog, who sniffed Thad's leg, then sat up on his haunches, his front paws tucked under his chin. The dog's tail whipped side to side.

"Well, hello there, little guy." He reached down and patted the dog, who then flopped over on his side, exposing his wide belly. "Have you kept out of trouble, Winston?"

"Mostly, except when he's begging for table scraps." Then Betsy laughed, the sound like soft musical notes.

"This guy is just lapping up the attention." Thad rubbed the dog's belly. "I love dogs. Never had time for one, with the hours I worked and living in an apartment and all. It wouldn't have been fair to him."

"I never have had a dog, either. He showed up one day and decided to live with me. So I kept him."

They continued walking toward the park, Thad keeping his stride short so Winston wouldn't have to keep up on his stubbly little legs. "I don't remember seeing many dogs in Pinecraft."

"There's not. There's another dachshund, it so happens, a few blocks away, named Belle." Betsy let out a low sigh.

"What's wrong? Is it your *Aenti* Sarah?"

Betsy shook her head. "No, she's doing well after her surgery. She's staying with us right now, since *Aenti* Chelle has the extra room, and everyone is taking turns caring for her. But I had to get out for a little bit. *Aenti* Chelle had the whole family over for supper, since she has the largest kitchen, and of course, because *Aenti* Sarah is staying with us."

"But . . . ?" They paused at the split rail fence and watched a few youths playing volleyball.

"I don't want to talk out of turn about anyone, but I'm worried about *Aenti* Chelle."

"What's wrong? I promise, I won't say anything."

"It's not so much her. It's Daniel Troyer. She smiles at him like she's one of the youth."

"Who's Daniel Troyer?"

"That's it. I don't know. He's older. Not old-old, like *Aenti* Sarah, but older than us. He's not married and he's here in Pinecraft for the winter. He claims to be a second or third cousin. I'm not good at our family tree, the older ones are, but none of them said anything."

"What do you think is wrong about him?"

"It sounds silly, but it's his watch."

"His watch?"

"It's not Plain. It's flashy, and gold. I think I saw a diamond at the spot for twelve o'clock." Betsy frowned. "I don't know. It's nothing. My sister thinks it's nothing. But she's engaged to be married and in love, so she thinks I'm just jealous of *Aenti* Chelle. And her, too. Anyway, for a Plain man, Daniel Troyer has a very fancy watch."

Thad grunted. He'd heard of some liberal districts where watches weren't frowned upon, as they were useful and not merely ornamental. "How can I help you?"

"I don't know. You know how to use the Internet. Daniel mentioned the name of the company he works for. I, uh, I wanted to try to check to see if he works there." Her cheeks shot with red, she looked him straight in the eye.

Thad suddenly realized how close they stood beside the fence, and noticed Betsy had three freckles on the side of her nose, her eyes weren't just blue, but had a hint of green around the irises. He wanted to make the worry crease between her eyebrows disappear.

"I . . . yes, I don't mind helping you. If you'd like, write down what you know, and give the paper to me tomorrow morning, before I leave the bakery."

"We're not open tomorrow. I . . . ." She licked her lips, then suddenly shot forward into his arms as Winston yanked on the leash.

He caught her as well as the whiff of lavender soap and felt the catch of her breath. "Are you okay?" His fingers itched to the point of distraction, he wanted to let his fingers run through her hair, to feel the length of it run through them. He'd never seen her hair down, but let himself imagine it for this instance.

"I'm—I'm fine," she blurted, stepping back and pulling Winston toward her. "Winston, don't ever do that again." Head low, ears flopping, the dog trotted back and stopped at her feet.

Thad hadn't minded so much. The thought thrilled, yet pained him. If he let his mind wander, he could see himself and Betsy, together. The pain came when he realized it was a dream. He'd have to give up so much—freedom, for one thing. His individuality, for another. The idea of a "bad boy" appealed to some women, Amish and otherwise. And Thad didn't consider himself "bad," not compared to some of the guys he knew. Guys who'd sweet-talk a young woman like Betsy, take what they wanted of her dignity and innocence, then toss her to the side when they got bored or someone more appealing walked up to them.

"So, like I said, write down what you know. Can we meet here, tomorrow morning then? I can start calling around. It's a holiday weekend, so I might not be able to learn much." He paused for a moment. "Maybe Imogene knows something. She knows a lot about everyone, it seems."

"Okay, I'll give you the information." Betsy wrapped the end of the leash around one finger, then unwrapped it. "It might be nothing. But I don't want to see *Aenti* Chelle hurt. Thanks, Thaddeus."

Her cheeks red, she strode briskly away from him, back in the direction they'd walked.

❧

Pete stood with a small cluster of men at Pinecraft park, watching a bocce game on the expanse of lawn. He glanced across the way. There went nosy Betsy and her dog down the street after talking to Thaddeus Zook, of all people. He ducked his head a little lower, letting the brim of his hat do the work.

One of his bearded cohorts sent a ball flying across the grass and almost touching the jack ball used as a target. The man's teammate clapped him on the back in triumph.

Pete scanned the area again. Betsy headed off down Fry, probably going back to the house. He thumped his stomach. What a meal. He'd never had the like. And Rochelle? She'd captured his attention the entire time, blushing as she'd introduced him to the rest of the family who hadn't met him before.

Thad still stood by the fence rail. Pete allowed himself a grin. The young Amish woman had tumbled into Thad's arms. The electricity between them, well, Pete could feel it all the way over here.

Right, Thad. Who could blame the kid for being attracted to the young woman. Innocence and sweetness was appealing. Pete had seen the same in Rochelle, and a quiet pain he had no business trying to coax out from her.

"Daniel, you want a turn?" one of his new friends asked.

"No, no thank you. I'm feeling a bit ill at the moment. I hope it wasn't something I ate. If you'll excuse me . . ."

"See you at the Gospel concert on Sunday afternoon?"

"Perhaps."

He slunk around the side of the nearly empty shuffleboard court. Thad had started walking, but continuing the opposite direction on Fry—closer to Pete. He turned his back on the street and looked to be headed toward the creek instead.

He'd been gone long enough, had made promises to his boss he'd come through, but the minute he'd set foot in this village, he didn't miss the bite of winter approaching Ohio. Pete watched a heron launch itself into the air and soar above the palm tree. A man could get used to this. He snuck a glance toward the street. Thad strode along, seemingly oblivious to anyone watching.

Now satisfied that Thad hadn't seen him, Pete followed a block's length behind. After he learned where Thad Zook was staying, maybe he could find a way inside and see if whatever Thad had stowed in his possessions had been worth the trip.

17

*F*or the remainder of the weekend, Betsy couldn't push past the memory of practically being in Thad's embrace. She'd never been so physically close to a man before. Of course, back when she thought herself in love with Jacob Miller, she allowed herself a dream or two, but never entertained the idea for long.

She'd burned two pies on Saturday by allowing her mind to wander, to imagine being in Thad's arms again, with him looking at her with those dark eyes of his as he removed the pins from her hair and let it tumble down her back. He would pull her closer yet, so close she could feel his heart beating when he kissed her.

There. She'd done it again. Worse, while sitting in church and listening to the local bishop preach.

Her sister planted her elbow in Betsy's side. "You awake?"

"Ow. Yes."

Mamm leaned forward and hushed them with a look. Some things didn't change. Betsy sat up straighter and focused on the service, but not before she caught a glance from Gideon across the aisle with the men.

Oh, right. She had promised to meet up with a group of them, and spend some time at the beach. She welcomed this day of rest, and especially welcomed it this weekend with more of her family and friends in the village.

Silly child. She chided herself. No imaginations about Thaddeus Zook would replace the security of her family and friends. Thaddeus was "off limits," with good reason. She dared not start imagining if only. If only he'd return, rejoin the church, then maybe . . .

Such decisions weren't made lightly, if at all. A cousin had left, and one of her friends from the district. Both were miserable in *Englisch* marriages, even with all the supposed "freedom" they enjoyed. Betsy didn't feel particularly restricted. Other families might not have even entertained the idea of allowing a young woman to open her own bakery.

After church, the women visited in the side yard of the church building, with the men lining the side of the building where they'd placed their hats on a table before going inside the church.

Betsy glanced over, admiring how nice they all looked in their black trousers and suspenders, with white buttoned shirts, and variety of hats. Even in slightly relaxed Pinecraft, the Sunday best still appeared on the Sabbath day.

There went Gideon again, looking her way. She snatched her gaze away from the men and back into the circle of chatting women.

"So we must hurry through the meal as quickly as we can," Emma was saying. "I can't wait to get back to the beach and look for more shells and sand dollars." Her face and lower arms already bore a sun-touched glow, aided by generous application of suntan oil—coconut scented, no less.

Betsy enjoyed having her sister nearby, but as usual, Emma had made herself the center of attention. She stopped her childish thoughts again. Life seemed to come easier for Emma. Maybe it was being the youngest. Betsy had enough to be thankful for in her own life.

"And what about you, Betsy?" Vera Byler was asking.

"Me?"

"The annual Pinecraft pie contest. I assume you will be entering."

The others looked at her—*Mamm*, Emma, Vera and her daughter Patience, as well as friends Miriam and Abigail.

"I suppose I will." She hadn't thought about it, her primary focus being the bakery.

"You should," Emma said. "I'm surprised you didn't enter last year."

No, last year she'd been working her first real job and waiting in Florida, hoping Jacob would realize she was the one for him.

"Maybe I will."

"You know, it might not be the best idea," Vera said. "I know you're busy with the bakery, where customers have ample opportunity to taste your pie all the time."

"Actually, I think it would be good publicity." The idea appealed to Betsy the more it turned itself around in her mind. The newspapers and media people would be there. The judges, however, were formidable, including a local Beachy Amish Mennonite woman whose palate for pie was unrivaled. The first time the woman had visited the bakery, Betsy had been shaking in her shoes. But the woman's warmth set her at ease.

"Publicity is a few hairs short of boasting." Vera punctuated her statement by sealing her lips into a thin line.

Betsy bit her own lip and considered her response. "I am simply trying to be a good steward of what my family has entrusted me with, and the more customers I can find, the better. What better place, than at a pie contest?"

Vera tugged on Patience's arm. "Come, we have much to do."

"Do?" Patience was asking, but Vera was already hauling her daughter away.

Mamm shook her head. "That lady. Pay her no mind. I think she is just jealous, but will never admit to such. I know I had my doubts, but your bakery is lovely and the food is *gut*."

"Thank you, *Mamm*."

"Well, is *Daed* ready to leave yet?" Emma scanned the group of men, still milling about and talking.

"I do not know." She glanced at Betsy. "You two can walk to Rochelle's home and see if *Aenti* Sarah needs any help."

Betsy nodded. She was past ready to leave and had been holding down her fidgets. "I'll start laying out the leftovers for everyone." Of course, the family would all descend on *Aenti* Chelle's home to plunge their forks into the remainders of the Thanksgiving meal and see *Aenti* Sarah.

Emma stepped along beside Betsy. "I've missed you."

"And I've missed you." They strolled down Kaufman in the direction of Shrock, toward *Aenti* Chelle's. A few passersby, also on their way from church, waved and nodded to the sisters. "This place is practically empty in the summertime, and I have no one to go to the beach with."

"The only one missing from Pinecraft is Eli." She frowned, her lips curving into a little girl's pout. "He doesn't get any time off from the machine shop until they close for two weeks at Christmas."

"He's coming to Pinecraft, though, isn't he?" Betsy caught a whiff of someone's supper, drifting across the street.

"Yes, but *Daed* and *Mamm* are heading back to Ohio the day after Christmas. *Daed* has end-of-the year reports to oversee." She cast a sideways glance at Betsy. "Maybe if you said something to them, I could stay with you and *Aenti* Chelle until New Year's, or even later. Starting now."

"Starting now?"

"I can help with *Aenti* Sarah. Besides, I feel like I'm staying with all the old people."

"Old people?"

"Yes, *Mamm, Daed*, our grandparents, all the *oncles* and *aentis* . . ." Emma shrugged. "*Aenti* Chelle is older than us, but she doesn't act old."

Betsy said nothing. Emma always seemed to have an ulterior motive. She probably did in this case, too. Emma thrived on being right in the middle of something happening. Here in Pinecraft, something was always happening, or about to happen. Especially in the winter seasons. But Betsy and *Aenti* Chelle spent the majority of their time working, not vacationing.

"I don't know if me speaking to *Daed* on your behalf would help. You're old enough; you can talk to him yourself."

"Well, all right. Maybe I can help you in the bakery sometimes, too. I know we'll have much more fun running it, instead of Vera looking over your shoulder all the time. I can't believe what she said about your bakery. And her, helping you, too!" Emma's words echoed off the side of one of the houses.

"Shush, not so loud." Betsy glanced around. "You probably heard about Thaddeus, and *Daed* not finding him suitable to help."

"He does have a point. Thaddeus didn't look Amish to me at all, the one time I saw him. Customers go to Pinecraft Pies and Pastry wanting to eat Amish food."

"You sound like *Daed* . . . and no, Thaddeus doesn't look Amish. You should have seen him before he started shaving regularly. He always had this, almost beard, but not a real beard." Betsy's earlier thoughts began dancing in her head.

Stop. He may have a kind heart and gentle, strong spirit, but everything else about him is wrong.

Emma stopped on the street and pulled Betsy's arm, tugging her to a stop. "You like him. Oh, my. It's all over your face, in your eyes. Won't *Daed* be shocked, his perfect one all mooning over someone like Thaddeus Zook?"

"I'm not the perfect one, Emma. And—" She wanted to add, "I don't think of Thaddeus like that," but it would be a lie. "Anyway, he has been a big help and I'm not sure how long he's planning to stay in Pinecraft. He's worked at fancy *Englisch* restaurants as a pastry chef. It wouldn't surprise me if he ends up going back in Ohio."

"Aha. Well, we must pray for him, then."

It was Betsy's turn to stare. Emma never spoke in such a way. Not free, irrepressible Emma. Truthfully, Betsy was surprised Emma hadn't run off, with such a curiosity of the *Englisch* and the world at large. Perhaps they had Eli to thank for it.

"You know, you're right. We should pray for him. He seems lost and sad. He's different from anyone else I've known."

"Why'd he leave?"

"I suppose it was to finish his education and go to culinary school. He's almost twenty-eight."

"Ah. I'm glad I didn't have to keep on with school."

At this, Betsy laughed. Trust Emma to bring the conversation back to herself again. Here they were, at *Aenti* Chelle's. An unfamiliar vehicle was in the driveway, parked beside *Aenti* Chelle's minivan.

"Oh, did I tell you?" Emma continued. "*Aenti* Chelle's nephew Steven—he's actually her cousin's wife's brother's nephew, so no relation—is taking a bunch of us out on his boat fishing. I can't wait. I've never been out fishing before."

"No, you didn't tell me that. I went last winter. I liked it, but I felt a little queasy from the waves."

"I sure hope I don't get seasick."

Betsy and Emma headed up the walk, the sound of a male and female voice coming through the screen door.

". . . should almost be home from church any minute. I stayed with *Aenti* Sarah today," *Aenti* Chelle was saying.

"Ah, I was bad. I skipped church this morning. I get migraines."

Daniel Troyer.

Betsy frowned as she pulled open the door.

"What is it?" Emma asked, entering behind Betsy.

"I'll tell you later," she whispered. Surely, Thaddeus would find out something about this man soon.

⁓❧⁓

Thad yawned his good morning to Betsy and her new shadow, Vera Byler, on Monday. After a few hours of prep, the apple and other fruit pie fillings were ready and waiting for the ladies to pop fresh pie into the ovens and get the fried pies going. That, and start the doughnuts, which were a surprising hit in the village. She'd discovered people much preferred the apple cider doughnuts over the plain sugar glazed.

"I'll see you tomorrow morning," Betsy said as she allowed Vera to enter ahead of her. She gave him a pointed look. Of course, she probably wanted to know if he'd learned anything about Daniel Yoder.

"Did you preheat the ovens?" Vera asked him.

"Fifteen minutes ago," Thad replied. "Betsy, I have an idea for a new pie, if you'd like to try it. I can prepare one and have it ready for you tomorrow morning."

"Oh, what's that?"

"Tiramisu."

"I'd very much like to try it. I had it in a restaurant once. Not as a pie, though." She stopped, then looked as though she were going to continue.

"I need to show you something about the coffee maker, for a moment."

"Certainly."

She followed him into the seating area of the bakery. "I need this cleaned out, tonight, if you could. I'd do it, but I'm afraid I'd never figure out how the pieces go together."

"No problem."

Betsy glanced toward the doorway to the kitchen. "Did you find anything out about Daniel Troyer?"·

"So far, I confirmed the company he works for is legit. But they've been closed for the holiday weekend. So I'm going to call them this morning, as soon as they open."

"All right." She frowned. "I still feel silly."

"No." He smiled at her, in spite of his resolve to keep a distance. "If it's nothing, it's nothing, and it'll be forgotten."

"All right."

He wanted to pour himself a cup of coffee after the brew was ready, and sit in the corner while munching on a fresh fried pie, but the desire for sleep won out. He yawned. If he stayed much longer, they'd probably find him slumped over the table and facedown on his fried pie.

Thad yawned again. "Don't worry. As soon as I know something concrete, I'll let you know."

She smiled at him and he felt its tug on his heart. But he gave her a slight wave as he left the bakery through the front door.

No way, buddy. He'd heard in a roundabout way of her unreturned interest in his second cousin Jacob, and he did feel sorry for her. Betsy would make any Plain man a fine wife.

He almost stopped short in the street. Not just any man. Not for Betsy. She had a spark, a creative spirit not always encouraged among her people like it should be. Pride lurked behind every doorway, with every delicious bite of food, with every accolade. He knew it and had seen it. The war against pride and self-promotion was a battle they were taught to fight since childhood. Again, the sensation of having one foot planted in the *Englisch* world with the other still glued to the Plain life set off an inner tug-of-war with him in the middle.

"Morning, Thaddeus." One of the three "preacher" brothers, James or John, greeted him as the older man passed by on his tricycle.

"Good morning." He nodded at the man, but the man had already zipped past on his tricycle.

Maybe he ought to purchase one for himself. Yet another thought to make him pause. But he already had a fuel-efficient motorcycle to take him away from here when the time came.

He turned the corner to *Mammi's* street and saw a vehicle in front of her house.

A police cruiser?

Thad broke into a run. A few neighbors milled outside on the front walk.

"*Mammi!*" He took the steps in one leap and stumbled through the front door and into the living room. A pair of Sarasota police officers stood in the center of the front room, with *Mammi* sitting serenely on the couch, her hands folded on her lap.

The three of them stared.

"It's all right, Thaddeus. Someone broke into the house." *Mammi* smiled at him. She might as well have said, "I weeded the flower garden this morning," with her matter-of-fact manner.

"Were you home? Are you all right?"

"I'm perfectly fine. I had gone for my morning walk with my friends and I had just come back for breakfast. The others left before you got home, the men deep sea fishing and the women on a bus trip to explore Tampa."

"And this is . . . ?" One officer—his name badge said Kitchens—glanced from *Mammi* to Thad.

"My grandson, Thaddeus. He's been living with me."

"Ah." The officer nodded. "Mr. Zook, we're going to need you to let us know if anything is missing from your belongings."

"Uh, sure." Thad remained standing, but he wanted to rush to *Mammi's* side. "How did they get in?"

"The kitchen window, by the table. They cut the screen." *Mammi* shook her head. "I've never had anything like this happen here, officers."

"*Mammi*, we're still in a city. I know it feels safe here, but . . ." Thad scanned the room. *Mammi's* living room was tidy, uncluttered. The drawers to her coffee table rested on the floor, their meager contents of pen and note pads and a package of chewing gum, along with several wrapped mints, scattered on the floor.

"They were likely looking for any cash you may have tucked away anywhere."

"But I don't have any cash hidden." *Mammi* lifted up her hands in surrender. "I keep it all in the bank."

"It's a safe idea, Mrs. Zook. And your grandson is right. It's best to remember your neighborhood is part of a city containing some people who don't follow the rules like you do."

"I, uh, I'll check my room."

"Hold on. The crime scene tech is arriving now. They want to see if they can get any prints on the doorknobs and drawer handles."

Thad forced himself not to fidget. "Can I sit down?"

"Sure, go right ahead." The officer's gaze narrowed as he studied Thad's covered arm, with the lower edge of the tattoo exposed. "So. Can you think of anyone around here who'd want to break into your grandmother's home?"

"No, I don't know anyone outside the village. I've only been here about five weeks or so." The realization he didn't know anyone outside Pinecraft village in Sarasota startled him. But then, it's what he wanted. To live quietly for the time being. To breathe.

What if he'd brought trouble *Mammi's* way?

However, Pinecraft, he'd pointed out and others knew, wasn't immune to the effects of the outside world, as much as the residents protected their peace and quiet.

They all fell silent. With the crime tech's arrival, the officers spoke to the lady in low tones. She nodded, her dark ponytail swishing as she put on a pair of latex gloves and opened her kit. Then, she started to work.

"So, Mr. Zook, what line of work are you in?"

"I'm a pastry chef by trade."

"You said you've only lived here for weeks. Where were you before this?"

"Columbus, Ohio, area." His palms itched and he tried not to wipe them on his jeans.

"So what brings you down to Sarasota?"

"Family."

Officer Kitchens nodded, then glanced at the tech, who was fluttering her attention to the window sill, the screen area, the door handles, and finally the coffee table.

"Mr. Zook, have you ever used drugs?"

"Now, what kind of a question is that? No." He looked over at *Mammi*, but dared not meet her eyes. "Not anymore. Not for a long, long time."

"How long?"

"Years, okay? More than five, at least. I don't appreciate this line of questioning." He tried to keep his voice even.

"We need to know. If there's anyone who might have an interest in you, or your family, for the wrong reasons."

Thad stared at the tile floor. He remembered hearing about Mitch's body on the tile floor of Dish and Spoon. Caitlyn had crumbled into tears when she'd told him and the others about it, her first day back at work after the murder.

"I've never seen so much blood."

"No, there isn't anyone." He didn't know it for sure. For a while at work, they'd all looked over their shoulders as workers speculated Mitch had been killed during a robbery in progress. Some, but not all, of the deposit money was missing from the bank bag, found at the scene.

"Well, if you happen to think of anyone, you'll be sure to let us know."

"Of course I will. If I knew something, I'd never want to bring my family into any harm."

This had to be nothing more than a creepy coincidence. Just like someone had broken into his apartment two days before his decision to leave Florida. But his apartment complex wasn't the safest place in the city.

At last, while Thad distracted himself by studying the variations in the shades of grout on the floor, the officers told him he could take a look inside his bedroom.

He headed down the hall, with the other officer following him. He tried not to glance over his shoulder, but the sensation of someone watching made his palms sweat.

He opened his bedroom door.

Whoever had broken in had yanked his mattress from his bed. His empty canvas duffel sat like a deflated balloon in the middle of the boxsprings. His dresser drawers, all three, had been pulled open, their contents in a heap on the floor. His closet door remained closed.

"I just came home when I saw a man run from the back of the house, then through my living room and dove out the torn screen." *Mammi's* voice grew louder as she approached his room.

"What other rooms did they search?" Thad asked. *Mammi* stepped into the room.

"My bedroom wasn't touched, as best I can tell." *Mammi* ran her hands over the sides of her prayer covering, her fingers tapping the hairpins.

"What did the man look like?" Thad had to know.

"Well, he wasn't Amish, like I told the officers. He wore a gray jogging suit and a black stretchy knitted cap." *Mammi* sighed. "I already told the police."

"Does it look like anything is missing?" the officer asked.

Thad reached for the duffel bag. Empty. His only valuables were his cell phone, the motorcycle, and his culinary tools, tucked away in their case on the closet shelf. He opened the closet door, then reached up onto the shelf. There. He pulled the case toward him.

"All here," he said as he scanned the knives. "I know they may seem like just knives, but this case has hundreds of dollars of culinary tools in it." He closed the lid and latched the case before placing it back on the shelf.

"We think your grandmother interrupted him before he got into the closet. Unless the intruder didn't know their value."

Thad nodded. Good thing. He couldn't afford to replace his knives and other tools of his trade.

"Well, if you can think of anything else, we'll leave our contact information."

Thad nodded again, feeling like a bobblehead. "Thank you."

He and *Mammi*, along with the officer, left his room. Of course his prints would be all over everything, and *Mammi's* as well. But *Mammi* had never been fingerprinted, nor had he.

As the door closed behind the officers, *Mammi* said, "I'm thankful nothing is missing. But if that man needed something so badly, he could have knocked on the door and asked."

Thad didn't respond. He still believed in a person's right to defend their property. Sweet, kind *Mammi*, though, full of grace for whoever had broken into her home.

"Are you all right?" he asked her, again.

"I'm fine, just fine." She waved off any offers of help. "I need to hang out the wash, since the washer's stopped. Been stopped for a while."

"Okay. Well, I'm going to make some phone calls and put everything away in my room."

He headed back to his room to clean. He shut his door, then put his mattress back on top of the box spring. He pulled out the number to Home Craft Cabinets not far from Shipshewana, Indiana.

The automated call system gave him an option to select for jobs and careers, so Thad chose that one.

"Human Resources, Diana speaking."

"Good morning, Diana. My name is . . . Thaddeus Zook, and I'm inquiring about one of your employees."

"Ah, for which purpose?"

"I'm verifying his employment with your company. I'm in Sarasota, Florida."

"Oh, Florida. Nice place to be this time of year. What's the gentleman's name?"

"Daniel Troyer."

He heard the sound of fingertips on a keyboard.

"Daniel Troyer, you say?"

"Yes, Daniel Troyer. He said he worked in the billing department."

"Well, we did have a Daniel Troyer employed in our billing department for ten years. But, unfortunately, he passed away in the spring. A tragedy, so young, barely forty years old."

❦

Pete Stucenski's heart still raced as he unlocked the door to his rental and slipped inside. Sweat poured from his body and his pores sighed with relief at the cool air. He didn't think anyone had seen him strolling the side streets of Pinecraft after his mad dash away from the Zooks' home. He'd removed the knit cap and the gray jacket of his jogging suit, and stuffed them inside the canvas tote bag he'd hidden behind someone's trash can around the corner from where Thad Zook lived.

It was early enough in the day, and not many people were out. Except for the old lady ruining everything by walking in on him. He'd kept his head ducked down as he ran through the living room, then the kitchen, and scrambled out the hole he'd sliced in the screen.

He should have spent the money and hired someone to do the dirty work instead of trying to do it himself. His right knee was already swelling from where he'd struck it on the Zook's back patio.

But he'd had to seize the opportunity, after the entire Zook clan—minus Thad and his grandmother—had piled into a gigantic van along with a cooler and other gear. Where they'd all headed off to, he didn't know or care, but the timing had been perfect to act.

Not hiring someone else meant fewer loose ends. He didn't want to turn into a loose end, either.

Perhaps he could risk it all by encountering the Zooks, then securing an invitation to their home, and doing his own investigation that way. He'd barely gotten started on Thad's belongings before the front door opened.

Pete hobbled to the kitchen and opened the freezer door. He could feel his knee joint tightening, the more he bent the knee. He found a plastic bag in a kitchen drawer and loaded it with a tray full of ice cubes.

He settled onto the loveseat and propped the bag of ice on his knee. He tried not to rub his itching chin, sensitive to the adhesive for his beard.

There had to be a better way to deal with the whole mess.

He could go back to Columbus and lie, say he'd searched through all of Thad's belongings and found nothing. Halfway true. He didn't know for sure. Then good old Murphy's law would be against him. If he told them all was well, then Thad would undoubtedly come forward with information, and Pete could likely end up on a tile floor just as Mitch had.

Rochelle Keim would no longer be a distraction to him. After this morning, his charade, at least with her, would need to become nothing more than a Florida memory.

18

"Did you hear about the break-in at the Zooks'?" Gideon asked as he walked into the bakery, not long before closing.

Betsy attempted to keep her expression even, not irritated, at seeing Gideon. He was a kind, good, gentle man and despite the zeal she found unnerving at times, there were worse men who could pursue her.

"Yes, I did. I'm thankful no one was hurt."

"I can't believe someone broke into the Zooks' house this morning."

"It's too bad. However, no one was home." Betsy shook her head. Even in peaceful Pinecraft, the ugliness of the world tried to intrude. Of course, such was the case when people were involved, even Plain people. Back in Ohio she'd heard of one or two Plain folk stealing from others, and the church handled matters itself without involving the authorities.

"I wanted to come, walk you home, for safety."

"For safety, huh?" Betsy pulled the last remaining pies from the case, half a cherry pie and two slices of lemon meringue. She paused. "Gideon, would you like the rest of this pie? I can't serve day-old pie tomorrow."

He brightened. "Yes, thank you. Thank you very much."

"It would be wasteful to throw out, and *Aenti* Chelle and I still have a few desserts from Thanksgiving. We certainly don't need more pie in the house."

"So . . ." he said as she reached for a box for the pie, "have you prayed any more about us? Sunday at the beach . . ."

Had she prayed? Yes, she had. She'd prayed for ways to keep telling him and showing him she wasn't interested in anything besides being Gideon's friend. Maybe giving him left-over pie was a bad idea. She'd couple the pie with another assurance that no, she was not interested in being courted by Gideon Stoltzfus.

"I enjoyed spending time with you and all my friends." She slid the two slices of lemon meringue onto the empty space on the cherry pie dish. "But no, Gideon, I don't want you to court me."

"Did you pray about it, though?"

Betsy tried not to sigh. She set the nearly full pie plate inside the box. "Yes, I did." She closed the box and snapped the tab inside the slot to hold the lid closed. "I prayed you would come to understand I don't want to be anything more than your friend. I'm sure there's a lovely young woman around for you, but it's not me."

Gideon frowned, pulling the box toward him. "But there's no one else who catches my attention like you. You're kind, godly, pure, hardworking, and you come from one of the best families in our district. A man would be daft not to see it. Not to mention to appreciate your cooking skills."

She wasn't sure how to reply to that. "Thank you."

"And me," he added. "I am a good, strong worker. I am devout, I cling to the *Ordnung* and our ways. There is nothing I would not do for you."

The idea almost made her shiver.

"I'm done in the back," Vera announced as she pushed through the door and entered the sales floor. "I left some hot soapy water for you to wipe down everything out here."

"Thank you, Mrs. Byler." She shifted uncomfortably on her feet. She'd been standing for several hours, and she wondered what the older woman would think of Gideon's obvious attention.

Vera gave Gideon a pointed look, then did the same to Betsy. "I won't leave until you're ready to lock up the store."

"I appreciate that." More than the woman realized, probably. "I'll just need a few moments to wipe down the case and make sure I grab the bank deposit bag."

"No rush. I've had supper cooking in the slow cooker all day." Vera settled back on a nearby stool, and crossed her arms. Another pointed look at Gideon.

Yes, Betsy was grateful for the older woman's presence. No tongues would wag about Gideon being "alone" with her at the bakery after hours, no matter how small a time period. Her family had given her their trust, not just with their financial investment, but more. Not that there was any danger of anything inappropriate occurring, especially on her part.

She excused herself and went into the kitchen to find a clean cloth to wipe down the counter and the bakery case. The bell over the front door gave its merry *ching*. Ach. She'd forgotten to turn the sign to "closed."

Betsy went back to the sales floor. An *Englisch* woman had entered. She wore jeans with a button-down shirt topped by a blazer. A small bag hung over her shoulder, and she clutched a narrow notepad and a pen. Gold bracelets clinked on her wrist and their flash matched her gold dangling earrings.

"Elizabeth Yoder?" The woman was probably closer to Thaddeus's age. She glanced from Vera to Betsy.

"I'm Elizabeth Yoder." Betsy set the damp cloth onto the counter. "How may I help you?"

"I'm Susan Cantrell, a production assistant with WSAS, a local Sarasota television affiliate."

"Hello." She stepped around the counter to shake hands with the woman.

"One of our producers had a chance to taste some of your pie, and he enjoyed it so much that he wants us to feature your bakery in our weekly segment 'Around Town.'"

"What? My bakery, on television?" A television station, talking about her bakery? No. It couldn't be. But she'd seen the company's posters on city buses, advertising the local network.

"We will come here and film, likely for several hours, to watch you bake, talk to you and your customers. 'Around Town' segments run about five minutes. We want to feature your bakery." The young woman smiled. Betsy had never seen teeth so white except on a toothpaste box.

Vera had stood up from the stool, her face wearing the expression of a thundercloud. She said nothing, but sealed her lips together into a thin line. She headed into the kitchen, the door swinging behind her.

"This sounds interesting. I'm, I'm glad your producer enjoyed the pie. When were you thinking of coming to . . . visit?" Making a video about her bakery. She couldn't go on camera. The village . . . what would they think? What would her family think? *Daed* would certainly say no.

Susan opened the notepad. "We'd like to come first thing next week, if possible. Shoot on Monday, edit on Tuesday, then the segment would run on Wednesday morning."

"Um, I should speak to my father first about this. Isn't there some kind of an agreement I'm supposed to sign?"

"Well, yes." The woman looked like she hadn't expected that question from Betsy. "I do have a copy here, in my folder."

"May I have a copy, to show to my father, of course?"

"Why, certainly." Susan pulled the form from a portfolio in the bag over her shoulder. "Here's my business card also. You have access to a phone?"

"Yes, I do. I'll call you as soon as I decide."

"Terrific. I'll need your answer by this time tomorrow. Otherwise I have to move on down the list, you see."

Of course, Betsy saw.

"We also need your employees and associates to sign similar forms. Is this your husband?" Susan glanced at Gideon.

The man needed no encouragement like that. "No, no Miss Cantrell. He's not." She looked over her shoulder. Vera still remained in the kitchen.

"Oh, pardon me." Susan's face bloomed red. "Sorry, Mr. . . .?"

"Stoltzfus. Gideon Stoltzfus. Millersburg, Ohio. Elizabeth's pies are the best in the village. You won't find one you don't like." He beamed at Betsy.

This was what she got for forgetting to turn the sign to "closed." Although she had a feeling Susan Cantrell would be persistent, despite whatever the sign hanging in the window said.

"I'll call you as soon as I have an answer for you."

"Fair enough," Susan said. "Don't wait too long."

⁓❧⁓

Daniel Troyer of Home Craft Cabinets didn't exist. Not anymore on this earth, anyway, except maybe in his family's memory. Thad carried the knowledge around all day, as he put the contents of his room back together, took the motorcycle out on the road, and even as he started making a tiramisu pie after supper.

Mammi had gone, leaving him the kitchen. He'd forgotten until returning from the market with all the ingredients that his *Mammi* didn't use an electric mixer. However, the lack of electric baking tools wouldn't hinder him.

His wrist had a muscle spasm the longer he beat the softened cream cheese. He stopped, set the wooden spoon into the bowl, then flexed and rotated his wrist as he pondered what to do next about the mysterious Daniel Troyer.

He needed more information about Daniel. One thing he knew, the Plain people kept track of each other, no matter what the distance. If a family moved to another district, the church would verify who they were, what occupation they held, and their standing in the fellowship. The sensation of living in a fishbowl chafed at him, even with the distance of time.

Troyer, a common enough name. Thad guessed there were likely dozens of Daniel Troyers in the Plain world, and perhaps a few who weren't. Before venturing to question the man himself, Thad figured there had to be another way to find out more about him.

Henry Hostetler might help him. But then, Thad didn't want to alarm anyone in the village, not if Daniel were a good man and the whole thing was a misunderstanding. However, why would someone pose as a dead man in Pinecraft? Was he on the run, or hiding from someone? Or maybe he'd merely committed the sin of wearing a fancy watch.

Thad had enjoyed his quiet for the past weeks, but he hadn't assumed another name. It wouldn't work, pretending to be someone else. Everyone in the village knew who he was, and some wouldn't speak to him. He refused to let it bother him. Because not everyone ignored him. He knew a few probably prayed for his mortal soul. If he was a sinner, at least he was honest about it. Daniel Troyer was likely no more suspicious than he.

The timer dinged, jerking his attention back to the pie. Thad removed the baked crust from the oven. Perfect. He knew his crusts rivaled the quality of any Amish housewife's.

Thad glanced at his phone. He ought to call Henry now, before it grew much later, and before *Mammi* returned home. She was out visiting a friend again and making plans for their food booth at January's Haiti auction. And before coming to stay with his *Mammi*, Thad had believed all she did was sit around her home most of the day and quilt or cook.

He picked up his phone and punched in Henry's number.

Henry answered after the second ring. "Good evening, Mr. Zook. How are you?"

"Doing well, Henry. I have something I need to speak with you about. While my *Mammi* is out tonight, preferably."

"I'm just turning onto Bahia Vista now. I can be there in about five minutes."

"Thank you, thanks very much."

"It sounds serious."

"Well, it could be. It might be nothing, but I'd rather get your opinion than be wrong."

"Ah. Fill me in when I get there."

"I'll get the coffee brewing, if you'd like."

"Certainly, it's getting chilly out here."

Thad ended the call, then started the coffee pot. No rush on the pie, as the crust needed to be completely cool before he layered the filling inside.

His recipe called for vanilla pudding mix and whipped cream. He made a stovetop vanilla pudding, which he allowed to cool beside the pie crust on the stove. A knock sounded at the front door just as Thad removed a metal mixing bowl from the freezer. Time to make some real whipped cream after he answered the door and let Henry in.

Thad opened the front door. "Come on in, Henry. I'm finishing a pie."

"As in eating? I can give you a hand with that." Henry rubbed his palms together.

"No. Making a pie." He grinned at Henry's glee. "But I know *Mammi* has some dessert on hand, if you want."

"Naw, I'm just kidding." Henry inhaled deeply as he entered the kitchen. "Love the smell of brewing coffee."

"Here's a cup. Pour away." Thad set a ceramic mug in front of the coffeemaker.

Henry helped himself to the coffee, then took a seat at the kitchen table. "What kind are you making?"

"Tiramisu, sort of like the Italian dessert." Thad poured the heavy whipping cream into the chilled bowl, then grabbed a nearby whisk. "Other than the crust, it's no-bake, but involves lots of stirring."

"So, what did you need to talk to me about?"

"There's a man in the village, visiting, supposedly from Indiana. But, well, someone is wondering if he's not who he says he is. And, it's important they find out if it's true or not. So they asked me if I could do some looking around on the Internet and make a few phone calls. And I did."

He kept whipping the cream with the whisk. Good grief, but he loved mixers with commercial grade motors. This manual stirring was for the birds. He bit his lip and had a flashback to culinary school, one of the old lessons, learning how to mix and blend by hand, without benefit of an electric mixer. He'd aced it then, but he'd also been much younger.

"Huh, you don't say. Wouldn't be Daniel Troyer, by chance?"

Thad nodded. "How'd you guess?"

"I had Thanksgiving with the Yoders and Keims. Daniel was there." He looked as though he wanted to say more, but he took a sip of coffee instead.

"Betsy is concerned about her aunt."

"Of course, she's protective of Rochelle. We all are. But then, we take care of one another here in the village."

Thad grunted and stopped whipping the cream for a moment to give his wrist a break. "I don't know if you can find out anything more, but I called the company he supposedly works for. Daniel Troyer died earlier this year."

"Maybe it's a different company."

"Maybe. It would be nice to be wrong. I know I've had people make wrong assumptions about me." Thad resumed whipping the cream. The consistency was thickening. Perfect.

"How so?"

Thad shrugged. "Because I didn't join the Order, I'm an evil person."

"Do you think you're an evil person?"

"No. But if there's no hope for me outside the Order, why try?" He whipped the cream faster. "I have nothing to prove to them, or anyone else. I have nothing to hide. But people still make assumptions when they look at me."

"Truthfully, Thaddeus, we all fall short. The Order? It's like the letter of the law. It was intended to keep people secure. But for the wrong reasons, in our own strength, we can't fulfill it all. Sure, people make up inconsequential rules for the sake of rules. But although we are made in God's image, because of the Fall, there is none truly righteous. We all stand on level ground, no matter what we wear or how we look. Beards and Plain clothing can mask a dark heart. But you need to decide for yourself what you believe."

Thad slowed his pace on the cream, now forming stiff peaks. If he kept up much longer, it would break down again. Religion, it was all the same. *God, if You are real, You wouldn't make it so impossible.*

He swallowed around the lump in his throat before continuing. "Tell that to the rest of them. You know how it is, growing up, doing anything to stand out from the others is discouraged. My *daed* hates I bake for a living. Women's work. Ach, yes, I have rarely heard of a *daadi* knitting socks or a winter scarf. Men don't bake for a living, and of course, they're not supposed to go get an education. I didn't want anything so wrong. I'm happy you gave me a chance to work for you, but in fact, construction's not my thing."

He shouldn't have opened his mouth about people making assumptions about him. Thad realized, too, his last spiel to Henry had been in *Dietsch*. The words had poured out, from somewhere deep inside. He didn't fumble or reach for them.

No matter how he talked, or how he covered up his arm, he still didn't belong.

"I left my Order as a young man, not long after my wife and I married." Henry stared at his mug as if he could see the memories unfolding. "We found grace, we didn't have to discipline ourselves to please God, but our love for Him makes us want to please Him. His commands aren't burdensome, either. I am reminded every day I need a Savior, and salvation isn't by my own strength. There are other reasons we left. But we didn't leave God. In fact, we know Him just as well outside the Order as inside, if not better."

"I'm glad it worked out for you." Thad tried to sound sincere, and part of him was. Henry had a peace steadily glowing from within, even in the most mundane of jobs. You couldn't help smiling at a man who wore a tropical print shirt along with suspenders to hold up his trousers.

You need to decide for yourself what you believe . . .

"Well, I didn't mean to start preaching at you. All I can do is share with you what it's been like for me. God always listens to a repentant soul, Plain or not Plain." Henry stood, then headed for the coffee pot for another cup. "Anyway, tell me all you know about Daniel Troyer and I'll see what I can find out. Like you said, if it's nothing but a misunderstanding, fine. We'll say no more. But if this man isn't who he says he is, I must go to the Amish bishop."

19

*I*t seemed half the male congregation from Pinecraft's Old Order fellowship had found their way to *Aenti* Chelle's house. Maybe not half, but judging by the number of beards in the living room, Betsy felt gravely outnumbered. Winston sat in the corner in his bed, blinking and looking around at the assembly. Betsy wanted to scoop him up and find a place to hide.

By the time she arrived at *Aenti* Chelle's after closing the shop, her parents were waiting for her. The expression on *Daed's* face made her insides quake just a little. Vera Byler must have told someone, Betsy wasn't quite sure who, about the news producer coming to the bakery and wanting to do a show about Pinecraft Pies and Pastry. Wondering wouldn't make the group in the front room or their questions go away.

Aenti Chelle waited in the kitchen, watching the coffee brew and slicing apple bread. She told Betsy she'd be praying, just before Betsy went to face the group.

"Hello," Betsy told them all, as she surveyed the room and the faces sorted themselves out. All right, the faces belonged to her *daed,* four *oncles*, and her *daadi*. Three other men she recognized from church, along with the local bishop. So it wasn't quite half the congregation.

"We understand the local television station wants to film in your bakery," said the bishop. "They want to record for several days and create an hour-long feature about the bakery, too?"

"Oh, no, that's not how it is." Betsy shook her head.

"Did you agree to this?" *Daed* asked before she could continue.

"No, *Daed*, I did not. I knew I'd have to speak to you and the family first. Also, the lady told me my part of the show will only last about five minutes."

"I don't know if it's wise to go on television." Uncle Joseph, usually the quietest of her *oncles*, spoke up. "We do want to sell as much pie as we can and turn a profit. But Pinecraft has had so many cameras and filmmakers coming through." He glanced at the bishop, who was nodding.

Betsy squared her shoulders. "A long time ago, one television company filmed part of a show at Yoder's about their pies, and it was nearly thirty minutes long." She didn't add that she'd watched it on *Aenti* Chelle's computer.

"It's not the show I'm talking about."

Betsy knew the one. Some time ago, a group of former Amish youths, none from her area, were being filmed for a television show. Rumor at the time had it they were trying to stir up trouble and get the Amish and Mennonites angry at them, then record the whole thing for television. She'd been horrified. Why would people do such things? For money, she'd heard. She remained silent.

"Did you tell this producer you weren't going to be filmed?" Now it was *Daadi's* turn to question her.

"No, not quite." She bit her lip. "We didn't talk about much because I didn't want to commit to anything before I talked to *Daed*."

The bishop said nothing as the men talked about film crews passing through the neighborhoods, journalists interviewing some of the residents. To Betsy's inner delight, she realized not all of them were against the idea of the news station filming at the bakery.

"All right." The two words from Bishop Smucker silenced them all. "Elizabeth, I assume you are interested in having the news station record at the bakery. What are the benefits of this happening, and how would you conduct yourself if we allowed it?"

She swallowed hard. "I'm not the first Plain person to run a business the *Englisch* will want to visit. Since I've returned to Pinecraft and opened the bakery, I feel the weight of responsibility with spending my family's investment. My *daed*, my *daadi*, and my *oncles* are counting on me paying them back and also earning a profit, like my *oncle* said."

Betsy glanced from face to face. Her family had to agree with what she'd just told everyone. Didn't they? Why invest hard-earned money in a venture if it would fail? Why not use every legal—and honest—opportunity to bring in more business?

"Go on," the bishop said.

"It's expensive to advertise on television. I've only been able to advertise in the newspaper twice. The lady who runs the Pinecraft Village site on the Internet has also been writing about the bakery." Betsy paused. "So, in a way, I think this five minutes of television time is like free advertising."

"Sometimes free things aren't free," *Daadi* interjected. "How do we know this won't cause trouble for us?"

"Being on television has been good for Yoder's. People come from all over the country to visit Yoder's when they are in Sarasota." Her words surprised her. *Gotte* must be answering *Aenti*'s prayers.

"What's going on in here? What's the ruckus about?" *Aenti* Sarah stood in the doorway and glared at her brother. "Jacob, why didn't you tell me we were having company?"

"A television station wants to visit the bakery and put it on the air," *Daadi* replied.

"*Aenti*, you should have asked for help getting out of bed." *Aenti* Chelle was at *Aenti* Sarah's side in a flash, her chide gentle.

"I heard voices. Anyway, it's time I do some getting out of bed on my own. The physical therapist wants me to use the rolling walker from the hallway to the kitchen."

"All right. But be careful." *Aenti* Chelle drew back into the kitchen but stood close by.

Betsy smiled for the first time since leaving the bakery that afternoon. *Aenti* Sarah might have had major surgery to repair a broken hip, but certainly her liveliness wasn't affected. No, she couldn't have borne the idea of *Aenti* being in an *Englisch* "rehab home" as she recovered from her surgery.

"Well?" *Aenti* looked at *Daadi* as she pushed her Rollator into the living room and made a beeline for the nearest open chair. She gingerly settled herself onto the seat.

"You were sleeping, Sarah. I didn't want us to bother you."

"No, I was only resting my eyes a bit after supper. Now, as you asked me to help with the bakery, I have. Until my hip broke. But I still consider myself part of the business." *Aenti* Sarah then switched her focus to Betsy. "Elizabeth has conducted herself properly and I believe she would do the same even with the television people visiting us all day." High praise, coming from her *aenti*. Betsy tried not to look triumphant. The bishop could still forbid her to go on television, or the bakery at all.

"Bishop Smucker, what say you then?" *Daadi* asked the man who had watched the exchange between brother and sister with an amused expression. Betsy tried to imagine her grand-father and great-aunt as children, debating over some matter of importance in a child's world.

The bishop stroked his beard, long wisps of snowy hair. "I'm not encouraging the bakery to go on television. However, since the television station contacted Elizabeth, I think she may proceed."

Betsy wanted to clap, but instead clasped her hands together in front of her. She opened her mouth, but Bishop Smucker continued.

"Please, consider carefully how this will be filmed. Make it clear that you will not be posing or parading yourself. And the Zook young man . . ."

Now Betsy's heart seemed to leap into her throat. "Yes, Bishop?"

"He may help you with preparations as he has been. However, he is not to be on camera."

"I understand." Betsy nodded. Too bad for Thaddeus. He deserved quite a bit of the credit for the bakery's success since *Aenti* Sarah's surgery. There was no way she could have enough doughnuts and pastries ready every morning, and not spend her time on the sales floor yawning at everyone.

"I have fresh coffee, if you would all like some. And, there's warm apple bread in the kitchen I'll bring in, too." *Aenti* Chelle stood in the doorway. Steam rose from a cluster of coffee mugs on a tray.

"Why, certainly," said Bishop Smucker.

As *Aenti* Chelle passed her, she said to Betsy, "Betsy, if you'd grab the sugar, cream, and some spoons, to put on the coffee table?"

"Right away." Betsy wanted to skip from the room. Despite what she considered meddling by Vera Byler, the bakery would get a chance to be on television after all. She thought about her favorite dress, which was a vivid blue almost matching the color of the Florida sky.

She wouldn't pose for the camera, but if the producer wanted to film over her shoulder, or somehow record her rolling out pie dough, the dress would be a good color. A smile tugged at her lips as she pulled some spoons from the silverware drawer. She could hardly wait to tell Thaddeus.

And maybe Thaddeus had some information for her about Daniel Troyer. She sealed her lips together. So far this evening he hadn't come by, and *Aenti* Chelle said he was supposed to walk her to Big Olaf's for some ice cream.

"Oh, Betsy?" *Aenti* Sarah's voice drifted into the kitchen. "I need some sugar, please."

"Coming, *Aenti* Sarah."

Betsy allowed herself a few bounces on her toes before settling her stride to something more appropriate for an adult. But Pinecraft Pies and Pastry was going to be on *television!*

⁓⧵⧵

Thad glanced at his phone, at not quite six in the morning. He'd been at the bakery since four, doing prep and making pie crusts. Today, instead of leaving when Betsy arrived with her grim shadow, Vera Byler, in a few moments, Thad would stay.

The tiramisu pie waited for Betsy's arrival in the stainless refrigerator. Thad had sampled each of the pie's components and smiled with each tasting. The dessert would make people's taste buds sing and he couldn't wait to see Betsy's face when she tried it.

Today, Friday, he hoped she wouldn't try to pay him again. He never asked for a paycheck and hadn't expected one. Betsy's venture had found a tentative footing at last. A rumor had drifted his way via *Mammi*—a television station would be coming to film at the bakery. Only, it wasn't a rumor.

He considered it a marketing gift and thanked *Gotte* for the provision and good timing for Betsy. Prayer. The idea made him give a sad smile. He knew there were plenty of churches all over Sarasota and plenty of them claimed to have the right path to follow. Their method of worship was the preferred method and the most correct. Even the *Englisch* couldn't get it sorted out, it seemed to him.

He liked Henry's peace and the easy way he spoke about *Gotte*. Or, God, rather. So much of what he'd known growing up in his Order was about appearances, looking right, acting right, and praying to God for mercy. He did believe in God, but had given up on the idea of religion in general several years after leaving his family. What good did it do anyone?

Enough of those thoughts. Today was Friday, and Thad had decided to investigate the job opportunities here in Sarasota. He'd sat around long enough and the time for lying low was over. Nobody had been after him, after all. Other than the people showing up, asking for him at Stacie's place, and Pete Stucenski looking for him to give him his old job back, they were all.

Thad didn't think working at Dish and Spoon again was a wise move. The place would never be the same after Mitchell's death. Even after the news died down, people would still say, "Oh, this is the restaurant where the owner was murdered." People wouldn't come primarily for the food, but for where a murder took place. Or the opposite could happen. Sales would slack off and the place would have to close for good. Either way, he didn't want to be professionally attached to it.

The back door opened and Betsy walked in. "Good morning." It seemed the sun's glow increased behind her as it streamed through the doorway.

She stopped just inside the doorway, the sunlight framing her from behind as she pulled a clean apron from the nearby hook. "I have some great news for the bakery—have you heard?" She smiled at him, her face fresh and clean, her eyes sparkling. He could barely make out the freckles by her nose. The first face besides *Mammi's* he saw every morning, before having a few moments of conversation.

So beautiful. So pure.

And he loved her.

The realization slammed into Thad and made him grasp the stainless work table with both hands. Funny how the most mundane, ordinary moment could freeze.

But he couldn't love her. It was the worst time, and he wasn't the best man for her.

Betsy kept talking as she tied the apron, glancing over her shoulder. ". . . and Mrs. Byler should be here any minute now. I'm planning to call the station first thing at eight."

Thad nodded. "Going on the Sarasota morning show. Awesome." His brain still spun inside his head as his heart hit overdrive.

"Now," she continued, placing her hands on her hips, "If you could get the coffee started—"

"I did." He gestured with his head toward the sales floor. "Already had a cup."

"Oh, okay. Well, did you bring the tiramisu pie? I can't wait to taste it." Betsy scanned the room.

"It's right over here, in the refrigerator." Thad placed a cloth over the bowl of doughnut mix he'd been preparing. What was he thinking? Anything between them would be impossible, as things stood right now. He didn't see it changing.

"I'll get some plates and forks. Because you need to eat a slice, too."

Insistent, wasn't she? He smiled at her confidence. Maybe the confidence came from her height, which didn't bother him as they stood almost eye to eye. She grinned and set the plates and forks down between them, then pulled a pie server from the utensil caddy.

"I'll have you know, I didn't use a single electric appliance to make this, not including *Mammi's* oven where I baked the pie crust ahead of time." He sliced through the pie and served up two slices. It was a tad early in the day for sweets, but he couldn't turn her down, not with the shine in her eyes.

"So the Plain and simple ways you haven't forgotten?"

He glanced at her as she spoke. Yes, she was teasing. He slid a plate in her direction. "No, I haven't forgotten."

She slipped the fork through the whipped cream topping, through the filling, then into the crust and pulled off a piece large enough for a generous bite. Then she picked up the fork and closed her lips around the bite of pie.

He watched her chew as he sampled his bite. Her eyes drifted shut. "Um, delicious," she said after she swallowed. "Sweet, but not too sweet, and the coffee flavor is something different. People will love this. Matter o' fact, I'm going to put this pie out for free samples this morning."

"I'm glad you like it. I'll make another one tonight, if customers like it."

"Better yet, give me the recipe, if you don't mind sharing, and I'll try making it, too." Betsy took another bite, looking thoughtful. "Thaddeus, may I ask you a question?"

"You just did." He couldn't resist. He also loved the way his full name sounded when she said it.

"Why did you leave the Order? I know it was to continue your studies and go to culinary school, because your *daed* didn't want you to be a chef. But why?"

Sure. Smile at him and use those sparkling eyes to hit a guy in his weak spot. "Have you ever seen things from an outsider's perspective? Probably not. I know you probably couldn't imagine it. But I'd realized that being Plain means everyone being the *same*. And I'm not. The last thing in the world I want is to be like everyone else."

He tried to keep his voice even, but she'd asked him for a real answer, and she would get one. If anything, it would help him hold her at arm's length and if she felt any spark between them, his words would extinguish it.

"I got to the point, I couldn't *breathe* anymore, every action, every look, being weighed and measured. I can't fit into their box. Because of it, and what I wanted to do, I left. I don't like the idea of being like everyone else. All the sameness, everywhere I look."

"Thaddeus Zook, you would never be the same as anyone else, never. You stand out in a crowd no matter where you are, and it's not because of your clothing." Betsy's face flushed. "You should give your family a chance."

"My family, except for *Mammi*, has hardly had anything to do with me since. I still don't know how we got through Thanksgiving." The admission tasted bitter to him.

"But people watch over each other only because they love each other. I know your family must love you and want to know your soul is safe."

"My *soul* can be safe in the *Englisch* world, too. There are people—people out there—who love God and worship Him, too. And they're not Plain. Sometimes it seems the Plain people think they're better than other people *because* they're Plain. Being proud of being humble. Doesn't it mean it's for nothing in the long run, the false humility?" He shook his head and stared at his slice of pie, missing a bite. The bitterness of the coffee took the edge from the sweet. He tasted the bitterness the most right now.

"I see. All the Amish, all the Plain people aren't like that. It's not all, or none." Betsy shook her head. "So, your life in the *Englisch* world. Were you able to love God and worship Him out there, too, like the others?"

He didn't say anything more. No, he hadn't worshiped in the *Englisch* world. He didn't buy the idea that the Plain people had the market on faith. He'd met plenty of people who weren't Plain and yet were good people, Christian even. Instead, his stance was more in the middle. Keeping untangled from both sides had allowed him to hold on to a bit of peace. And no one was yammering at him about rules. Yet loneliness had been a bitter price to pay.

"Henry Hostetler and I were talking last night, and he said something that made me think. He told me, 'You need to decide for yourself what you believe.' That's just it, Betsy. I don't know."

"Well." She took another taste of pie, then set down her plate and fork. "I think you need to take some time, while you're here in Pinecraft, and decide. It would be a shame to— to not be all God intends for you to be."

Right now, though, the idea of deep soul-searching stung his soul. "Since I've met you, Elizabeth Yoder, you've made me want to do so. But it's not easy."

"I have? How?" Her eyes widened.

If he tried to explain why, he'd fumble the words. "You make me almost want to be Plain again."

He looked down at their hands, two of them clasped together. She squeezed his hands, a gentle strength against his palm. He gave a soft tug and then she was in his arms.

"Betsy . . ."

She closed her eyes and he lowered his head so his lips met hers. They were as sweet as he'd imagined, probably with the help of the pie and whipped cream. She showed no resistance as her arms crept around him. He'd kissed a good number of women over the years, but this kiss held the longing of innocence.

If only he could let himself return to what he knew. But he couldn't, wouldn't. He didn't think so. He wasn't sure. And it was a wishy-washy answer at best.

They stepped back at the same moment, Betsy's cheeks flushed. She glanced his way.

"I . . . I almost wish we could do that again," she said.

"We shouldn't." He frowned. "And I wish we hadn't. I'm sorry."

"Thaddeus—"

"I need to go. I'll be back early tomorrow, and I'll have the recipe written out for you. And don't worry, I'm still checking on Daniel Troyer."

"All right." Her voice was barely above a whisper.

"Good morning." Vera Byler's voice trumpeted through the open back door, and she entered the kitchen. "What have we here?" Her eyes narrowed slightly as she looked from Thad to Betsy, then to the pie.

"A tiramisu pie sampling. Help yourself to a slice, please, and let Betsy know what you think of it," Thad said as he turned away from Betsy. "Have a good day, ladies."

He had checked online last evening and saw a job opening at a Sarasota restaurant in Siesta Key, advertising for a part-time pastry chef and prep cook. He lost no time in e-mailing them his credentials and contact information. If it wasn't Providence, he didn't know what was.

20

*T*haddeus had left her, gaping after him, while Mrs. Byler descended on the tiramisu pie and finished off a generous slice.

After she'd eaten it all, short of licking the plate clean, she proclaimed, "Well, I've had better."

Betsy said nothing in response other than to state Thaddeus had prepared it and it was a no-bake pie. Then she straightened her spine.

"Today I'm going to give samples to customers and see how they like it." Betsy went to the sink and washed her hands. Time to get busy, not keep remembering the kiss over and over and over. It counted as her first kiss and the idea of it made her breath catch. Thaddeus's words following snapped her to reality along with the job at hand.

Yes, a mistake. Yes, a bad idea. They both were to blame for the kiss. But, she realized as she dried her hands on a clean towel and went back to the pie plate, she could see how it appealed to other young women, the idea of a forbidden man sweeping her away to a life of adventure.

No adventure, no matter how appealing, would be worth giving up her bakery, leaving her family. Uprooting herself alone and planting in Sarasota had been adventure enough.

Straightaway at eight o'clock, during a lull in customers, she left Mrs. Byler on the sales floor. She stepped out the back door and dialed the phone number to the news station to accept their offer. Television. Her bakery would be on television.

Mrs. Byler hadn't mentioned it so far this morning, although she'd been unusually quiet after coming in and seeing Betsy with Thaddeus, then sampling the pie. A wave of horror rolled over Betsy. Had Mrs. Byler walked in on their kiss? She didn't think so at the time. The two of them had been talking when Mrs. Byler stepped through the back door.

If Mrs. Byler had begun talking about the television people visiting the bakery, what would she say about Betsy and Thaddeus?

"WSAS, Susan Cantrell."

"This is Elizabeth Yoder, with Pinecraft Pies and Pastry." Just then, Winston decided to pitch a fit from the security of his pen.

"Miss Yoder, thank you for calling. So, have you decided?"

A lump lodged itself in Betsy's throat. "Yes, you're welcome to come film your show at the bakery. There are certain things, and people, you cannot film. I hope you understand. Winston, be quiet. I'm sorry, my dog is noisy."

"No problem. So you have a dog, too? Interesting."

"Yes, he's a dachshund. So, you're going to come on Wednesday?"

"Right. And I understand about being respectful when recording. I've been reading up on the Amish."

Betsy wasn't sure she liked the sound of that. "All right. You said you would come Wednesday morning and spend the day, or part of it?"

"Right. What I'll do is stop by Monday and leave some release forms with you to sign. Also, anyone we film, whether they're a customer or whoever, we'll need a release form or a waiver. What we'll do is fade out some of the faces if there are those who don't want to be on film."

"I see. Well, I'll watch for you on Monday, then."

"Terrific."

They spoke for a few more moments about pies, and how long Betsy had lived in Sarasota full-time. Betsy ended the call. Susan Cantrell had a kind warmth about her, although enthusiasm like hers could wear one out in short order.

She stepped back into the kitchen and heard voices in the front of the bakery. A woman's voice filtered under the crack beneath the swinging door and the tile floor.

"I'm here, doing a favor for the family," Mrs. Byler was saying. "Truthfully," and here her voice lowered, "since it's just you and me in the room, her pie is nothing to write home about, as they say. But she's the one with family who can afford to fund this idea. I wish I had people like that. Young people just don't know how to work like some of us older ones. You know I'm not one to complain or be envious, but it doesn't seem fair my pies aren't more in the forefront."

Another female voice, one Betsy couldn't quite place, responded. "It's all right, Vera. God will reward your generosity. Speaking of pie, are you entering the Pinecraft Pie Contest?"

"Yes, of course, I am. If I have a chance for my pie to beat Elizabeth's pie, all the better in a public setting."

Now Betsy's face flamed for a different reason than Thaddeus's kiss two hours ago. Should she push through the door and end the woman's spiel of words? However, there was plenty for her to do back here, inventorying supplies so she could place an order for more flour and such.

Mrs. Byler, a friend of her family since childhood. In her mother's circle of friends? Why, she'd made Betsy sound like a privileged and spoiled young girl.

"Oh, I meant to ask: what do you know about this young man, Thaddeus Zook? He works here early in the morning, but I'm not keen on the way he looks at young Elizabeth. He's trouble, I tell you. From one of those fancy *Englisch* restaurants back home. I imagine he must want this place for himself."

"I don't know much about him. His family doesn't say much, him being shunned and all."

Shunned? Betsy had assumed so, judging by the way he'd left his family and how they treated him. Shunning, she knew, was in the eye of the beholder—or in the case of the Plain people, in the eye of the *Ordnung* or the family.

Her heart sank. Unless something changed drastically, it would be better for her and Thaddeus not to see each other at all. Truth be told, the more she saw him, the more she wanted to be with him, to hear stories of working as a chef, to cook and bake together. She found him absolutely fascinating. And it scared her. She could never pay the price he paid by leaving everyone and everything he'd known behind him.

⁓☙⁓

Rochelle glanced at her phone as she opened her client's stainless dishwasher. Nothing. Daniel had never shown up the other night to walk with her to Big Olaf's for ice cream sundaes. She didn't call him to see why. It wasn't the way she did things. If he was interested enough in her, he would call. Anyway, she didn't know him well.

But a man ought to call, ought to keep his promise, even if it was simple as taking a walk for ice cream. However, she knew from past painful experience certain men were no good at keeping promises. Rochelle pulled out the silverware basket and set it on the counter.

She worried, too, about Betsy and the questioning she'd had to face the other night about going on television. Rightfully so. Rochelle understood the village's need to stay true to its beliefs. What was compromise, and what was merely doing business?

This morning Imogene had called Rochelle before she left for work, concerned.

"Someone is saying Betsy contacted the television station and asked to be put on TV," Imogene had said.

Betsy had blossomed during her time in Sarasota and become more confident, but Rochelle knew the young woman would never do something like arranging a television interview without consulting her family, especially since they'd put up the money so she could open her store. What a blessing to have family supporting her.

When Rochelle had opened her cleaning business, all she had was the proverbial shoestring. But now, the Lord had shown over time how He'd taken care of her through the ups and downs of running a business. The same was happening for Betsy now, yet Rochelle knew some in the village were likely jealous of the attention.

Her phone warbled. *Daniel!*

"Stay strong," she told herself as she picked up the phone. "Slow down and relax. There is an explanation, I'm sure, and it shouldn't matter so much to you anyway."

Rochelle punched the button. "Daniel, hello."

"Rochelle, there are no words to tell you how sorry I am for not being able to meet you the other evening for ice cream."

"Apology accepted. And it's all right. Things come up sometimes." *But you could have at least called.* "I understand."

"Wouldn't you know, I took a slip the other morning and fell on the driveway."

"Oh, my. Are you all right?"

"Smashed my knee but good on the concrete. It swelled up pretty bad, but I've been icing it."

Rochelle paused from putting silverware into the drawer. "Do you need anything? I can come over and run the vacuum, take out your trash, and do some dishes, if you need me to."

Ah, there she went again. But she truly did love to help people, and loved the satisfaction she received when seeing a home put right.

"No, no. But thank you for the offer. It's sweet of you."

"You're welcome."

"You're . . . you're the best thing that's happened to me since coming to Pinecraft. I'll . . . I'll always think fondly of the time we spent together."

"Oh. I'm . . . flattered. Are . . . are you leaving soon, then?"

"Uh, soon. Maybe before Christmas." His voice held a flat tone instead of his typical animated tone.

"Will . . . will I get to see you before you leave?" She had to ask. *Gotte, help me. Why did I get attached so quickly?*

"I, um, I hope so." He fell silent. "Well, I wanted to let you know why I wasn't there the other night."

"Okay, thank you." Rochelle hung up the phone without saying good-bye.

❧

For the first Sunday morning in almost ten years—or maybe nine—Thaddeus put on a pair of trousers with suspenders. He had told *Mammi* on Saturday evening he would like to go to the church meeting with her on Sunday, if he could. But he had no proper clothing for an Amish service. Inside of five minutes, she appeared in his doorway with a folded stack of clothes once belonging to his *daadi*.

Mammi looked sheepish as she handed him the folded clothing, the trousers, hand-sewn white cotton shirt, and ancient suspenders with still enough grip to hold up the trousers. She even had a straw hat.

"I should have done something with these a long time ago, but, I didn't get rid of them, for some reason. You are welcome to wear them as long as you would like. The sleeves might be a bit short, but the shirt is still good."

He'd nodded, accepting the clothing. No shoes, but his black sneakers would have to do. He hadn't paid much attention if the younger men wore certain shoes on Sundays. Of course, they wouldn't wear beach shoes.

This was what he didn't miss about the Plain life. He could understand the need for consistency in clothing when working for a restaurant, and there was something special about wearing his chef's jacket that made him stand a little straighter. In fact, it hung now in his closet as a reminder of what he'd left behind in Ohio. So no, maybe wearing the Plain clothing on Sundays wasn't such a big deal after all.

He slipped the suspenders over both shoulders. *It's time for you to decide what you believe.*

Well, Henry Hostetler, he was about to do it. He finished his outfit by slipping on his *daadi's* black vest.

When Thad stepped into the front room, his *mammi* stood there, a slight smile on her face.

"You will do nicely. You look much like your *daadi* did at the same age."

"Ah, I do?"

"Ya, except for the haircut, and no beard. By your age, your *daadi* was married and had already fathered three sons."

Thad nodded, and they left the house for the short walk to the Old Order meeting. Humidity hung in the air.

"Maybe it will rain today," *Mammi* observed, nodding to a couple as they left their home.

"Maybe." Sweat trickled down Thad's back. He squinted ahead of them. More Plain people, dressed in their Sunday clothing, walked along the empty streets toward the church.

He didn't ask if his parents or other family would be there today. The Old Order people had several choices of places to worship on Sunday, but most went to the main Old Order church, or to the "overflow" church, which met in the large garage in a private home not two blocks from the other congregation.

"Your parents will be there this morning," *Mammi* announced, as if she knew his inner question. "Your siblings have already gone home. They have to work through January."

No wonder they hadn't come around. He almost wanted to apologize to *Mammi*, for the family not visiting much, if at all, while Thad stayed at her home.

A family passed them on tricycles, the *daed* of the family pulling a small trailer behind him, heading for the service as well. They wished him and *Mammi* a good morning. If anyone recognized him in his new garb from around the village, he couldn't tell.

This morning they passed the main church and continued in the direction of the overflow church. Whether it was because the building was already full or whether it was because Thad accompanied *Mammi*, he wasn't quite sure.

When they arrived, *Mammi* introduced him to Bishop Smucker in short order. "My grandson who's been living with me this winter. He's a chef."

"Good morning, and welcome."

"Thank you." So far it felt he'd passed the test, and the *Dietsch* flowed easily from his lips. Of course, the clothing probably helped. Thad found a seat on the men's side of the room. He saw his *daed*, two rows ahead.

Gotte, what am I doing here? If this is how I'm to find my way, please show me. He didn't know if God would listen to him, a wayward "sinner," but it didn't hurt to try.

The songs began and the words tumbled from Thad's mouth of their own accord, like he'd flipped some type of internal switch. But what were words, if you didn't quite mean them, or even understand what they meant?

No, he would find no redemption in the songs. As his mouth sang the words, he was reminded of going to the singing with *Mammi*, and the longing the songs had ignited inside of him. Maybe not longing for the way things were—he didn't want that again—but maybe for the way things ought to be.

21

$\mathcal{Y}$es, there was Thaddeus, standing at the edge of the group of men after the service. The men gathered in their typical spot, in the side yard of the house where they met. If someone had told Betsy Thaddeus had shown up to the service today, she wouldn't have believed them. She didn't recognize him, either—not at first.

All the young women who'd attended the service this morning noticed him straightaway. His eyes, his posture, the way he scanned the crowd.

"I can't believe it's Thaddeus Zook," Emma said beside Betsy. "Here. At service. And he's not dressed *Englisch*."

No, he wasn't. And in the Plain clothing, he appeared more handsome, even with his *Englisch* haircut, cropped close and worn longer on the top. Lately, he'd taken to shaving more, as an unmarried man should. Betsy noticed the change.

He shifted his weight from one foot to the other, his hands stuffed in his pockets like he wasn't sure what to do with them.

"Ouch, my nose hurts." Emma touched her red nose and cheeks.

"So you went fishing again on Steven's boat?"

"Yes, I did. If you'd listened to me the other night, I told you we were going yesterday."

"We?"

"Oh, a few of us, and Steven, and some others from the local Mennonite church."

Betsy nodded. She felt a pang of envy. But she'd chosen this responsibility of operating a business on her own. She knew the hours would be long. She knew the price would be not running around with other young people.

Emma hadn't mentioned missing Eli. Not lately. That much she did remember. Nor did she mention her offer to help Betsy in the bakery.

"So," Betsy asked, watching Thaddeus conversing with a few of the young married men in the group, "how's Eli doing? Is he still coming for Christmas?"

"He's doing well. And yes, he's still coming." Emma fell silent, then frowned.

"Is everything all right?"

"Yes, of course, I'm fine."

Betsy dropped the questioning. Emma joined a group of friends. Emma would tell her, in time, or she hoped her sister would. What concerned her was, thus far, no one had brought up the upcoming visit of the television station to her bakery.

Wednesday was still three days away, three more nights of trying to get some sleep. Part of her wondered if she'd made a foolish choice in agreeing to allow the station to come to the bakery. Part of her knew it was good business sense and no true compromise on her part. She didn't watch television. She did want to see the segment and how it looked. *Aenti* Chelle could help her find it on the Internet.

Mrs. Byler stood with some of the older women, chattering away.

The pie contest happened to fall next Friday, only two days after the news people would visit the bakery. Likely the film crew would be there for the contest, too.

Mrs. Byler made it clear she considered her pies to be the best, both in her open admission of the fact as well as her undisguised disdain for others' baking. Betsy had stopped herself several times from approaching her *daed* and insisting they find someone else to help in the bakery until *Aenti* Sarah was finished with her physical therapy.

What would Thaddeus do, if this were his bakery? She glanced his way again. He made eye contact with her, and half a grin appeared on his face as their glances locked.

She knew what he'd do. He'd tell Mrs. Byler to leave and her help was no longer needed at the bakery.

If they were anywhere else, she would cross the expanse of grass between them and ask his advice about Mrs. Byler, and find out what more he knew about Daniel Troyer. Surely he'd found out more by now.

"Betsy," her mother was calling not a dozen paces away, "have you decided what you're going to bake for the pie contest? Others are curious."

She joined her mother by a group of bicycles, where some of the ladies chatted. "No, I haven't. I'm sure I'll think of something. But I've been busy."

"Right, the television people are coming to the bakery this week," one of Mrs. Byler's talkative friends interjected.

"Yes, they are."

"Have you chosen what you're going to bake for them?" the lady asked.

"No, I'm planning to do my everyday baking."

The woman made a noise that almost resembled a grunt.

"Enough about that," said another older woman—Thaddeus's *mammi*, Mrs. Zook. "What I would like to know is what else we can do for the Haiti auction. January will be here before we realize it. Maybe some of us can gather to put in a quilt or two? I have several pieced tops only needing to be put together."

Betsy nearly sighed with relief. She hadn't liked the sudden turn of conversation, and thankfully, Mrs. Zook had changed the subject. However, Betsy would rather find something else to do for the Haiti auction besides quilt. Her fingers felt more at home pinching pie crusts than feeling the prick of a needle.

Melba Stoltzfus approached them and stood beside Mrs. Zook. "Hiram is asking the men, but I'm also asking you ladies." She stared at Betsy.

"What is it?" she heard herself ask.

"When was the last time you saw Gideon?"

"Friday afternoon." Betsy wanted to add, "making his daily visit to the bakery," but didn't. Gideon hadn't visited her yesterday, which she found odd; however, the day had been so busy, preparing pies for people to take home to serve as dessert today.

"He left our house last night after the singing. We walked by this morning on the way to service, to see if he was going to walk with us, but he didn't answer his door."

"I didn't see him at all yesterday, and he usually stops for a cup of coffee. But we were busy at the bakery."

"Well, maybe the landlord can let you into his apartment, can't they?" *Mamm* asked Mrs. Stoltzfus. "I pray nothing is wrong."

"Me, too." Mrs. Stoltzfus frowned. "Thank you, thank you all. We are going to go straight to the Kaufmans' house on our way home, to see if they can lend us a key. Maybe he's sick."

Maybe. No, Betsy didn't have any romantic attachment to Gideon, but she didn't think ill of him in the least. She hoped nothing bad had happened to him.

❧

Thad turned on his cell phone after he arrived home at *Mammi's*. She was pulling dishes from the refrigerator, making plenty of clanks and clunks he could hear all the way into his bedroom.

He had a voice mail message. The manager of Palm Trees, the restaurant in Siesta Key Village looking for a part-time employee, invited him to come first thing tomorrow morning for an interview.

"Please bring your knives because we need to see your knife work, too," the manager said.

Thad phoned the office and left a message confirming he'd be there at nine to meet with the executive chef and head pastry chef.

Unfortunately—or fortunately—if he landed this position, he'd have to give Betsy notice and leave her bakery. The place had been a quiet sanctuary for him, where he could work in the wee small hours of the morning and think.

Ever since tasting the tiramisu pie, and sharing their kiss, Thad had run figuratively, and almost literally, in the other direction. Still, he couldn't help a smile at her this morning after the church meeting. Getting some distance between the two of them would be better, especially for her.

He yawned. He'd agreed to meet Henry at the park in the afternoon, before the concert at two.

"You should come," Henry had said the other night. "A few boys from Ohio are in town, and they're going to play guitars and sing. I think you might know one or two of them. Aw, I shouldn't call them boys, they're all around your age, give or take a few years."

So Thad agreed. He shifted himself from his bed, then joined *Mammi* in the kitchen.

"You're still welcome to come with me to Abe's." *Mammi* was headed to his cousin's house, where the family would be. No, Abe hadn't invited him, had told him years ago he would never be welcomed in his Ohio home if he left the Order. Thad figured the same would be true here in Pinecraft. *Mammi* probably didn't know.

"No, I'll eat here. But thank you, anyway."

"There's a concert in the park this afternoon." *Mammi* looked hopeful, her hands clasped in front of her.

"I'm going. I promised Henry I would go." He wanted to hug her for her unconditional love, the way she always tried to include him. But he'd never hugged his *mammi* and wouldn't start now.

"Good. I'll look for you." She smiled at him before she left on her three-wheeled cycle.

Thad scrounged through the contents of the refrigerator and found some leftover cheesy vegetable casserole and a few slices of meat from a roast *Mammi* had prepared. It should be plenty. He polished it all off with a glass of milk. Not quite one-fifteen now. Arriving forty-five minutes early wouldn't hurt.

It took him less than ten minutes of strolling through the sleepy streets to arrive at the park, where a few families had already arrived. A brood of children, different ages, climbed and ran and played in the children's area. A Plain woman sat on a bench, watching them.

The closer Thad got to the pavilion and the children's area, the more the woman came into focus. *Mamm?* The little ones on the swings and slide were his nieces and nephews, known to him only as the faces of innocence.

Mamm turned to look at him as he approached. Even from the short distance, he saw the longing in her eyes.

"*Thaddeus.*"

"*Maam.*"

"I brought the children early. The others will come before the music starts."

"I see. I'm early for the concert." He focused on the slowly drifting waters of Phillippi Creek a stone's throw from them, and took in the sight of the lone fisherman sitting on its bank.

"You're here for the concert, then? Does this mean you might be coming back to us?"

"No. I'm not going back to Ohio." As far as his faith was concerned, he was still trying to figure that out. Maybe today would help, seeing the mixture of Plain people and others.

"I wish you would."

"I . . . I can't." The idea of having to compromise part of himself, well, he couldn't do it. Not for anyone else.

"Well, I'm glad you're here anyway. I wanted to tell you something, only, there has been no chance for me to do so, with others around who might wonder why."

Her tone made him face her. "May I sit down?"

"Of course, Thaddeus."

He settled onto the bench beside her and waited for her to continue.

"Someone came by the farm last month, looking for you."

"Who?"

"I don't know. It was a man. *Englisch.* I was afraid something had happened to you. But I knew if something did happen, it would be the police who came."

"You're right. When did he come?"

"Very early in the month. He said he wanted to find you because he heard you were looking for work. Were you looking for work?"

"Sort of. The restaurant I was at in Columbus had been closed after the owner was murdered." The cold, hard fact reminded him of the news, photographers with their cameras, reporters asking about Mitch and any so-called enemies, if it was just a robbery gone bad, and if so, why had the robber left a bank deposit bag with eight thousand dollars on the floor?

"Oh, how terrible. So you were out of work, then."

He shook his head. "I had something temporary going, but one of my bosses had asked if I'd like to go back to work there when it opened again."

"But you came here instead."

"Right."

They both fell silent and he mulled around his *mamm's* words. Someone looking for him. About a job. Just like Pete, Mitch's partner, had. He liked to think his culinary skills would be in demand, but for someone to track him down, all the way to his family's farm?

The feeling of being watched came roaring back onto his shoulders. He glanced around the park. A few more had arrived, some walking and some chaining their bicycles to the split-rail fence.

"What did you tell them?"

"I hadn't heard from you in months." Her words sounded accusatory. But how could he go where he wasn't wanted?

"Okay."

"But it's not all. He asked if we had any other family around. I told him we had family in Florida."

22

*T*had tried to inhale at his *mamm's* words. "You told them about Florida, about Pinecraft?" But it was nothing. Didn't she say the man had stopped at the farm earlier in the month? And December began next week. Surely, someone would have already found him by now, if they wanted to and had the right resources. Zook wasn't a common name, not in most places outside the typical Amish communities.

"I didn't say where in Florida. But I couldn't lie to him and tell him we had no family anywhere else. And, I didn't know you were here."

No, he didn't fault her for being honest. He wouldn't have wanted her to lie for his safety. "No, *Mamm*, of course. You did the right thing."

"You had probably go soon, find somewhere else to sit. I don't . . . I don't want the others to see me talking to you. They'll have questions. The children won't wonder so much, they're too busy climbing and playing tag."

"Oh. Okay." Thad sighed. This was why it was better to avoid everyone, why he'd dreaded his family traveling to Florida this winter. The pain of exclusion he thought he'd overcome. The frustration at not being what they wanted, someone he couldn't be. He rose. "Thank you for telling me."

She nodded and stared across at the playground. *Mamm* didn't say anything more, so Thad trudged away from the bench and back over to the pavilion.

He found a vacant picnic table in the back, far from the long, low benches making up the seating area in front of a low stage. A trio of men stood at by the stage, talking and laughing with each other. One pulled out an acoustic guitar, another a banjo. The third rummaged through a cardboard box and pulled up some small flat squares. CDs?

The man going through the CDs looked familiar. No, it couldn't be. His old friend, Benjamin Esh? Taller and more muscular, of course. But yes, Benjamin Esh. Thad figured Ben would be married and working on child number two or three by now. Thad had left before he knew what had become of his old friend. Judging from Ben's *Englisch* denim jeans and blue plaid button-down shirt with the sleeves rolled up, he'd left the Plain life behind him.

Thad headed toward the men. "Ben Esh?"

The man's focus snapped up from the CDs to Thad. "Wait . . . I know who you are." He squinted. "Thad? Thaddeus Zook? I can hardly believe it." Ben stepped around the side of the table and extended his hand.

Thad shook hands with his old friend. "You . . . you're not . . . Plain."

He shook his head. "Not anymore. I go to a Brethren in Christ Church. One of the more, ah, 'liberal' ones." As he spoke, he leaned closer and made quotation marks in the air. "I left the *Ordnung* not long before I was due to be baptized. Went to live with some second cousins."

"Ah, I see." Thad tried to recall the last time the two had spoken face-to-face, and the memory had been lost, like much of what happened right before he left the Order.

No, it wasn't quite a coincidence, him seeing someone from "before" in Pinecraft, considering he was in the winter haven for most Orders of the Amish and Mennonites.

"So you've been gone longer than me. What brings you to Florida? Vacation?"

"Not exactly. I've been staying with my *Mammi*. She's hear year-round now."

"Well, Jim and Ray and I are traveling, visiting different churches and singing, playing our songs."

"Good, good for you." He had a vague memory of Ben having a decent singing voice. "A friend of mine invited me today, so I thought I'd hang out here for a while."

"Excellent. Have a CD."

"Oh, I couldn't."

"I insist."

"Okay, since you insist." He accepted the plastic case from Ben. *Songs of Faith* read the title, and the graphic was a photo of the three friends standing by a fence in front of a field. "Nice."

"Maybe you could come over one night. We'll be here until Wednesday night, until we head for Orlando. We're staying in the RV park, lot twenty-three."

"Sure, why not."

"I mean it, man. Come on by. I'd love to hear what you've been up to."

Thad nodded. "So, you keep in touch with your family?"

"As regularly as I can. They still hope I'm going to come back, but they understand I still have faith in God, and I walk the same walk they do, only a little . . . different. If that makes sense."

"They . . . they didn't shun you?"

"No." Ben stepped over to a guitar case. "I've never been baptized into the church, so they didn't shun me. I guess they think I'm running around, so to speak. But I'm not. A few of the older ones don't see it so kindly."

Not shunned? Benjamin Esh had never been shunned?

"Ah, I see." Thad watched as Ben took out an acoustic guitar. "I'll, ah, try to come by on Wednesday sometime."

"Awesome. Remember, lot twenty-three. Hey, it's good to see you." His smile glowed. The man radiated contentment, peace, joy. He hadn't been shunned. The thought ricocheted through Thad's mind.

Betsy smoothed the apron over her favorite blue cape dress, then ran her fingers over her head covering. Not a hair out of place. It didn't matter. She wasn't going to be on camera, not her face, anyway. As much as she appeared to be Plain, she didn't feel Plain sometimes.

She studied Susan Cantrell's large leather tote, trimmed with a brightly colored fabric. It was a beautiful bag, and definitely large enough for carrying plenty of things.

"It's a Dooney & Burke," Susan Cantrell said.

"A what?"

"My bag. It's a Dooney & Burke. I love it. It's beautiful and it carries everything I have to haul around with me every day." Susan scribbled something on her notepad. "The photographer is almost here. He's recording some shots of the neighborhood."

"The neighborhood?" Betsy's spine stiffened. "You need to be careful with how they're filming. There are people here in the village who aren't happy about recording. Pinecraft has had a lot more news attention in the past few years, and not all of it positive." The television producer had arrived around eight-thirty, without a cameraman.

"Our editing department can take care of that, especially if we don't have signed releases from our subjects. We typically blur out faces, including those who don't wish to be on the air. Speaking of which, I have a release for you to sign, and any of your workers. And any customers we film."

Betsy nodded. "Where do you want to start?"

"We'll begin by filming your display case, then have you slice some pie and serve it to a customer. We'll also record someone, likely you, rolling out pie crust in the kitchen. Also, we'd like to get some shots of the outside of the building and your sign."

"All right. If you could, keep my face out of the filming. Please. Otherwise, I can't do it. I appreciate you choosing my bakery to feature on the show, but I'm trying not to offend anyone here. I live here. This is my home."

"Of course, I understand." Susan nodded. But it didn't mean she understood.

Part of Betsy wanted to cancel the whole thing. Part of her knew this opportunity would help her business immensely. Part of her imagined what some might be saying about her, and the bakery. Vera Byler hadn't shown up this morning. Instead, she sent a note carried by one of her fresh-faced little granddaughters.

I'm sorry. I can't come today. I'll see you tomorrow morning.
Sincerely,
Vera Byler

Betsy would manage, somehow. She should have asked Emma to help her, if Emma wasn't running off to the beach yet again or out fishing with friends on *Aenti* Chelle's nephew's boat.

The front door opened, the bell clanged, and in stepped Emma, her face flushed, her nose peeling. "I'm here, I'm here. I meant to tell you to wake me this morning, but I knew I'd never get up in time." She skidded to a stop when she saw Susan.

"Miss Cantrell, this is my youngest sister, Emma."

"Well, it's nice to meet you, Emma."

"Nice to meet you, too. How can I help?" She glanced from Betsy to Susan, then back again. "I can take cash if you need me to mind the register." Emma usually worked a day or two every week in a gift shop back in Ohio.

Betsy nodded. "Yes, if you could help customers, I can concentrate on the kitchen and talking to Miss Cantrell."

Emma stepped behind the counter. "So if you run low on pies, I can just get another one from the kitchen?"

"Yes, let me know ahead of time, though, especially if it's pie, since it takes a little longer to restock. Unless it's a refrigerated pie." Betsy didn't have time to explain how she kept her inventory as fresh as possible, because she was still figuring out a system that worked. She hadn't quite noticed a pattern yet with customers, other than the coffee crowd who would come for their free cup in the morning.

They'd already gone on their way.

"Oh, good." Susan looked out the front window. A gray-haired *Englisch* man, camera on his shoulder, headed for the door. "Here's Barry now. We can get started on the indoor work."

She met the cameraman at the door, and Betsy joined Emma behind the display case.

"I'm so glad you came." Betsy almost sighed with relief. "Mrs. Byler sent word she couldn't help today."

"She's probably staying away because of the television people." Emma shook her head. "You know some people aren't happy about this, so Mrs. Byler probably doesn't want her name attached to the bakery while they're here."

"I know." Betsy studied Emma's face. Yes, she appeared to have been hurrying to get here, but something about her eyes, a hint of pink. "Emma, have you been crying?"

Her sister shrugged. "I . . . I . . . Eli and I aren't getting married anymore."

"What? When did you decide this? And why?"

Emma switched to *Dietsch*, her voice low. "This morning. We talked on the telephone. He's . . . he's not coming to Florida for Christmas after all."

"So you called it off because he's not coming for Christmas?" Betsy glanced at the television people. They were still talking, the cameraman nodding as Susan Cantrell read something aloud from her notepad.

"No, I've realized, since I've been here in Florida, I don't want to marry Eli. It's not fair to him. I don't want to always wonder . . ." Emma paused, her eyes filling with tears.

"Wonder what?"

"If there's more than him for me. I always wanted to get married, keep house, have a family, but now, I wonder."

Betsy had no words for Emma at the moment. She'd always thought Eli a quiet and kind young man, a bit bowled over by Emma at times, but he clearly adored her. They seemed happy enough and both sets of parents had given the couple their blessing in October. Of course, she'd missed a lot in the last year being gone from Ohio and had only heard updates from Emma or secondhand from their mother.

"Have you prayed?"

"Ya, I have. I have no answer."

Betsy still didn't know what to say, but here came Susan and the cameraman back to the counter. "Let's talk later," she whispered. "It's going to be all right. You'll see."

"Thank you, Betsy. You're so strong. I feel better just being here with you."

Sometimes Betsy didn't feel strong. "Well, I'm glad it helps."

"Oh, I meant to tell you. You'll never guess who showed up back home. Gideon Stoltzfus. He got a ticket and took the bus straight back to Ohio."

"What?" Relief washed over her, and thankfulness. "How did you know this?"

"Eli. It's another reason I called the wedding off. He kept saying it was your fault, that there was something wrong with you for not accepting Gideon's offer. I told him what he could do with his idea."

"*Emma.*"

"Well, I did." She gave a sharp nod.

"All right," said Susan Cantrell, returning to the counter area. "Our guy here will take some shots of the interior. And then we'll wait for a customer to come in. I can talk to Betsy in the kitchen and record audio while Emma, you watch the front of the store. And relax. We want to film you as natural as possible, so try to forget the camera is here. Pretend it's your grandmother watching the bakery while you work."

This made Betsy want to laugh, so she did. "All right, Susan. Let's go to the kitchen while Barry and *Mammi* watch the store while Emma works."

Betsy smiled at her sister before leading Susan into the kitchen.

Dear Gotte, please let Emma do well on film.

23

T had arrived fifteen minutes early for his interview at Palm Trees and found a convenient spot to park his motorcycle. An ocean breeze drifted down the main drag of Siesta Key Village, footsteps from the edge of the white sands of Siesta Key Beach. A guy could get used this, fast.

He'd missed the trips out on the cycle. Why hadn't he made more time for this lately? He shook his head. He'd allowed the village atmosphere to suck him in with the power of a vacuum. For a time, he'd been content to lose himself in the fantasy he could be not-Plain among them. There were some who still spoke to him and associated with him. Those outnumbered the ones who didn't.

He swung his leg over the bike and popped the kickstand, before unstrapping his knife case from the back of the cycle. His chef's jacket was neatly folded in a bag. Before he went to the kitchen, he'd ask the way to the men's room and prepare himself for the interview to follow.

Gotte's will be done. The thought came, unbidden. Did he want *Gotte's wille*? He'd long ago tried to free himself from thoughts like that. However, this thought came because it was what he wanted, not what someone else was trying to force on him. Divine guidance would be most welcome.

Daed had thought he should have studied a more traditional trade, yes. So had the others. They had begged and pleaded with him for hours to reconsider, to bend to their will, to at last join the church and participate in its baptism.

He couldn't. It wasn't truthful.

But back to *Gotte's wille* again. If *Gotte* gave him a talent, oughtn't he to use it? In Plain terms, what he did might not be traditional, but it in no way contributed to dividing people or drawing people away from the Order.

No, it was that he wasn't like everyone else. It's what *Daed*, and the others, had wanted him to be—like everyone else. He remembered his nearly eighteen-year-old self realizing the fact and it being the last thing to send him packing, literally.

A passing car honked at someone, jolting Thad back to the very-present priority of moving on with his life. As the days had passed, the heebie-jeebies had left him.

He held the knife case in one hand, his helmet in the other, and pulled open the door to Palm Trees.

The restaurant atmosphere, one he'd called home for years, surrounded him again. The host desk, the menus tucked into the holder, an expanse of bar to the left with an accompanying patio. He glimpsed a simple raised stage in the courtyard outside. The place was probably hopping at night.

"You must be Thaddeus Zook," a young woman in a dark blue chef jacket said. "I'm Beth Waller, head pastry chef." *Beth. Betsy.* Two female pastry chefs, two completely different women.

"Nice to meet you." He shifted the helmet to his hip, the knife case to his left hand, and shook her offered hand.

"You bike, huh?" She glanced at his helmet appreciatively, her nut-brown hair scraped back into an efficient bun.

"Yes, I do."

"What do you ride?"

"A Harley Sportster, 2008."

"Sweet. I own a hog myself." She grinned, assessing his arms. "Well, when you're ready, head straight back to the kitchen and I'll let the manager and executive chef know you're here."

Thad glimpsed a men's room sign past her shoulder. "All right. I'll be a moment."

She smiled at him, a dimple appearing in her left cheek. "I can't wait to see what you can do."

Did she just hit on him?

Thad shook his head and headed for the men's room. The attention didn't make him exactly uncomfortable. Hey, she was a pretty lady. But now, the attention didn't seem as welcome to him. Which was okay. He wasn't looking to meet anyone. Not with Betsy claiming his thoughts and the aggravation of what to do about it.

He entered the men's room and set his things inside an empty sink. He pulled his chef's jacket from the small bag and shook it free of a few wrinkles. The few minutes in the bag as he traveled from Pinecraft hadn't done much damage.

There. He settled the jacket over his black T-shirt and buttoned it up. The sturdy weave felt good, like he'd put on a part of himself he'd laid aside for a while.

Stop thinking so much. If he wanted to get this job, he needed to be focused. Lack of focus meant mistakes, bad food, poor-tasting desserts, all of which led to unhappy diners.

Thad stared at himself in the mirror and tugged the hem of his jacket, then his cuffs. *Thaddeus Zook* was embroidered on the left upper chest, along with the insignia of a plate covered with a spoon.

"Here goes." He left the restroom, then headed through the dining room and straight to the back and the kitchen. The fluorescent lights glowed in the gleaming room.

Thad set his helmet on the nearest edge of stainless prep table and approached the trio waiting for him.

Beth grinned. "And this is Thaddeus Zook. This is Brad, our manager, and Antoine, our executive chef."

"Nice to meet all of you. What would you like me to show you?"

Brad spoke first. "We need a part-time pastry chef to help Beth, and Antoine needs a sous chef on occasion. So the right person for us needs to be versatile."

"Okay."

"Let us see your knife work," Antoine said, with a hint of an accent. "Please, dice an onion, filet a fish, and shuck the bowl of oysters."

He could do those things, but he should have practiced. Why hadn't he thought of it before? Because all he'd be thinking about was the pastry part of the job. He had recipes in a journal, twists on traditional restaurant favorites as well as new concoctions all his own. Those were more valuable to him than his knife set, which he would never have the heart to part with.

Thad placed the knife set on the prep table and opened the case, before stepping to the nearest sink to wash his hands. He'd pulled out each knife in turn last night, sharpening each of them, before sliding them precisely into their individual lined pockets.

He dried his hands on a clean towel, and pulled his favorite knife from its sleeve and turned his attention to the onion in front of him. It was almost like his hands remembered how to maneuver the onion, and he made quick work of dicing it into tiny cubes, then scooping the bits into an empty bowl.

Next, for the fish, a run-of-the-mill trout. Thad slid the filet knife from its spot and something else slid out too. A small keychain, without a key. He paused as he stared at the keychain.

"Is something wrong? Because the onion looks terrific," Beth said.

"No, not at all. Thank you." He took his time filleting the fish. They'd probably judge this more strictly than the onion.

Someone had stuck a keychain in his knife case. A keychain with no key. It made no sense. It also meant someone had gone through his stuff, back in Columbus.

The last time he'd looked at those knives, other than last night, was when he left Columbus and packed up his things at Dish and Spoon.

❧

Thad zipped along in the stop-and-go traffic all the way back to Pinecraft. His gut told him he'd done a decent job at the interview.

"I'll give you a call," Beth had said, sending him off with a grin.

Somehow he'd gotten through the interview with the old feeling coming back, as he answered every question and they drilled him about possible scenarios in the kitchen.

But what if it had been a mistake, and someone had stuck the keychain into his case, thinking it belonged to someone else. He was making a big deal out of likely nothing. Thad decelerated as he turned onto Bahia Vista.

His attention turned back to the job. What would people in the village think if he took a job at an *Englisch* restaurant? He wasn't so much concerned with what they thought, but whether their opinion ought to matter to him.

He'd grown tired of doing next to nothing around here, and Henry hadn't mentioned needing help with any tile work. Maybe after the first of the year. What else could he do, except what go back to what he knew? Part of him wanted to help Betsy in her bakery, but he knew the odds of her business succeeding. *Mammi* had told him about a television station coming to do a story about the bakery. Good news for Pinecraft Pies and Pastry.

Thad grinned as the Harley growled past the bakery. A WSAS van sat in the lone parking space beside the shop. Thad nearly decided to check in and see how the television filming was going. However, it could wait.

He continued along to the house and found it empty. He headed for the refuge of his room and set his helmet and knife case on the dresser, then opened his small backpack.

Thad took out the keychain again, turning it over with his fingers. The key fob was a dark gunmetal gray rectangle, smaller than a skinny pack of gum. It looked like one end— the end not attached to the chain—came off like a lid or a cap.

He pulled off the end, exposing a USB connector. Computer file storage, on a convenient keychain. He wasn't totally computer illiterate, and his curiosity made him wonder even more about why the keychain had ended up in his knife set.

Someone had tucked it there, for safekeeping, maybe? Or maybe they'd confused his set with someone else's at the restaurant. But he couldn't see that happening. He never left his knives far from his reach.

He set the keychain on the dresser. He'd have to make time to go over to Rochelle Keim's, yet again, and see if she minded him using her laptop, to see if there was anything on the USB drive.

Then again, maybe it would be better to find another computer to use besides Rochelle's. The temptation to visit with Betsy would be strong, and he didn't need it now.

He supposed he could ask Henry if he knew of anyone who would mind him using the computer. Either that, or Imogene. A former Amish woman who was now a shutterbug likely had a computer. He hadn't seen her lately, either.

Thad figured he'd check with Ms. Keim if he could use her computer. If there was nothing on the USB drive, then nothing. He needn't spend much time there, especially if Betsy were home.

He called Rochelle's number and the call went straight to voice mail, so he left a message, asking if he might borrow some time on her computer for a few moments, when it was convenient for her.

Thad ended the call, and the fidgets began. He burned off some of the energy by washing the few dirty dishes in the kitchen sink, then by sweeping and mopping *Mammi's* floor. Then he sharpened the few utility knives in the drawer.

Ben Esh came to mind. His old friend had extended an open invitation to stop by the RV park and visit before he and his musical group left Sarasota. Who knew when this chance would come again? More than anything at the moment, besides Rochelle Keim letting him know about using the computer, was having his questions answered about Ben's life after leaving the *Ordnung*.

Rochelle looked at her calendar. Christmas, so close, less than a month away. And Daniel Troyer, leaving before Christmas. It was just as well she hadn't let her defenses down with him, not completely. If he was leaving, then so be it. Silas Fry had made his own choice years ago.

She wondered how he'd been dealing with Belinda's death. She didn't dare consider asking anyone to find out, save her sister Jolene. But if she enlisted Jolene's help, then everyone would know why Jolene was asking questions about Silas.

This quick affection for Daniel Troyer was borne out of nothing except sheer loneliness, and Rochelle knew it.

Lord, I don't want to be with someone because of loneliness alone. I would rather suffer loneliness than be committed for a lifetime to the wrong person.

She tore her focus away from all things Daniel and Silas, then back to the calendar and her laptop. The aroma of supper in the oven made her mouth water.

The front door banged open.

"*Aenti* Chelle, I'm home. And . . . you have a visitor." Emma entered the kitchen with Daniel following her. "Steven was dropping me off, just as Daniel arrived. I have some fish, too." Emma held up a string of mullet.

"Hello." Daniel stood in the entryway to the kitchen. He clutched his hat in one hand, and paper sack in the other. "I brought something too, but not fish."

"Oh?" She didn't get up from behind the laptop.

"Ice cream from Big Olaf's. I asked if they could dish up a couple of quarts for me." The man's shoulders drooped. He glanced at Emma, who scurried onto the lanai with the fish.

"I see." Her quiet home had turned into a three-ring circus, with *Aenti* Sarah napping in her room, Emma traipsing in sunburned after an afternoon of fishing with her friends, and now Daniel looking like a schoolboy in trouble. Now all she needed was Betsy and Winston to show up and the effect would be complete. She begrudged none of it, although her first instinct was to send Daniel home.

"Well," she found her voice worked, "the least I can do is offer you supper, since you brought dessert."

"Thank you."

"You can put the ice cream in the freezer." Rochelle gestured with her head in the direction of the refrigerator. "I made slow cooker chicken curry. Have you ever had it before? It's a bit spicy, but it also has coconut milk and sour cream in it."

"No, can't say as I have." He stepped over to the refrigerator and opened the freezer door. "I thought you might be done for the day. It's nearly five-thirty."

"I am. Just wrapping up a few accounts."

A familiar step-click, step-click sounded in the hallway. *Aenti* Sarah and her walker. Beautiful timing. Rochelle smiled at the older woman. She almost opened her mouth to chide her about asking for help, but *Aenti* showed she was a stubborn bird. If Rochelle were in her nineties, she expected she would be, too.

"Supper ready yet?" *Aenti* Sarah sniffed the air, then studied Daniel. "You're back."

"He brought Big Olaf's ice cream, and yes, supper is almost ready." Rochelle rose from her chair. "I need to check the rice."

"Huh. What are you making with rice? I was in the mood for some meatloaf and mashed potatoes."

Rochelle tried not to sigh. "I'll make some of that tomorrow night. I was busy today, so I put supper in the slow cooker before I left this morning."

The front door opened again. It would be Betsy, home from the bakery.

"Hello." Betsy trudged into the kitchen and set her tote bag on the table beside Rochelle's computer.

"Hello to you, too." Rochelle scanned Betsy's face. "How did the television interview go today? Well, I hope?"

"Yes, it went well." Betsy frowned as she sank onto the nearest chair. She cast a glance at *Aenti* Sarah continuing her step-click to the front room and a cushioned armchair, then glanced over to Daniel. "They were careful about how they filmed, but now I'm not sure if it'll even make it to television."

"Why not? What happened?" *Aenti* Chelle took the chair across from Betsy. "Daniel, please, sit down."

"I can come back. This is family business, after all." The man shifted from one foot to the other.

"No, you don't have to leave."

"Yes, it's okay." Betsy wanted to cry, but she didn't. Crying was for little girls and she'd done enough crying over things she had no say about. "Somebody—I don't know who—called the television station and told them I have someone baking for me who's not Amish."

"Well, whatever is wrong with that? For a while, you've had Thaddeus Zook helping you prep in the early mornings. But Vera and you do the baking and frying." *Aenti* Chelle shook her head. "Of all the nerve, calling and trying to ruin things for you."

"I know. But the newswoman looked nervous, said she needed to tell me and she'd have to run things by her bosses and let them know. She said the caller said it wasn't right some people were pretending to be Amish and trying to get other people's money."

Daniel Troyer sat up sharply in his chair, so much so that the feet scraped on the tile floor. "Pardon me. My knee had a spasm. From when I fell the other morning."

Betsy paused. She didn't like the man. Not at all. Not with his fancy watch—now missing from his wrist—and his Plain-looking hair and beard. She heard Winston scratching at the back door leading to the lanai.

"Oh, I'll let Winston in. Sorry," *Aenti* Chelle said as she stood, "I was so wrapped up in my work when I got home I didn't let him in." She headed for the sliding glass door, and Winston skittered onto the tiles.

He slid to a stop when he saw Daniel, and the hair on his back rose. Then he growled.

"Winston, be nice." Betsy shook her head at the dog, but she found it hard to blame him. "He's a little protective."

"It's a good quality in a dog, even a small one." Daniel reached down. "Here, boy. C'mon." Winston didn't budge.

"So, when will this newswoman let you know?"

"Tomorrow morning. I'm trying not to let it bother me much, but I can't help it. I know it has to be someone in the village who called her, it must be. And then I don't want to think about it, because it's horrible to think someone here would do such a thing."

Aenti Chelle sighed and headed for the stove. Winston followed, looking over his shoulder. "Winston, it's just rice. Nothing interesting for a dog."

At any other time, Betsy would have laughed at Winston. But not now. She wondered what her *daed* would tell her about this latest development. He'd warned her about Thaddeus Zook.

"Here, let's eat. Help me with the plates. I know you're tired, and it's been a busy day. I know dealing with the camera hasn't been easy, either."

Betsy joined *Aenti* Chelle by the cabinets. No amount of her *aenti*'s untraditional cooking would soothe the disappointment tonight.

If only Thaddeus were here. The idea of having his listening ear, along with the rest of him around her, helped a little.

24

*T*had and Ben Esh chatted the afternoon away under a tree dripping with Spanish moss. He met Ben's wife, Tisha, a nurse. The couple had attended the same college near Lancaster in central Pennsylvania and married not long after graduation.

He and Ben were on their third cup of coffee after an early supper when the subject of being Amish or not Amish came up, along with the whole shunning thing.

"Don't you know, if you were never baptized, you technically aren't shunned? Sure, if you ever went back, you'd have to go through proving. But no, they shouldn't have shunned you." Ben Esh shook his head.

"But, your family—they still speak to you and welcome you into their home?" Thad asked.

"Yes, they do. I haven't left my faith, either." Ben's tone grew more serious. "I'm sorry your experience has been far different than mine."

Thad shrugged. "I can't change the past. What's done, is done."

"God has gifted you with a unique talent, Thad. But whether you're Plain, or not, you're the one who has to 'work out your own salvation with fear and trembling.' I can't judge you. As long as you believe Christ's work on the cross saved us all, well, we have plenty of common ground."

Thad nodded slowly. He was still trying to get his brain to catch up with the idea of shunning versus not shunning hinging on baptism. It seemed he had run off on *Rumspringa*, so to speak, and hadn't returned. As far as what Ben said about Jesus, he already knew all about it. He'd been raised on the story of the cross and condemnation. But salvation and redemption? Those things seemed too hard to worry about.

Thad's phone buzzed. Rochelle Keim, calling him back.

"Excuse me, Ben. I've been waiting for this call."

"No problem."

Thad pushed the button on his phone and headed toward the base of the tree, away from the picnic table beside the RV. "Hello, Ms. Keim."

"I got your message, Thaddeus. If you'd like to come by this evening to use the laptop, you're more than welcome. I know Betsy will be glad to see you, too."

"All right, thank you. Thank you so much." *Betsy will be glad to see you, too.*

"Come by, anytime. But we generally close up around nine during the evenings around here."

He glanced at his phone. The time was heading past six-thirty now. "I'll be there soon."

"Everything okay?" Ben asked as Thad returned to the table.

"Yes, I need swing by another friend's house on my way home." Friends. As reluctant as he'd been when first coming here, yes, he did have friends in Pinecraft.

"I've enjoyed catching up with you." Ben stood, and the two shook hands. "Let's keep in touch, okay? You're going to be staying in Sarasota?"

"Yes. I think so, if I get called back on the job in Siesta Key Village."

"Well, I'll be praying you find your way."

"Thanks, Ben."

As Thad rode off on his motorcycle, it felt as though the future loomed ahead of him, as uncertain as ever. But for now, he could focus on one thing—seeing what was on that USB keychain.

He roared up on his Harley to Rochelle Keim's house, and parked in front. Another vehicle occupied the space in the driveway beside Rochelle's van.

Betsy answered his knock, along with Winston, who gave Thad a boisterous greeting. "Hello, come in. My *aenti* said you'd be stopping by." He'd missed her wide smile lately. Something in her eyes, though, made him pause.

"How did everything go today?"

"It went well, I think. Although Emma left halfway through the day when some of her friends came by, to go fishing." She made a face like she'd just sucked a lemon slice, then opened the screen door and he followed her into the house. Whatever had been supper smelled terrific. He thought he caught a whiff of curry powder in the air.

"Ah, I see." He glanced around the kitchen, then heard voices coming from the opening sliding glass door from a covered lanai beyond. "Oh. I saw the car out front. You have company?"

"Daniel Troyer."

"Huh. I should get a look at this guy."

Betsy reached out and clutched his arm. "No—they're talking. If we start introductions, he'll stay even later. I'm hoping she's going to send him off soon, anyway. And I can't keep this from her much longer. I feel like she knows I don't care for the man. Neither does Winston."

She kept hold of his arm and he couldn't resist the chance to gently take her hand between his. "Betsy, if things were different . . ."

"But they're not." She pulled her hand from his grasp.

He nodded. "Uh, about Daniel. I should tell you . . . I called that company he supposedly works for in Indiana. They told me the Daniel Troyer who worked for them passed away this spring."

"No. Unless we have the wrong Daniel Troyer?" She shook her head.

"I hope you don't mind, but I was visiting with Henry the other night, and he promised me he'd ask around, too. I don't know as many people as he does in the Plain communities. Well, they'd talk to him a little more quickly than me."

She frowned. "All right. I know he won't say anything. Maybe I should have asked him first. But. . ."

"I'm glad you asked me." He saw Rochelle's laptop on the kitchen island. "I guess I should let your *aenti* know I'm here."

"I'll tell her. Go ahead, the computer is on island." Betsy headed for the lanai, and Thad stepped over to the kitchen island. He pulled up a nearby stool from the corner.

Thad heard the murmur of voices, a deeper male voice, and the female voices. He popped the USB stick into the slot on the computer and waited while the computer recognized the storage in the drive. Video files, several of them.

He clicked on the first video and turned up the volume.

He recognized the setting immediately, the interior of Dish and Spoon. Mitch, the dirty dog, had set up hidden surveillance cameras throughout the restaurant. This first file was in the dining room, nearly empty. A group of men sat around one table. One of them he recognized straightaway. Mitch and his business partner, Pete something. A Polish name he couldn't recall at the moment.

Another man looked vaguely familiar, and Thad wasn't sure if it was because the guy was a regular customer. Maybe not. Even if he were, Thad didn't see diners too often.

They all wore suits and the table was covered with dirty plates holding the remainders of their meals.

He could barely hear them speaking, but it was enough.

"So, we can guarantee you a spot in office if you help us get Ohio in the next presidential election. It's going to be a key state."

"There's no way I can do it, gentleman," the man said, steepling his hands. "There's the matter of something called the electoral college."

They kept talking about business dealings, money owed to this one and that, in addition to campaign funds guaranteed to the guy running for office.

Thad paused the video file and opened an Internet browser. A quick search told him the identity of the would-be senator, Channing Bright. The elections had come and gone, and the guy had won by a landslide. It looked like he'd had some help from the men around the table.

If this file were given to the wrong, or right, people, depending on how you looked at it, Bright would be in trouble. The election was over, but he didn't take office until after the new year.

Was this what Mitch had been hiding? Surely, the police knew about the surveillance files. What about these?

He closed that file, then opened another.

Mitch, talking to the would-be senator himself.

"You know my situation, Mr. Bright."

"I do."

"Well, look over your shoulder right there."

The future senator glanced toward the camera. "At what?"

"Smile, I've got this place wired and bugged, if you catch my meaning. It would be a shame if word got out about your activities in my restaurant."

"You're not serious."

"I'm a million dollars serious."

"It'll take time for me to get so much together. I can't believe you're threatening me."

"Oh, this is no threat. Come to think of it, my requirements just doubled. Look, two million is enough to give me some breathing room here. I ain't gonna be going to Tahiti or anything. Paying off some bills and staying afloat. The restaurant business is tough."

"Get a loan, then, and leave me out of your business."

"I couldn't dream of it. Desperate times, as they say."

"All right, I'll work on it."

"You have one week. I'll get you a bank account number for you to wire the money to, and you do the rest."

The senator-to-be shook his head. "One week isn't long."

"It's long enough." Mitch stood. "A pleasure doing business with you. Smile big when you leave. I have cameras everywhere. And good luck on election day."

The man glowered at Mitch, then stomped from the vacant restaurant.

Thad had seen enough.

❧

Pete sucked in a deep breath and tried not to look triumphant for no reason at all. "Thaddeus Zook? No, I don't believe I've met him."

"Betsy's quite taken with the young man. I like him. He's a bit brooding, a bit of a wayward soul, but I think he's on his way back."

"Back?"

"To his faith."

"Ah, I see." But he didn't. "So, are they dating or something?"

"Dating?" Rochelle's jaw dropped. "No, Betsy wouldn't date him. She's Amish and wouldn't be able to court someone who's not baptized into the church."

He was making mistakes. "Ah, so that's not why he's visiting tonight."

"No, he's borrowing my computer, checking some files."

"Ah, I see." Pete's brain floundered for what to do next. So maybe Thad did find something. If only he could peek over the guy's shoulder. He heaved himself to a standing position, taking care to mind his sore knee. "I should get going. I need to put some ice on my knee. Thank you for supper."

"Thank you for the ice cream."

He wasn't going to act now, not with Rochelle's family all around her. Better he leave and deal with Thaddeus in due time. Not too much time, though. He stood in the doorway, squinting toward the kitchen island where Thaddeus sat with his back to them, Betsy beside his elbow.

"See? This is my former boss, and his business partner. That other guy is now a senator in Ohio. And the fourth guy, I'm not sure who he is."

Thad fell silent. He pushed a button. "Betsy, you probably shouldn't watch anymore. I'm sorry."

There was no way Pete could leave now. He reached for his sore knee. "Aw, Rochelle, do you mind if I sit a moment? It's my knee."

"Of course. Would you like another cup of coffee?"

"Please." Pete limped back to the patio chair he'd occupied moments before. His phone buzzed in his pocket. Bright, probably. He let the call go to voice mail. He'd pay for it later, but for now he was handling things the way he wanted to.

Betsy tried to blot out the images, the angry words on the video as she washed the supper dishes. *Aenti* Chelle had wanted her to load the dishwasher instead, but tonight Betsy had energy to burn off before she could sleep.

Thad told her he used to work at that restaurant, and the owner had been murdered. Also, someone had tucked the keychain with the video files into his culinary gear. He had paused the video because one of the men—not his boss, but another man he didn't recognize—made threats against his bosses, striking one of them in the face.

Yes, *Aenti* Chelle didn't have a television in her home with good reason. Once you'd seen something, it was nearly impossible to forget what you'd seen. Those were some evil men around the table in the video, men who tried to buy an election unfairly. Trying to use violence and threats to get what they wanted.

Thad left not long ago, his brow furrowed. She didn't blame him. He said something about calling the authorities in Ohio first thing, which probably meant he'd end up going back to Ohio to give witness about the files and discovering them.

She turned the hot water on and filled up the pot, sticky with residue from cooking rice.

If Thad left for Ohio, all the better. He'd been right, tonight, when he said, *"Betsy, if things were different . . ."*

Things would have to be a *lot* different. Thad seemed to be softening some. He'd also mentioned something tonight about spending time with an old friend he knew before they both left the Order.

Lots of the time, people who'd been gone as long as he had didn't fare well after returning to their Orders. Quite a few left again.

She didn't like how she felt now, not seeing how they could be together, or even seriously consider being together, unless he made some changes.

"*Gotte*, please help Thaddeus. He came here to Pinecraft for a reason. Help him for his sake, not mine. I would rather he be somewhere else and be who You intended him to be, than be here near me for the wrong reasons." She'd whispered the words aloud, but glanced to the lanai where *Aenti* Chelle sat, alone.

Truly, she had enough to fret over with the bakery without adding whatever feelings she had about Thaddeus to that stack of worries. *Aenti* Chelle had always been good to offer wisdom. Tonight, though, Betsy thought her *aenti* had her own battle to fight.

Also, her *aenti* probably welcomed the quiet time, and when Daniel departed not long after Thaddeus had roared away on his motorcycle, *Aenti* Chelle had headed to the lanai, her eyes rimmed in red.

Betsy, too, welcomed the quiet business of doing dishes and didn't mind Emma leaving after supper, saying she was meeting up with some of the others at Big Olaf's. This in spite of the fact Daniel had brought plenty of ice cream for all of them.

Another worry niggled her brain. Emma certainly didn't act as if she'd just called off a wedding. The uproar hadn't rippled through the family yet, giving Betsy the idea Emma hadn't told their parents. She shook her head as she rinsed the silverware. But then, it was better to not marry than to marry with doubts.

So much swirling through her mind, much like the dishwater curling into a tiny circular current as it disappeared down the drain.

She did her best to leave all her burdens at God's feet in prayer. Many of them she could do nothing about.

Please, Gotte, sort it all out.

25

*T*haddeus jabbed the button on his phone to end the call.

"Stupid officer."

First thing Thursday morning he'd called the Columbus Police Department and asked for the criminal investigation department and Detective Kincaid, the officer handling the Mitchell Gabryszeski homicide. The officer was out sick, so Thad's call was shuffled to another officer helping with the caseload today.

The man's tone made Thad feel like he was a bother, an armchair detective who did nothing except watch CSI reruns. Yes, he'd listened to Thad's story. Thad tried to explain he had recordings of video files to possibly tie the new Senator Bright to Mitch's murder, but the officer sounded bored.

"I get several calls like this a day on every case I work," the man had said. "Look, I'll take a message for Detective Kincaid. He's going to be back tomorrow morning well. I'll have him get back with you then. If it's something notable, I'm sure he'll follow up."

Thad left his number and forced his irritation away. Of course, Mitch's murder wasn't the only case on the officer's desk. With every day that passed since Mitch's death, his case slipped lower and lower on the priority list. With no new leads and fresh cases, it was understandable.

Well, he'd done what he needed to do. But just in case, Thad added the keychain to his own plain keying.

He yawned. He'd seen Betsy in the morning before he left the bakery, and she looked as though she hadn't rested well. She basically told him someone had called the news station and badmouthed the bakery, telling them someone who wasn't Amish did the baking.

"I'm sorry," he'd said. It was the truth. He wasn't Amish. "If it's going to cause problems for you, I'll stop working for you. I'd hate to have to do it, but I might have to give notice anyway if I get the job I interviewed for."

She'd looked conflicted when he told her about the positive interview he'd had at Palm Trees.

"I understand if you have to work somewhere else. You're talented, Thaddeus." She'd given him a tired smile.

"Here, this is for you." He handed her a folded piece of paper.

"What is it?"

"My recipe for tiramisu pie."

"Thank you." She gave him a hint of smile in return. "The customers enjoyed it, so I'm definitely going to add it to the menu."

"Great." He'd left before the conversation continued, and after sneaking a dog treat to Winston.

Thad's phone bleeped, and he jumped.

"Thaddeus Zook."

"Thad, it's Pete Stucenski."

"Hey, Pete. How are you?" *Stucenski.* He needed to write that down.

"Good, good. Listen, I'm calling because I'm hoping you've taken some time to decide if you're coming back to Dish and Spoon."

"Uh, I don't believe I am. I've actually moved."

"Ah. You don't say. Where to?"

"Florida."

"Nice, nice. Especially this time of year."

"It's been definitely different than Ohio."

Silence hung on the line.

Thad broke it first. "I may have another job here, I think."

"Oh. Where at?"

He paused. "I, uh, rather wouldn't say just yet."

"I see." The two syllables sounded crisp. "Well, if you need a reference, feel free to put me down and I'll give a good word for you."

"Thanks, Pete. I appreciate that."

"You're welcome." The call went dead.

His gut tightened. Strange, or coincidence, Pete would call right after Thad found the video files?

Time would drag until Detective Kincaid returned his call tomorrow. If he didn't hear anything in the morning, he'd show the Columbus PD his persistence.

✦

Aenti Chelle burst into the bakery on Friday, not long before one in the afternoon. She carried her laptop computer case.

"It aired, it aired!" *Aenti* Chelle's smile made her appear younger than her years. She marched up to the counter triumphantly.

"What?" Betsy looked up from the case. She'd been counting the fried pies and was preparing to let Mrs. Byler know how many fresh pies to fry.

"The bakery. On television."

"Oh. Susan said she'd let me know if they were going to air it or not."

"Well, whatever the issue was, I guess the powers at the station didn't think it was big enough to prevent the segment from broadcasting." *Aenti* Chelle moved to the nearest table and set her case on top. "Here. I downloaded it from the web site so you can see it. I'm sorry. I couldn't wait, so I came right over after I finished lunch."

Betsy's vision swam for a moment. Television. Her bakery was on television. She grabbed the edge of the counter to steady herself. Thousands of people probably saw the show. She had no idea how many. The thought of the number of viewers made her stomach churn.

"Here. Just a moment and I'll get it to play." *Aenti* Chelle beamed.

Betsy joined her at the table and watched as her *aenti* clicked on a file. It opened and the image filled the screen. The words "Around Town" drifted into view along with some happy-sounding music.

"What's this? What's going on?" Vera Byler said as she emerged from the kitchen. "I didn't know you were going to start playing the television in the bakery."

Betsy turned to face Mrs. Byler. "No one has said anything about television in the bakery. This morning, the television station showed the video story they made about the bakery. *Aenti* Chelle is here so I can see it. We all can."

Mrs. Byler was probably the one who told the television people about Thaddeus doing prep work in the bakery. Betsy immediately regretted her suspicion, but then it made sense, as much as Mrs. Byler had made some hurtful comments about the bakery, even after beginning to work at the shop.

"Ready? Here goes." *Aenti* Chelle reached down and clicked a key on the laptop.

"A new bakery opens in Sarasota's Amish village of Pinecraft, and its young owner serves up a variety of tasty treats for every palate," came the broadcaster's voice.

"I've always loved to bake. Some women are better at quilting and such. I leave it to them, but I'd much rather find myself making pies, doughnuts, or fried pies." There she was, with her back turned slightly to the camera. She could see her jaw line, but not quite her face.

The narrator did a good job at explaining how the Amish didn't like to be recorded or photographed.

Betsy had never imagined herself on television. Her stomach quit churning and instead wound itself into a knot. What if some of the others didn't like even seeing this much of her on television? She listened to the conversation, mingled with commentary from the newswoman.

Now a shot of her hands and forearms as she rolled out a fresh pie crust, then carefully folding the crust in half and sliding it onto a clean pan. Fingers, fluting the edges of the crust.

" . . . I am thankful to my family for helping me, as well as local friends who help me with making pie filling, working the cash register."

A shot of pies in the display case.

Henry Hostetler on camera. "I've known the family for years and I've had Betsy's pie before at local haystack suppers. Nothing better than a slice of cherry pie and a good cup of coffee."

A shot of the coffee display, with a customer, face blurred, pouring themselves a cup of the fresh brew.

"Here at Pinecraft Pies and Pastry, the coffee is always free, but a donation jar is always nearby, and Betsy says all donations go to the local Haiti mission fund."

"We're open every day except Sunday," came Betsy's voice, with a shot of an Amish couple, their backs to the camera, walking up to the bakery.

"*And when you stop by Pinecraft Pies and Pastry, make sure you say hello to Winston, Betsy's charming dachshund.*" A shot of Betsy, back to camera, talking to the announcer as Winston sits up on his hind legs.

A flashback to the studios, to the morning show announcers. "Now, that just made my mouth water and gave me a sudden craving for pie," said the male announcer. "I've never been over to Pinecraft before, either, although I've heard of it."

"The village is primarily a winter vacation destination for the Amish and Mennonites from all over the country, especially Ohio, Indiana, and Pennsylvania," said the newswoman, now in the studio. "Betsy and a few other residents live there year-round, but the population can grow to as high as seven thousand in the winter."

"I hear there's a pie contest this weekend—"

The video ended.

"Oh, my." Betsy's hands trembled. "I don't know how they managed to put it all in order. And they mentioned Winston, too."

"You did well." *Aenti* Chelle patted her arm. "There. Relax. The best thing now is to just keep doing what you're doing. Making good pie and caring for people."

"They talked about the pie contest, too." Vera Byler, hands on hips, stood beside Betsy. "Time for me to make sure my recipe is in order."

"I finally figured out what I'm making." Thaddeus had given Betsy his tiramisu pie recipe this morning. Until then, she wasn't sure what she'd make for the contest.

"Betsy, I have to leave." Vera rubbed her forehead. "I have a headache and I don't think my breakfast sat well with me. I'm sorry."

"All—all right. Of course. Just sign out, and I'll take it all from here."

"Thank you." Vera untied her apron and headed for the kitchen.

Aenti Chelle's expression narrowed as she watched the kitchen door swing shut behind Mrs. Byler. "I think she's jealous."

"Jealous?" Betsy nearly voiced her suspicion minutes ago, but thought better of it.

"Yes. It's obvious to me." *Aenti* Chelle's eyes softened. "I feel sorry for her. I know how it feels, to see someone else getting the dream she had. Or, maybe I'm wrong. Maybe the attention bothers her."

Betsy opened her mouth to ask what *Aenti* Chelle meant, then closed it. She could never imagine her *Aenti* Chelle jealous or saying harsh things.

"Maybe. I hope she feels better soon. But right now, I have pies to fry, and they're not going to take care of themselves." If only Emma would stop vacationing long enough to help her.

"Your sister should be here, helping you." *Aenti* Chelle shook her head. "Your parents are coming for supper tonight, by the way. Emma's going to make her big announcement to them."

"You know about her breaking her engagement?"

"Yes. And, she's asked if she can stay here, like you did."

"Why . . ."

"I have the room, or will, after *Aenti* Sarah moves back into her home, which I know she wants to do. She's getting tired of my *Englisch* food." Her aunt closed the laptop. "Ah, don't look now, but here's some customers. I wonder if they saw the program? I don't recognize them."

An *Englisch* couple was walking up to the front door, talking to each other and glancing up at the sign.

Betsy nodded and moved over to the counter and display case. She had much to do today, instead of thinking about Vera Byler's jealousy, her sister's decisions, and the pie contest in the morning.

⤳ℚ⤲

Pete Stucenski trailed Thad Zook from Wednesday night on. If he could only get the guy alone, out of public places, or areas not chock-full of people in hats and suspenders. Then, Zook hopped his motorcycle and headed for Siesta Key Village.

All he had to do was get Thad to hand over the USB drive, and all would be well. The others, like the Amish girl Thad had the hots for, wouldn't say anything. She probably had no clue what was on the drive, or what a USB drive was.

If only he'd gotten to Thad before the guy left Ohio and disappeared.

Bright had given him a deadline. This weekend had to be it, or he'd send people to handle it himself. They wouldn't be as kind or gentle as Pete.

Pete almost regretted the whole thing would be over, one way or the other. He liked Florida. He considered cashing in all of his investments and uprooting himself to the Sunshine State. This time of year, hearing about four inches of snow on the ground in Ohio, the idea sounded brilliant.

Those Amish were pretty smart, keeping this vacation spot a secret.

He watched Thad pull into the parking lot of a snazzy-looking restaurant with an unoriginal name: Palm Trees. Now how hokey was that? Not much better than Dish and Spoon, a name Pete had gone around and around with Mitch about.

Thad headed into the restaurant.

Pete swung into action. Time to force his hand, a bit. Wearing gloves, he took the note he'd composed and printed at a copying store and securely tucked it to an obvious spot on the motorcycle.

If Thad wondered about anyone following him, he wouldn't wonder anymore.

Pete hopped back into his car and headed for Pinecraft.

26

*T*had checked his phone after leaving Palm Trees. Nobody had called. He was glad he went with his gut and sent a copy of the video file to the detective in Columbus via overnight mail. Detective Kincaid should receive it by tomorrow afternoon, at the latest. E-mail would have been better, but his attempt to send the file via e-mail was rejected, saying the file was too large to transmit.

The joy over having a new job—without Pete Stucenski's recommendation, thanks much—was dampened not a little by the knowledge Thad had.

He could call the papers or talk to the news in Columbus, but what would they do? Would anyone take him seriously? Nut jobs called the news all the time, he was sure.

Now that Senator Bright had secured his spot in Congress, he became a bigger target for critics of all kinds. Nothing new, trying to run a guy's name through the mud. His charming personality had the media shaming any critics.

Thad's best bet was getting the detective to listen. The police couldn't possibly have closed Mitch's case, not by a long shot, although by this time it had low priority. Maybe receiving a copy of the video files would put it to the top of the detective's to-do list.

He squinted out across the parking lot as he put his helmet on. A nice place to work, and you couldn't beat the view. Looking down, he saw a white paper tucked into the edge of the seat. Probably an ad, but then didn't they have laws against people sticking flyers on vehicles?

He opened it.

Give me what you have and you won't get hurt.

Someone knew. They'd followed him.

If they followed him here, they knew where he lived. They knew about Pinecraft.

He could run, again, this time knowing for sure he'd been followed.

He would never want to bring harm to anyone, his *mammi* or Betsy or any of them.

Gotte, what have I done? He couldn't go back, not right now.

Thad tried to think of who he could call, someone who could help without him dragging them into this.

He paced the parking lot. He was due to start work Monday. He wouldn't give it up. And it wasn't like whoever had been following him didn't know about this location.

Time to find a place to hole up until he figured out what to do.

Maybe Beth might know somewhere around here.

He went back inside the restaurant and found Beth, ordering supplies at her desk.

"Thad, hey, did you forget something?"

"No, I'm curious. I need a place to stay this weekend, close to here if possible. Know anywhere cheap?"

"My aunt. She's near Turtle Beach. Has a shop with a room upstairs. You might ask her. I'll give you her number." She scanned his face. "You okay?"

"Yup. I just need a room for a couple of days. Like tonight and tomorrow."

"Ah, okay. Well, she might have a vacancy. If you can stand her religious and outdated stuff everywhere, it's pretty nice." Beth grabbed a scrap of paper and scribbled a number.

"Huh." He reached out to take the paper from her. "Thanks. See you Monday."

తోపా

The family lined up around *Aenti* Chelle's table, with the extra leaf included. Supper had been cleared away and someone had the dominoes handy. Betsy nudged Winston with her toes. The dog had been busy cleaning up the crumbs from the floor and had settled onto her feet.

Aenti Chelle glanced at Emma. "Well, Emma, I know you've been bursting to speak to your parents."

"Yes, I have."

"What's this all about?" *Daed* frowned. "You're staying until New Year's and taking the bus home, aren't you?"

"I've, ah, I've decided to stay in Pinecraft." Emma blurted out the words.

"But your engagement. And the wedding. What?" *Mamm* shook her head. "There will be much to do, getting your house set up."

"Eli and I aren't getting married."

Betsy almost had to lean forward to catch her sister's words. She braced herself.

"Not getting married?" *Mamm's* voice squeaked. "But why, why not?"

"I—he—I—We're just not. I'm not . . . not sure."

"Better to let the dog go now, before it runs away on its own." *Daed's* expression remained flat. "What do you plan to do while you're here? Pinecraft is vacation for some of us, but for others who live here, it's work year-round. Your sister knows that."

Did they blame her for Emma's decision? Betsy didn't know if she ought to contribute anything to the conversation or not.

"I've decided to clean houses, like Betsy did. *Aenti* Chelle needs someone, especially with Betsy opening the bakery." Emma sounded matter-of-fact and resolute. "Once I can start taking in sewing work, I'll do that, too."

Something had changed, though, for Emma to make such a drastic decision. Emma despised cleaning, if her demeanor about housework were any clue. Emma was a good seamstress, so the idea of taking in sewing wasn't such a bad one.

However, Betsy was relieved she hadn't left *Aenti* Chelle in a tight spot with extra work. She'd managed to take on one account from Betsy, but still needed help with two others.

More discussion followed, but Betsy waited for them to bring up the subject of the bakery on television. At last, with Emma's jaw set, she fell silent. *Mamm* still appeared ready to cry and *Daed* looked ready to walk over to Pinecraft Park and play some bocce.

"So," *Daed* said, turning his gaze on Betsy, "I understand the television station did put on the show about the bakery."

"Yes, they did. *Aenti* Chelle has the recording for you to see."

"I do want to see it." Betsy couldn't gauge her father's expression.

"If you'd like, before we start the dominoes game, I can show it to you." *Aenti* Chelle glanced at Betsy before continuing. "I believe they did a good job, everything considered."

"Everything considered?" *Daed* asked.

"Um, well . . . someone called the television station on Wednesday and told them I have help baking the pies from someone who's not Amish." Betsy hadn't wanted to tell them that.

"See, I told you nothing good would come of allowing . . . that man to help in the bakery." *Mamm* shook her head.

"I think it's someone who's jealous and just wants to make trouble," said *Aenti* Chelle. "I also have a good idea of who might have made that call." Better her aunt say the words than Betsy, although they were true enough.

"Well, what's done is done." *Daed* shook his head. "As far as the young Zook man is concerned, if he has skills and stays out of trouble, I say we have his help. Better his help than from someone who'd sooner put salt in your sugar bowl."

"Do you mean, ah, Mrs. Byler?"

"Ya. Her husband came and told me she'd called the television station. He apologized. He knows how hard you have worked on the bakery, and how we've helped you."

Betsy nodded slowly. *Daed* was okay with Thaddeus helping her. The thought cheered her, but the idea that he'd likely get another job didn't make her smile.

"Another thing," *Daed* added. "Henry Hostetler came to me with a warning. He said there's an imposter among us, he has confirmation of the fact, and he's going to bring the person to Bishop Smucker straightaway."

⋞✦⋟

"I'm so glad you find the room suitable. It's not fancy, but then I'm used to taking in people who aren't used to fancy," Beth's aunt told Thad as they stood on the balcony and surveyed the inside of the one-room studio, complete with kitchenette. "I usually put missionaries up who are visiting my church, or the occasional wanderer in need of a place to lay their head."

The sun was headed down in the western sky, lighting the room above Gulfside Treasures Gift Shoppe at Turtle Beach.

"Ah, it's nice of you." Thad wanted some peace and quiet. If he was being followed, they'd have a good view of the ocean tonight instead of the snug streets of Pinecraft.

"Well, if you need anything, here's my cell phone number. I'm sorry I didn't have time to pick up anything for a snacks basket, so here." She handed him a folded-up bill. "There's a corner store a few blocks down where you can get a few munchies."

"Thanks, but you didn't have to."

"No, but I want to." She looked at him intently, reminding him a little of Betsy's *Aenti* Rochelle, so adept at taking care of people. "I pray you find what you're looking for, and what you need most."

"Um, thanks." He watched her head down the stairway attached to the side of the building. A unique lady, to put it mildly.

Thad scanned the street paralleling the Gulf. Its crisscrossing traffic didn't have room for anyone to park. He studied the gift shop parking lot below. No cars, save for Beth's aunt backing out slowly into traffic, making the approaching vehicles all slow down to a crawl.

Nobody had followed him here, at least that he knew of. Good. If they returned to Pinecraft, they wouldn't find him there either.

What to do, what to do? Once inside the studio apartment, Thad resumed the pacing he'd commenced in the restaurant parking lot earlier. Beth's aunt had a television set, but no cable. A DVD player, but the collection was all movies like *The Three Stooges* and somebody called Shirley Temple. A few kids' cartoons.

The only book, a Bible.

Thad wanted to laugh. During his visit with Ben Esh, his friend had talked about reading the Bible, how over the years it had "come alive" for him.

"I never knew, Thaddeus, the Bible could sound as if it were a message for me. Not just for everyone else, but it was for me. God tells me what I need to hear, to know, partly through my studies."

Wouldn't it be nice? Thad still couldn't grasp the idea that it was okay to study the Bible. In his home, *Daed* would talk about it a lot, but for the most part, the bishops and other elders did the teaching. He wasn't sure if his parents even had a Bible, although he'd heard some families did. But with some, a Bible was used more for recording family events, births, deaths than actual study. Too much studying could make one proud, he'd been told.

He decided to burn off his fidgets and hopefully fight away the willies with a trip to the corner store Beth's aunt had mentioned. Within thirty minutes, he'd made the walk, bought an armful of junk food, large bottle of pop, and a hot mini-pizza, and returned to the apartment. No vehicles.

Thad climbed the stairs, then locked the door and used the deadbolt once he was inside. He then set up the food and snacks on the little kitchen counter but brought the pizza and pop to the table.

Now, to cure his grumbling stomach.

Thad thumbed through the Bible while he ate, careful not to get any grease on the pages. Ben said something about the Psalms being good reading, an example of pouring out your heart to God. Thad never imagined anyone could do so, or if God would be interested.

He skimmed one of the chapters, ninety-one.

Living in the Most High's shelter,
    camping in the Almighty's shade,
I say to the LORD, "You are my refuge,
    my stronghold!

You are my God—the one I trust!"
God will save you from the hunter's trap
  and from deadly sickness.
God will protect you with his pinions;
  you'll find refuge under his wings.
  His faithfulness is a protective shield.
Don't be afraid of terrors at night,
  arrows that fly in daylight,
or sickness that prowls in the dark,
  destruction that ravages at noontime.

Good words. He needed some safety and assurance right now, a stronghold, a refuge, protection.

"*Gotte*, can I trust You? I know I haven't followed the ways of the *Ordnung*, but to follow You? Show me the way, the path I need to follow. Please." The words bounced off the walls and he felt a little foolish. He didn't deserve *Gotte's* help. He wasn't bad, but in the eyes of many, he wasn't good, either.

He kept reading as he ate his pizza. Not as good as Village Pizza by Emma, but it would do for tonight.

The night fell, and Thad turned on a lamp and kept reading. Then he arrived at a long chapter, one-hundred-nineteen, but it was broken up in to easy bits to read.

Your word is a lamp before my feet
  and a light for my journey.
I have sworn, and I fully mean it:
  I will keep your righteous rules.
I have been suffering so much—
  LORD, make me live again
    according to your promise.
Please, LORD, accept my
  spontaneous gifts of praise.
  Teach me your rules!

Though my life is constantly in danger,
  I won't forget your instruction.
Though the wicked have set a trap for me,
  I won't stray from your precepts.
Your laws are my possession forever
  because they are my heart's joy.
I have decided to keep your statutes
  forever, every last one.

It read like someone's private journal of thoughts. Thad tried to understand the concept of comfort in protection and rules. But then, who got to set those rules? Betsy bowed to the will of her elders, even if they didn't agree with her. She found it "comforting," she'd once said her family was on her side, so to speak.

Thad wiped his fingers on a napkin after he ate the last bite of pizza. He had the feeling, somehow, *Gotte* didn't mind so much if he were a pastry chef. He'd had the basic "rules" drilled into him his entire life, except for the last almost ten years. The rules still prodded him at odd moments.

If he were to go back to the Amish, he wouldn't in Ohio. Everyone would expect him to be the Thaddeus they knew. But that wasn't him anymore. Florida, though, had opened up possibilities and even freedom.

He thought of people like Henry Hostetler, Ben Esh, even Imogene with her semi-Plain clothing and the digital camera. They'd all "found God," or "came to their faith," whatever language people used for it.

He didn't have much to leave if he forsook the *Englisch* world. Somehow, being in Sarasota he could be in the *Englisch* world, but not of it.

The idea followed him to a restless night of sleep, even as he dreamed of being back in Dish and Spoon, with the senator, Mitch, and Pete all chasing him with carving knives.

27

$\mathscr{P}$ete Stucenski had driven all over the place last night, trying to see where Thad had gone off on his Harley. The guy had never returned to his grandma's house; his parking spot remaining empty. Saturday morning right at dawn, before anyone rolled out the streets of the sleepy neighborhood, Pete drove by at a crawl. No red motorcycle.

Had he left town? Or moved?

Pete should have asked a few more questions the other night at Rochelle's, but he didn't want to arouse anyone's suspicions about why he was so interested in what Thaddeus Zook was up to. He paused the car for a moment, the sound of the engine masking the soft whoosh of the breeze through the palm trees.

An early morning thunderstorm left the streets damp, but it would soon burn off once the sun rose.

Pete figured Thad would show up at the pie contest this morning to cheer on his girlfriend. Pete might as well grab breakfast, then resume his search for Thad.

Wearing his Plain garb, he headed for Yoder's restaurant, where the first few customers lined up for a hearty meal. His chin itched and he tried not to rub it and remove the beard.

This was the last time he'd do anything like this. Mitch's fault, all of it.

Within a few blinks, he'd gotten his breakfast of eggs, toast, and hash. A familiar-looking figure stopped at his table. The Mennonite handyman, Henry Hostetler.

"Good morning. Daniel, isn't it?"

"Right."

"Mind if I sit for a moment?"

Yes, he did mind.

"No, go right ahead. I'm kind of in a hurry to get this eaten, so I can get over to the pie contest."

"Yes, big news today. Are you entering anything?" Henry's eyes twinkled, but something in their depths made Pete pause.

"Nah, I'm better at eating pie than making it."

"I know what you mean."

A waitress stopped at the table. "Coffee, Henry?"

"No, thanks, Mary. I'm on my way out."

Pete kept eating, feeling as though he were on display. Thankfully, he'd ditched the watch a while back. The nosey Amish girl had made him aware of how out of place *that* accessory was. He ought to be grateful to her. If Thad and she ended up together, she'd definitely keep the guy on his toes.

"So, do you have any family coming to visit this winter?" Mr. Hostetler asked.

"No. They, ah, don't like to travel in winter. My trip has been cut short. There's been a problem at home, so I'm needed to go help them."

"You're from Ohio, right?"

What was with all the questions?

"No. Indiana."

"Okay. My mistake. I thought Rochelle had said Ohio." Henry studied him with an even expression. "Rochelle is like a daughter to me. We're only related by marriage, through my late wife's family, but I stay close to them. It's good to have people watching out for you, you know?"

Pete didn't know. The question made a sensation of longing echo somewhere deep inside him. "Yes, there's nothing like it. As far as Rochelle goes, I don't want to hurt her."

"I certainly hope not."

Pete polished off the last of his biscuits. "Truthfully, I wasn't looking to meet someone like her."

"She's special." Henry paused. "Mr. Troyer, if you don't mind, would you mind joining me somewhere where we can talk? It's important. But not here."

"Sounds serious." Pete picked up the check, and his hat. "Sure, where at?"

"How about the park? It'll be fairly empty, with the rain earlier."

"Certainly."

After Pete paid his check, he followed Henry in his vehicle to the park. The man was right. A lone fisherman sat on the banks of Phillippi Creek, oblivious to the rest of the world.

They began to walk. "This park brings people together, all kinds," Henry said as they approached the shuffleboard court. "It's unique, Pinecraft is."

"It's true."

Henry stopped and faced him. "Daniel, I wanted to tell you before I went to Bishop Smucker, but I'm concerned."

"Concerned, how?"

"Some people think it would be easy enough to come into our community with, shall we say, ulterior motives?"

"As in, how?" Pete wasn't sure he liked the direction this conversation was headed. He glanced around the neighborhood. The street beside the shuffleboard courts was empty, but wouldn't be for long.

"People think they can hide out from the law, or try to fool people into thinking they're someone they're not."

"Huh." Pete glanced into the opening to the shuffleboard court, where the wooden long-handled paddles hung, waiting for players to come.

"So, what I'm trying to say is, Mr. Troyer, if that is your real name, I've done some checking on you. And I know you're not who you claim to be. I'm not the only one who thinks so. Who in the world are you, and why are you here?"

"Hang on, I'll show you why." Pete gritted his teeth. What came next would be this nosy man's fault. Pete stepped over to the shuffleboard paddles and yanked one down.

❦

Betsy's palms were sweating a river, and so slick she was afraid the tiramisu pie would slip from her hands. The Pinecraft Bank parking lot was lined with a set of tables covered in white cloths.

"Where do I put the pie?" she asked the lady at the registration desk.

"Over on the end, with the single crust pies." The woman gave her two stickers covered with the number twenty-nine. "Put one sticker on the pie plate, the other you keep."

"Okay." Now her hands shook.

A few people stopped her, saying they'd seen her on television. She nodded and gave her thanks, but hurried to the table.

The crowd swelled to at least one hundred people. Everybody seemed to like pie, from the news reporters to the photographers who paused at the tables, photographing the entries.

Betsy scanned the faces. No Thaddeus. Surely he hadn't for-gotten? She wanted to surprise him, and if the pie won any kind of ribbon, she'd give him the credit for the recipe. Her heart sagged a little when she didn't see his face. But then, he hadn't shown up at the bakery this morning either. Unless he'd left before she arrived.

She'd already begged Emma to mind the bakery for her, just in case someone stopped by for a doughnut. Maybe it was silly to stay open, with a lot of the village coming to the contest.

Betsy set her pie on the table, and gave it a backward glance. There was her heart, her love for what she did, sitting on a plate.

Oh, she so wanted to win. Something, at least.

Vera Byler didn't acknowledge her as she passed, carrying her own pie covered with a topping of intricate latticework.

"Mrs. Byler, what kind of pie did you bake?"

The woman skidded to a stop in her sensible sturdy black shoes. "Strawberry-rhubarb." Then she kept on her journey to the pie table.

Evidently word had gotten around that Betsy and her fam-ily knew about Vera's phone call. After the flash of anger, Betsy felt pity. Sorry the woman felt so threatened and jealous of Betsy's situation. *Gotte, I'm so thankful. For my family. For Aenti Sarah's help. For Thaddeus.*

She reminded herself of the prayer she prayed for Thad each night, that he'd find the way *Gotte* had for him, a way of peace, comfort, safety. A way of assurance. Even with her roundabout journey here because of Jacob Miller—whom she'd see in passing and it no longer stung—*Gotte* had shown her the path to walk.

Here came the welcome, the judging, and tasting. The for-midable judges—someone from Yoder's restaurant, a local food writer from the newspaper, a Beachy Amish Mennonite woman from the village who authored cookbooks, and the Pinecraft Bank president—all had a chance to nibble a sample from each of the pies.

The judges laughed and joked as the cameras did their job of documenting the event. The pie contest was only a few years old, but its popularity seemed a fun way to celebrate during December.

An ambulance screeched by on Bahia Vista, its siren blaring. Betsy glanced up—the vehicle was headed down Kaufman.

∽✑

Thaddeus woke to his phone alarm shrieking at him.

"Ow." He rolled over and reached for the phone. His head ached, and he might as well be having a hangover from the old days. "Stop." He punched the button.

He took in his surroundings. The little apartment on Turtle Beach. The night alone and fitful sleep.

He swung his legs over the side of the bed and headed for the coffeepot. How in the world would he fill his day? *Mammi* was probably plenty worried he hadn't come home. And Betsy; he'd let her down by not going to the bakery.

But this morning was the Pinecraft Pie Contest, and he was missing it. He'd told Betsy he'd do his best to be there, and he had a hunch she was entering the tiramisu pie.

His phone rang out again. He picked up the phone. Henry Hostetler? It also showed Henry had called early this morning, and left a message.

"Hello, Henry—"

"Thaddeus, it's Rochelle Keim. Henry's just been admitted to Sarasota General. He was found in Pinecraft Park, inside the shuffleboard court. Someone attacked him, hit him on the head."

"Oh no. I'll—I'll be right there. Is he awake?"

"No." Rochelle's voice shook. "He's lost a lot of blood. They have him sedated because his brain is swelling. It doesn't look good."

"I'll be right there."

"He called you this morning, right before he was attacked."

"I'm going to check my voice mail now, then head your way. Thanks for letting me know."

"Let me know what you find out."

"I will." He jabbed the phone button and checked his voice mail.

Call at six-forty-five a.m.

"Thaddeus, it's Henry. You were right. Daniel Troyer is a fraud. I'm going to find him and talk to him now. He's here at Yoder's. And then, we're going to the bishop. I was going to ask if you'd come with me, but you're probably asleep." The message ended.

Thad couldn't get to the hospital soon enough.

28

Second place overall, first in single crust pies.

Betsy clutched her red ribbon. She'd always liked red better than blue, anyway. The man with the microphone even told the crowd about her bakery, and how it had been on the "Around Town" show the day before yesterday.

Ida Mae Graber, the first-place winner from Shipshewana, Indiana, beamed as she accepted her blue ribbon and certificate. Vera Byler stood nearby with her third-place ribbon. According to the judges, it had been a "tight" contest for overall winner.

The crowd lined up to congratulate the winners and to taste samples of all the pies. One woman at the edge of the crowd stood frowning. She'd been disqualified for bringing a pie baked from a box mix. The idea of bringing a commercial pie to a homemade contest made Betsy shake her head.

Aenti Chelle hadn't arrived yet. She'd said she would after running a quick errand, but she too was absent. All the same, Betsy smiled and accepted the congratulations from those who came down the line.

At last, the pie samplers drifted off to eat. One more stepped up to Betsy. Daniel Troyer. His hat was askew, his hair sticking out wildly from under the brim of his hat.

"Betsy, you need to come with me. Quickly. It's your aunt. She said something's happened to Henry."

"Henry?"

"Just come, quickly. He's been hurt."

Should she go with him, alone? Well, Daniel was old enough to be her father, and she could always explain later.

Betsy saw Vera Byler standing a few steps away and called out to the older woman. "Vera, I'm off to meet *Aenti* Chelle. Something's happened to Henry Hostetler. Could you please call the bishop?"

Shock registered on Vera's face. "Oh, goodness. Of course I will." The woman might be jealous, but she was efficient.

"Come. Now. It doesn't look good." Daniel grasped her elbow and led her off to a vehicle parked under a spot of shade in the far corner of the bank lot. With a flick of the button, the door locks clicked up.

"What happened?"

"I'm not sure, exactly."

She hesitated a moment. Something didn't feel right. And, why hadn't *Aenti* Chelle simply phoned her? Betsy opened the door. "If you don't mind, I'll sit in the back."

"Suit yourself." His words sounded clipped.

They shot out of the parking lot and zoomed off along Bahia Vista.

"So what happened? You said you weren't exactly sure?"

"I don't know if he fell, or what. But it's some kind of head injury. He's lost a lot of blood."

"I should call *Aenti* Chelle."

"*Don't.* I mean, she told me she was turning her phone off. To save the battery."

Betsy nodded, then glanced at the street sign as they went through an intersection. "Daniel, Sarasota General is in the other direction."

He remained silent.

They passed through the world outside, filled with sunny and happy people. What was wrong with this man?

"You're not Daniel Troyer, are you?"

"Aren't you the smart little—" Then he used a word that made Betsy's eyes widen, the kind of word she heard when some of the rougher kids from the city would play basketball in the park.

"I—I don't have money to give you." But her family had some money.

"Just be quiet. It's not about money. Not yours, anyway."

They came up to a red light and the stop-and-go traffic. Betsy reached for the handle. She could run if she made it out while they were stopped, or leap out of the car as it started to move.

Daniel glanced into the rearview mirror. "Don't bother trying the handles. Those are child safety locks. They only unlock when *I* want them to."

The light turned green and Daniel, or whoever he was, turned the corner and headed south. The beach. They were heading for the beach. But which one?

"Oh, right. I almost forgot. Take your cell phone out of your bag and throw it in the front seat."

Eyes stinging, Betsy complied. *Oh, Gotte, please. Protect me. Help me find my way home.* She wiped away a tear. No, she wouldn't let him see her cry.

"Good. I thought you'd melt into a puddle of saltwater. Don't bother crying. This has nothing to do with you."

She fought to find her voice around the lump in her throat. "Then, who?"

"Thaddeus Zook. He has something of mine, and I want it back." He pulled something out of the console between the front seats. A gun. "Now, be quiet for a while."

⤫

Rochelle sat in the waiting room of Sarasota General's ER, ignoring the stares at her cape dress and *kapp*. When she'd passed the park and saw the ambulance, she'd stopped to see if she could help. They were wheeling an unconscious Henry, his face ashen, from the shuffleboard court area.

She'd never seen so much blood since her *daed* was injured in a farming accident when she was nine. *Daed* . . . He'd recovered, but slowly, and her parents had paid a hard price for leaving their *Ordnung*, being shunned, yet living so close to family.

Gotte, not Henry. Please. He's been like a second father to me.

Thaddeus burst into the ER. She waved at him and he shot over to where she sat.

"I know who did this," he said as he took the seat beside her. "Daniel Troyer."

"No. No. It couldn't be." She shook her head, trying to wave away his words. Not Daniel.

"Miss Keim, please, listen to me. Henry called me early this morning. He's been helping me do some checking around on Daniel, thanks to Betsy. She was worried about you, and she didn't trust he was who he said he was. Turns out, she was right."

Daniel. No, not Daniel.

And the other night, she'd been changing her mind about her resolve not to see him anymore. To let him go back to Indiana, and not expect to hear from him again. And Betsy?

"Why didn't she tell me?"

"Because she loves you and she didn't want to hurt you. She wanted to be wrong, so she came to me. She had me do some calling around. But then I reached a point where I couldn't find out more, so I asked Henry to help. He called me this morning, saying he verified Daniel isn't Daniel, and he was going to talk to him and take him to the Amish bishop."

"Oh, no. So he met Daniel, and then . . ." Rochelle shook her head again. "But what could Daniel have done that was so bad that he didn't want anyone to find out who he was?"

Her stomach plummeted into her feet. What kind of man was this Daniel? To hurt a kind, generous, caring man like Henry Hostetler? And she'd trusted him, too.

Thaddeus's phone started to buzz, so he pulled it from his pocket. When he saw the number, the blood drained from his face.

"Pete." He frowned at Rochelle and shook his head.

"Zook, I've got your girlfriend here. And you have something I want, and I want it now."

"Put her on the phone." He motioned to Rochelle to find a pen. She pulled one, and a notepad from her bag. "I want to talk to her."

"Hang on."

"Thaddeus?"

"Betsy, are you all right?"

"Yes, I'm all right."

"Good. Where are you?"

"I'm—"

"I'll let you know where to meet me. You have the video files, I assume?"

"I do, but listen—"

"No, you listen. You've cost me weeks and weeks I can't ever get back. Don't call the police, either."

He then chose *not* to tell Pete he'd already sent a copy of the files to Columbus. Likely, they would be delivered today by two p.m.

He scribbled on the paper. *Get police on phone. Tell them a man named Peter Stucenski has taken Betsy. Tell them to call Columbus PD about Mitch*—He stopped writing.

Rochelle nodded and pushed some buttons on her phone. "What do you want me to do then? I don't want to keep the files, Pete."

"I'll call you in ten minutes and tell you where to meet us." The line went silent.

"Yes, please," Rochelle was telling the dispatcher. "My niece, Elizabeth Yoder, has been taken by a man named Peter Stu—" She frowned.

Thad took the phone from her. "His name is Peter Stucenski. Hello? My name is Thaddeus Zook."

"Could you please explain? Where is Miss Yoder? Where are you calling from?"

"I am at the Sarasota General ER with Rochelle Keim, who you were just talking to. We believe Mr. Stucenski assaulted a man named Henry Hostetler, who's being treated here for a head injury. Then he took Elizabeth Yoder against her will. He just called me and said he has her."

Finally, Thad felt like they'd made themselves understood without sounding like raving lunatics. After Rochelle gave a description of Peter and his vehicle, the dispatcher said they'd begin a search, and contact the Columbus Police Department.

A man in scrubs approached them. "Ms. Keim?"

"Yes, I'm Rochelle Keim." She rose from her seat.

"We're going to do surgery on Mr. Hostetler to relieve the pressure. I'm confident we'll be successful. However, he also has a skull fracture and a contusion on the frontal lobe of his brain. We'll let you know when you can see him and we've moved him from recovery to ICU."

"Thank you, thank you." She nodded, glancing at Thad. He debated going to find Betsy or waiting at the hospital. He decided to wait.

A stream of Plain people entered the ER, from the Amish bishop to Betsy's parents. Thad stood, but froze in front of his seat. No, he wasn't going anywhere. Henry was his friend, too.

Together, he and Rochelle explained everything to them, about Henry, Betsy, and the recording. It dawned on Thad, if he hadn't come here, none of this would have happened.

"And, what I wanted to say was, I'm sorry, Mr. and Mrs. Yoder. I—I care for your daughter very much. She's a . . . a special person. If I'd have known this would have happened, I would have never come here. I never wanted anything like this to happen." His throat caught.

"Thaddeus." Mr. Yoder's voice boomed deep. "We don't hold you responsible for a wicked man's actions. What he did isn't your fault. You've done the right thing and notified the authorities. And now, we must pray for *Gotte's wille* to be done, in our friend Henry, and in Betsy, in you, and in your old boss, Mr. Stucenski."

Thad nodded. They huddled together, praying silently.

Oh, Gotte. I ask forgiveness for anything wrong I've done. I have sinned, both before leaving the Ordnung, and since. Please, forgive me. Don't hold any of my wrongdoing against Betsy. Protect her. Take care of Henry. Guide the surgeons. Like the psalm writer, I put myself at Your mercy, and all of them, too. Even Pete.

He felt his phone buzzing and withdrew from the group. Pete again.

29

$\mathcal{B}$etsy had never been to this beach before. They'd gone all the way down Harbor Drive to somewhere called Castaway Beach. More remote and not close to the usual tourist areas, their presence wouldn't attract much attention.

They sat in the parking lot, the engine still running.

"Lie down on the seat while we're parked. It looks weird with you sitting in the backseat."

The man had a gun. Betsy lay sideways on the seat. *Gotte, I don't want to die. Not yet.*

"Please. You can let me go. I'll make sure Thaddeus gives you what you're looking for. I promise."

"I'm sure you would."

"You told him not to call the police. I'm sure he already has."

"And after he takes an hour getting them to understand his story, well, I don't know if they'll come running."

"They will. They have to. They're the police. And they know about Henry."

She could see from his profile she'd made him pause.

He growled into the phone. "Why isn't he answering? Oh. Thad. It's about time. What? You were all *praying*, with her family? Imagine! You've gone back to your roots. Trying to win over your sweetheart here, huh?"

Sweetheart? Daniel—or Peter, rather—had called her Thaddeus's girlfriend also. Yes, he had feelings for her, and she for him. They could sort it all out later. But praying. With her family. She sucked in a gulp of air.

"Does she know about the other women? You didn't tell her about them. What was her name? Megan? What did I hear about you two in the walk-in freezer? I'm not the only one on video, you know." He then started describing horrible things, making Betsy plug her ears. Her heart hurt. This was an evil, sick man. He must be hurting to hurt others like this.

Now the tears did come and her ears hurt from the pressure of her fingers. *Gotte, please, make him stop.* Thaddeus had claimed her heart. It didn't matter what he'd done in the past. It shouldn't. But the words, though muffled, jabbed into her.

There. It sounded as though he ended the call. Betsy removed her fingers from her ears and wiped the tears away. Be brave. *Gotte, protect me.*

At last, Peter looked at her in the backseat and said, "He's on his way."

❧

Thaddeus wanted to run a red light just to get a police officer to follow him, but it wasn't the best idea. What if they stopped him, and then arrested him for some reason? He'd never make it to Betsy in time.

He'd never been to this beach but followed Harbor Drive until he couldn't go anymore, then found a parking lot, empty except for a few cars, one of them a silver sedan. Pete's.

Thaddeus parked near the vehicle. It was empty. He called the police and was put through right away.

"I've found them. He called me back."

"Don't do anything. Don't approach him or try to negotiate. We want Miss Yoder unharmed."

"Me, too." But no way was he going to sit here and not talk to Pete. Pete would talk to him.

"Stay on the line until the officers arrive. We're sending three units."

Good. They were taking this seriously. He clutched the phone carefully and headed for the beach path. Thaddeus glanced down at his phone. The called dropped. Signal lost.

As he scaled the dune path, he saw them at once, a Plain couple on the beach. Betsy moved stiffly, her face looking out at the water. He wanted to get her attention, but she'd know he was there soon enough.

"Pete," he called out. They both turned. Betsy tried to bolt from Pete's side, but he had his hand clamped on one arm.

"You made it."

"Yup. I sure did." Thad held up the keychain. "Is this what you wanted?"

"Yes."

"You could have just come to my *Mammi's* front door, as yourself, and asked for it. I would have given it to you."

"Would you, if you'd have known what was on it?"

Thaddeus hesitated for a moment. No, if he'd seen those files months ago, he'd have gone straight to the authorities.

"Mitch *died* because of those files, Pete. It wasn't right."

"He died because he got greedy and stupid. I'm going about things the right way. I'm getting paid handsomely to make this problem go away."

"Betsy, are you okay?" Thad wanted to run to her, but, instead, took a few steps closer.

"Close enough." Pete let Thad see the weapon tucked into his belt.

"I'm fine, Thaddeus. Mr. Pete here, though, is a sad, hurt man." Betsy faced him. "I'm going to pray for you, Pete. God shows mercy to all of us, especially if we're repentant. He is good and just and loving—"

"Don't start with the God talk. I don't want to hear it. The longer this takes, the longer it takes me to get out of here and back to Ohio. No one's going to believe you, Thad."

"What if I threw this into the waves?" Thad spun the keychain on his finger.

"What if I shot Miss Betsy in the leg?" Pete lowered the muzzle of the gun. Betsy flinched.

Thad stopped spinning the keychain. If Pete had attacked Henry, he'd hurt Betsy, too. And he'd probably been the one to hurt Stacie the day Thad had talked to her on the phone.

"All right. Here. You can have the keychain. But let me have Betsy."

Pete looked up, scanning the dune behind Thad. "Cops? You called the police?"

"Of course, I did. Here." Thad held up the keychain. He tossed it a few yards away from Pete, and it bounced onto the wet sand. Pete cursed as he threw the gun down, then ran for the keychain. More footsteps on the sand. Officers running. Shouts.

Thad ran for Betsy and pulled her into his arms.

She sank against him. "You came for me."

"Of course I did."

"I was so scared. I didn't know. Then I heard about Henry. But he's the one who did it, right?"

"Right." He planted a kiss on the top of her head, not caring who saw them. "He's in surgery now."

"Were you praying with them?"

"Yeah, I was. I really was." He could stand like this forever, it seemed. But he had a feeling there was an officer or two wanting to talk to them both.

Betsy's head ached. She'd told her story at least twice to the officers there at the beach. She didn't let go of Thaddeus's hand the entire time. He told his story, too.

"And, officer, if you contact Detective Kincaid with the Columbus PD, he should have a copy of the files on the keychain Pete was after. I sent them to him by overnight mail."

Betsy couldn't help but smile at Thaddeus. So smart. So handsome. So much for them to work on.

"Good," said the officer. "We'll need you both to come make statements again at the office. But this is enough for now."

Thaddeus nodded. "If you don't mind, I'd like to take this young lady for a walk on the beach until her ride gets here." He'd already phoned a relieved *Aenti* Chelle, who would come to pick Betsy up.

"Go right ahead."

Betsy let Thaddeus lead her along the shore. "Now, what?" She had to ask.

"Well. There's something you should know. I'll probably have to go back to Ohio for a bit. Not long, though."

She tried not to frown. "Yes, you probably will."

"But, Elizabeth." He stopped tugging her closer, holding her hands in his. "I want you to know this. I love you. I've loved you for quite a while. But I also know, I'm not the man you need me to be. Not yet. You deserve better. I always thought it would be someone like Gideon."

"Oh, *no*. Not him." She reached up, hesitated, then touched his face. "I love you, and I need you. And I'm willing to wait. But . . . does this mean you're willing to . . . ?"

He nodded. "I'm going to talk to Bishop Smucker about joining the church. Here. In Sarasota. It's different than my family's. I can still be me, be a pastry chef, and it's okay. I'm not afraid of being like everyone else, because everyone is so different here."

"Good. It's very good." She smiled at him. "But you'll be giving up so much."

Thaddeus shook his head. "No, I won't. Not when I see how much I have to gain."

Epilogue

Six months. Thaddeus Zook couldn't decide if the time had gone by in an instant, or if it dragged. When he saw Betsy's face in the congregation, the 180 days, give or take, might as well have been 180 years.

He had passed his proving time. And he didn't mind at all. Not for the joy set before him. Betsy had waited. He knew she would. Of course, there would be doubters who might question how long it would be before he left. But this time, there would be no leaving. He'd sought to meet with God, and God had met with him right back. The more time he spent in Pinecraft the rest of the winter and into the spring, the more Thaddeus saw his place as here. He met with Henry regularly as the man recovered from his head injury and started working part-time again at his contracting business.

The staff at Palm Trees wished Thaddeus well, but hoped he'd still consider being a pastry chef for them. Nope, the idea wouldn't fly, not with his Old Order brethren. Anyway, business was booming at Pinecraft Pies and Pastry. Thaddeus also had it on good authority from the bakery's owner that his skills were desperately needed. And him, too.

During Thaddeus's proving time, Bishop Smucker's combination of kindness with expectant accountability didn't make Thaddeus feel as though he were entering a prison in joining the Sarasota *Ordnung*. They all had much in common, yet God had made them all different. The bishop thought Thaddeus being a pastry chef a bit nontraditional; however, Pinecraft wasn't quite a traditional Amish village, either.

As long as Thaddeus kept to their *Ordnung*, all would be well. Thaddeus didn't feel forbidden to ride his Harley anymore. He simply chose not to. Even if he were *Englisch*, a Harley wouldn't be practical for a man who would eventually have a family, with *kinner* of his own.

Pete would be going to jail, and had already pled guilty to the charges for what he'd done in Florida. When Thad returned to Ohio to give a statement for the attorney general in the new case against the Ohio senator, he sold the Harley to a young chef fresh out of culinary school. The man sped off gleefully from the parking lot. Thad would miss the feeling, just a little.

Then after a brief visit with his family, he returned to Florida, via the Pioneer Trails bus, and Betsy had waited with Rochelle in the parking lot of the tourist church to welcome him home.

He'd had ample opportunities to back out, even after all the classes he attended. Now, though, he knelt along with two other young people, quite a bit younger than him, for the baptism ceremony.

He answered the questions the bishop asked before everyone: Yes, he was committed to living the Christian life. Yes, he was committed to Christ. Yes, he had forsaken the world. At this last statement, it was as if he was walking into a home and the entire family had assembled to feast on the fatted calf—for him. Yes, he accepted the *Ordnung* of the local district.

Water poured over his head and down his shoulders, but not to make him clean. He knew he was already clean on the inside. This symbolic act committed him to his people—the *Ordnung* in Sarasota—as long as he would live. There were far worse places to be than home. And home was here.

"Now, please stand."

Thaddeus and the others stood. Bishop Smucker grasped him by the shoulders and gave him a kiss on his cheek, a fatherly kiss of acceptance. He had a long way to go with his family, but Thaddeus knew he had plenty of time to sort it all out. He was among a group of people who accepted him, loved him. Not perfect, but then neither was he. God had plenty of grace to dish out. He thought for an instant of all that he'd left behind him, and saw all the treasure in front of him.

After the service concluded, the most precious treasure of all approached in her favorite blue cape dress matching her sparkling eyes.

"You're not supposed to talk to me just yet." Thaddeus couldn't resist teasing Betsy for breaking with tradition. "Aren't you supposed to stay on your side of the yard with the other women?"

"Maybe. But I wanted to be the first to welcome you home."

He smiled at her. "I'm glad you're the first."

"Welcome home, Thaddeus Zook." He felt a kiss from the expression in her eyes.

"Home for me will be wherever you are."

Glossary

Ach—oh
Aenti—aunt
Daadi—grandfather
Daed—father
Danki—thank you
Dietsch—Pennsylvania Dutch
Dochder—daughter
Englisch—non-Amish
Gotte's wille—God's will
Gut—good
Kaffi—coffee
Kapp—prayer covering
Kind—child
Kinner—children
Mamm—mom
Mammi—grandma
Mudder—mother
Onkel—uncle
Ordnung—set of rules for Amish living.
Rumspringa—running around; time before an Amish young person has officially joined the church, provides a bridge between childhood and adulthood.
Ya—yes

Group Discussion Guide

1. Betsy longs to have her own bakery but needs her family's financial backing. Share about your favorite small family-owned business.
2. What was your favorite scene in *A Path Made Plain*?
3. Thaddeus doesn't like the idea of being like everybody else. What would you say to encourage him to stand out—in a good way?
4. Betsy struggles with the concept of understanding God's will. How do you understand God's will for your life?
5. The longer he remains in Pinecraft, the more Thaddeus struggles with the feeling of letting his family down yet feeling conflicted about returning to the Order to please them. How do you handle it when a family member lets you down or you disappoint another family member?
6. Betsy adopts a dachsund that she names Winston. Share about a time you unexpectedly adopted a pet or how a pet has enriched your life.
7. What's your favorite pie recipe or the most unusual pie you've ever tasted?
8. Someone tries to stir up trouble for Betsy's business and sabotage the opportunity for her bakery to be on TV. How do you deal with saboteurs like that in your own life?
9. At first, Betsy dreads having her *Aenti* Sarah help in the bakery. Over time, she welcomes the older woman's help. How has an older individual helped you, either now or in the past?
10. Who was your favorite character in *A Path Made Plain*? Why?

Want to learn more about author
Lynette Sowell and check out other great
fiction from Abingdon Press?

Check out
AbingdonFiction.com
to read interviews with your favorite authors, find tips
for starting a reading group, and stay posted on what
new titles are on the horizon. It's a place to connect
with other fiction readers or post a
comment about this book.

Be sure to visit Lynette online!

facebook.com/lynettesowellauthor

We hope you enjoyed reading *A Path Made Plain* and that you will continue to read Abingdon Press fiction books. Here's an excerpt from Lynette Sowell's *A Promise of Grace*.

༺❧༻

1

*T*he minivan's air conditioner gave one last puff of cold air not long after Silas Fry drove across the Florida state line. Silas merely lowered the front windows without saying anything to the children.

How many more hours to Sarasota? Two? Three?

"I wish we were back in Africa." Lena sighed and fanned herself where she sat in the front passenger seat. She leaned toward the open window. Her sigh sounded as if her world had suddenly crumbled. At nearly nineteen, she tended to see life in extremes. And Belinda had been the one adept at handling her moodiness.

"Me, too." Matthew's echo was born of always wanting to follow in Lena's trail.

"I know you do, I know." Silas forced his voice to come out around the lump in his throat. Africa, his home. Their home. It would never be the same without Belinda. None of them would be.

Despite what Belinda had done long, long ago, he'd loved his wife until the very end. Until the day a semi had plowed into the van in which she and some other ladies had been riding home from a quilt auction. And he'd loved her for a long time after.

None of those who died had suffered, the families were told. Suffering was left for the rest of the families left behind, spouseless husbands, motherless children. For them, the wounds ran deep and healed slowly.

Silas filled his lungs with the fresh, humid air blowing into the van. "Your great-uncle said we'll have plenty of time to go to the beach after supper tonight."

The seashore. The ocean had been the one constant where they'd lived in Africa, not far from the coast in Mozambique. And, one big reason he'd chosen to move them all to Florida. In landlocked Ohio, the children had balked and he even found himself feeling a bit constricted, his only refuge in the air, flying a Cessna.

Life with Belinda as their hub had fallen apart. Somehow, with God's help, they'd find a way to put it back together again.

Someone had told him children were resilient.

Children?

He often needed to remind himself that Lena wasn't a child anymore, her studies had ended long ago, and she was planning to continue her education, not to become a teacher like her mother but a medical assistant. She'd already completed her high school equivalency certificate and planned to enroll in college in Sarasota.

Matthew was not a child either, all of fourteen and idolizing his older sister with her take-charge view of the world. They'd already discussed him finishing school in Pinecraft at the Mennonite school, after seeing where he compared to other students his age. He had a good eye for building and construction, as well as taking motors apart and putting them back together. Silas wasn't sure where he'd come by his skill.

But Silas couldn't help thinking of both of them as children. He'd been there from the beginning, when their first cries rang out. He'd seen them grow and thrive, through first words and first stumbles, through the first days of "I can do it myself." Especially with Lena, who seemed to have come from her mother's womb sure of herself and the world.

Lena shifted, her tanned feet now tucked up in the corner between the door and the dashboard, her chin resting on her hand as she gazed at the palm trees they zipped past along the highway.

Silas cast a look in the rearview mirror. Matthew, wearing his favorite shirt Belinda had sewn with the help of an ancient sewing machine before they'd left Africa. Not long from now, the sleeves would be too short and the last of Belinda's lovingly sewn clothing would be ready to donate to someone else's growing child.

"I miss the beach, and fishing," Matthew continued.

"We'll have plenty of time for it here."

"But you're going to work."

"I am. I need to earn money for us, just like other fathers do." He'd explained to Matthew before. Lena accepted, and truthfully, she was more concerned with her own studies. Maybe it was her way to cope. He understood, part of him wanting to be at the controls of a plane instead of a minivan towing a small trailer with all their worldly goods.

Silas relaxed his grip on the steering wheel and decelerated. He wasn't flying, doing what made his heart soar the most. God hadn't taken it away from him. He would fly again, soon, enough.

The Aviation Fellowship friends—like family, after his and Belinda's more than a decade serving overseas—had sent them off with a generous check and the beginnings of setting up a household.

"One day, you'll be back, Silas," Levi Brubaker had told him before they left Ohio. "God has you called to missions."

"My mission is in Florida now, with my family."

"I understand. We'll be ready to have you back when the time is right."

A lump had swelled his throat as he'd cut ties with the ministry he'd poured himself into. What would he—they—do now? Life for his fellow missionaries and pilots would go on. They all promised to keep in touch, of course. But things had changed too much for Silas to continue to subject his family to more uncertainty.

Which is what they were doing right now, the van limping its way to Sarasota and the Amish and Mennonite village of Pinecraft, their new home.

And, where Rochelle Keim lived.

He'd thought of her, several times, over the years. Each time he'd pushed the thoughts away. Deliberately trying to discover how Rochelle fared wouldn't be good, for anyone. Now, though, he wondered how she'd aged, if her brown eyes still were soft, expressive, warm, and kind. Her beautiful hair—

"Are you okay, Dad?"

He blinked, and glanced at his daughter.

"Mostly. It's been a long trip."

"I wish we could have flown. I wish you still had a plane."

"Me too. But this has been a good way for you to see some of the United States you've never seen before."

Lena shrugged. "That's true." She paused. "The air conditioning's not working."

"No. It's not. I'll see about getting it fixed after we get settled."

God, we need a lot of things fixed.

He thought they'd been fine, as fine as they could be. Until losing Belinda. Had it been almost a year?

He always believed when you didn't know what to do, do the next obvious thing God expected of you. And so, he was. Being a father, providing for his family again, soon, piloting for a small private airport that often needed pilots on call for short chartered flights. His one concession to the children had been moving to Florida, to the coast, to the small Plain village within a thriving city.

Whatever came next, he had no idea.

⁂

Of all days for the washer to break down, and her with a pile of laundry. Rochelle Keim hauled the laundry basket from her house to the van, and plunked it into the back. Part of her *kapp* caught on the edge of the van's hatch and the *kapp*, including hairpins, nearly slid off her head. *Ow.*

The village of Pinecraft had its own Laundromat, the only one Rochelle knew of with its own set of clotheslines—bring your own clothespins.

Betsy and Emma, her Amish nieces a couple of times removed, were busy with a morning of wedding planning. How Rochelle wished she could have joined them. But no, she said she'd take care of all the household laundry, including bedsheets, towels, and clothing. Afterward, she had one cleaning client to visit, Emma had her own clients to serve, and Betsy was needed back overseeing business at Pinecraft Pies and Pastry.

Rochelle tried not to sigh. The action wouldn't change anything. Some days, she was tired of cleaning up after other people, herself included.

She fetched two more baskets of laundry, one of them sopping, from the house, then slammed the van's hatch closed.

She had already placed a call to Henry Hostetler, one of Pinecraft's handymen and contractors extraordinaire, about checking the washing machine if he had a spare moment. But the older man was busy finishing replacing a roof, and promised to stop by on the way home just before suppertime.

Rochelle drove through Pinecraft's sunny streets, giving the occasional three-wheeled adult cycles wide berth. Most people walked or bicycled the village's streets, nestled on both sides of Sarasota's busy Bahia Vista Avenue, and flanked on one end by the meandering Phillippi Creek.

Thankfully, she tucked her van into one of the few parking spots. She wouldn't have to lug her laundry too far. An Old Order Amish woman, Rochelle couldn't recall her name at the moment, moved her tricycle with its little trailer out of the way. The woman waved and smiled, then mouthed a *gut* morning.

Rochelle returned the wave and smile. She reminded herself she was blessed to live in such a place as Pinecraft, where Amish and Mennonites of all orders and fellowships converged, most of them during the winter months. A few, like her, called the village home year 'round. Right now, the place was what some might call the proverbial ghost town.

But she couldn't imagine herself living anywhere else. The only other home she'd known was Ohio, and she'd severed ties with that part of her life a long time ago. Her parents, formerly Amish, left their order when she was but a girl, and joined the Mennonite church.

Even her father didn't quite understand why she'd uprooted herself and moved to Florida when she was barely twenty.

"God will guide your path; don't be hasty," her father had said.

Rochelle smiled at her father's words as she tugged the first load of laundry from the back of the van. She'd used those same words when providing counsel to her younger Amish nieces. However, haste hadn't goaded her to leave her family in the Midwest.

With the age of forty growing closer, day by day, month by month, with half a lifetime of years behind her growing up in Ohio, she wondered if she'd have listened to herself when she was her nieces' ages of twenty and twenty-two.

"Good morning," said Nellie Bontrager, the owner of the three-wheeler and trailer. "I see you have a household's worth of laundry there."

"Washer's broken." Rochelle shrugged.

"Here. I'll get the other basket for you."

"Thanks." She also tried to shrug off the unsettled feeling she had after hearing the washing machine clunk to a halt, belt screeching.

She wasn't just tired of cleaning other people's messes. She was tired of cleaning.

Period.

At least today.

Nellie huffed as she trudged along to the nearest empty washing machine. "Good thing it's not washday."

"Good thing," Rochelle agreed. If it was Monday, wash day for many in the village, she'd have to wait her turn for an empty washer. She ought to be thankful the calendar read Tuesday. Instead, her agitation simmered inside her, as if she were an unhappy three-year-old.

Instead of stomping her foot, she sighed, and set the basket she carried on the floor. The clomping noise the basket made didn't quite mask her sigh.

"Is everything all right, Rochelle?" Nellie's expression didn't quite pierce Rochelle, but the older woman studying her was enough to make Rochelle stare at the sopping wet bedsheets and undergarments. She needed to get the detergent and bleach from the van.

"Yes. No. I, I'm not sure." She had to force the confession out. Rochelle never liked to be unsure of much. Uncertain decisions like choosing which flavor of pie to order at Yoder's Restaurant for dessert—now they were a nice uncertainty. No matter what the decision, the results would have a delicious outcome.

Of course, everything was all right—with her—other than the fact today she hated cleaning, and her, a professional cleaning woman.

"It's—it's the weddings. I shouldn't talk about it, because it's not my business." She'd already said too much.

"Is it Betsy and her tattooed baker?" Nellie shook her head and clicked her tongue.

"No, no. Betsy and Thaddeus are doing fine." Of course, a few still doubted Thaddeus'S baptism into the Amish faith, despite his proving time, baptism, and him settling once and for all into the Amish fellowship in Pinecraft.

"Ah, young Emma and Steven, then."

Rochelle nodded. "Emma is young." She didn't add that Emma had broken off her engagement last winter to Eli Troyer back in Ohio, and chose to remain in Pinecraft with her older sister, Betsy, the two of them occupying Rochelle's spare bedroom. She didn't add Emma never seemed to be able to make up her mind on matters and sometimes it changed with the breeze.

Despite her seeming indecisiveness and the rumblings throughout the community, Emma had joined the Mennonite church and planned to marry Steven. Emma attended services with Rochelle regularly, but little things made Rochelle worry if the union between Steven and Emma ought to take place.

Rochelle could clean and organize, but the matters of a twenty-year-old young woman had Rochelle's hands tied. Perhaps it's why God had willed her no family of her own.

Although with Betsy's easygoing ways, Rochelle had wondered more than once what it would have been like to have a young woman like Betsy as a daughter. Emma, though, would have caused her to build up calluses on her knees over the years.

"I hear they'll be here today, likely, and are renting a home from John Stoltzfus," Nellie was saying.

"Oh, who'll be here today?"

"Silas Fry, and his family."

"In Pinecraft?" Of course, Nellie meant Pinecraft. John Stoltzfus, an Amish man who lived in Lancaster County, Pennsylvania, owned property in the village and leased it with the help of Nellie's neighbors, a Mennonite couple who lived in Pinecraft.

"Yes, Pinecraft. You know his wife died almost a year ago. Tragic. The van accident."

"Yes, I remember." Rochelle nodded and kept her hands steady as she poured laundry detergent into the machine. She still remembered the day her sister had shared the news with her.

More than once, she'd prayed for Silas and his family, as she ought to. More than once, she'd poured out long-restrained tears about losing Belinda, her one-time best friend. However, she'd lost Belinda years and years ago, before the semi-truck ended her time on this earth.

⁊⊙⊱

Rochelle, 19

"My grandmother's turning eighty," Belinda Miller announced. "Almost four times our age."

"You make it sound ancient." Rochelle shook her head, and laughed from her place at the sink. A few more dishes to wash, then she and Belinda could leave to go shopping for ingredients for Estelle Miller's gigantic birthday cake.

"Well, eighty is ancient, almost. Momma says she looks great for her age, and Grandma says she doesn't care how she looks for her age, she's happy to still be here to keep Grandpa out of mischief."

"There, I'm done." Rochelle set the last plate in the dish drainer, then wiped her hands. Their fellowship would celebrate the birthday of the matriarch of the Miller family during the coming weekend, and both she and Belinda had volunteered to make the cake. Belinda had taken several cake decorating lessons at a local bakery supply shop, and she was eager to show off her skills.

Rochelle was just along for the ride on this one, she'd assured Belinda, who'd designed a three-tiered round cake, white frosting, and multicolored wildflowers made of sugar.

"Did I tell you John Hershberger is picking me up for the party?" Belinda's cheeks flushed.

"So, you two *are* courting! And you didn't tell me?" Rochelle threw the dishtowel at Belinda's head. "I knew you'd been giggling and looking at him at youth meetings for months now."

Belinda ducked. "No, silly. We're not courting. Yet. I'm sure we will be soon."

For the past few months, all Rochelle had heard was John Hershberger this and John Hershberger that. Rochelle had been tuning her best friend out, because her college studies had kept her busy. Too busy for many of the activities the young adults participated in at Hope Mennonite Church.

However, one meeting not long ago had captured her attention. A missionary group, visiting from overseas, told them all about the great need for workers. Teachers. Doctors. Nurses. Pilots.

At the word nurse, Rochelle's ears had perked up higher than her father's dog, Patches, did. She was already studying hard for her nursing degree at their local college.

"There is great need here in the United States for good nurses, and nursing care, but all members of the medical field are needed in Africa, especially in developing countries and where the gospel isn't always welcome," the speaker had said.

"Anyway," Belinda continued, "John said his best friend, Silas Fry, is riding along with him. You should come too. We can all ride to the party together."

Daring, riding together, just the four of them in a vehicle.

Rochelle adjusted her *kapp*, then smoothed her apron. "I know Silas Fry."

Well, knew him in a roundabout way. Silas was the kind of young man everyone noticed. The other young men all liked to be his friend. The other young women liked to smile at him and the boldest struck up conversation. They'd grown up together and participated in the same youth group, but in the last couple of years, childhood friendships had changed into something different as couples began to pair off.

Rochelle had spoken to Silas recently, entirely by accident. She'd gone up to him, thinking he looked like her cousin from behind and called him by her cousin's name. He swung around, with laughter in his eyes and she felt a tug of aware-ness in their blueness reminding her of a happy summer sky.

"No, I'm not Levi," he'd said. "I hope you're not disap-pointed."

"No, I'm not." She choked out the three words as her face flamed all sorts of hot. Belinda would tease her, probably as much as she'd teased Belinda about her budding romance with John Hershberger.

But nothing was budding with Silas Fry. She'd tried
keep herself from noticing him, because other young wome
couldn't help but notice him. However, from this momen
she didn't think she'd ever succeed at pretending not to notic
Silas Fry, ever again.